MW01245566

PRAISE FOR *THE MEMORY WARD*

"This book scared the shit out of me so much I had to close
my blinds one night while reading. It's also funny as hell.
And that's where Jon Bassoff gets you, in that bizarrely tense
space between unsettled and funny and heartwarming.
I don't know what or who is real anymore. I'm still shook!"
—STEVEN DUNN,
author of *Potted Meat*

"*The Memory Ward* is a nesting doll of horror
and suspense. Bassoff artfully crafts a novel that questions
morality, free will, and what makes us human.
Compelling from the first page to the last."
—ERIN E. ADAMS,
Bram Stoker Award finalist
and Edgar Award-winning author of *Jackal*

THE
MEMORY
WARD

BOOKS BY JON BASSOFF

The Memory Ward
Beneath Cruel Waters
Captain Clive's Dreamworld
The Drive-Thru Crematorium
The Lantern Man
The Blade This Time
The Incurables
Factory Town
Corrosion
The Disassembled Man

JON
BASSOFF
THE
MEMORY
WARD

BLACK
STONE
PUBLISHING

Printed in the United States of America

First edition: 2025
ISBN 979-8-212-91210-5
Fiction / Thrillers / Suspense

Version 1

Blackstone Publishing
31 Mistletoe Rd.
Ashland, OR 97520

www.BlackstonePublishing.com

For Tobey

Remembrance of things past is not necessarily the remembrance of things as they were.

—Marcel Proust

PART 1

HENRY "HANK" DAVIES

CHAPTER 1

Mailbag slung over my shoulder, sun helmet tipped back on my head, I walked slowly down the empty and sun-bleached streets of Bethlam, Nevada, and I couldn't help but feel uneasy, couldn't help thinking *those* thoughts. All around me were rows and rows of pretty houses with pretty lawns and pretty decorations, but still, there was something menacing about it all, as if the town's caretakers were busy gathering and hiding secrets, burying them beneath the red dirt.

Every day, the same mailboxes outside the same houses. The Browns, the McCabes, the Thompsons, the Ellisons. Sometimes, a little boy would appear in the distance bouncing a red ball and laughing, and sometimes, a couple would pass, walking hand in hand and smiling, and sometimes, an old model Ford would drive down the street, windows cracked, radio playing the faint melody of another time. But most of the time, Bethlam, Nevada, was quiet. Most of the time, it was empty.

I'd been delivering mail on this same route for a few months more than five years. Had it really been that long? In a lot of ways, the five years all seemed like one long day. I guess that's what happens when we live a life of routines. Each day becomes inextricable from the others. Five years becomes no different than ten, no different from twenty, no different than a lifetime.

But on this day, something different *did* happen. Something strange and unusual and unsettling.

I was walking down Spruce Street, humming some nameless melody, thinking about days gone by, when I stumbled over a branch that had fallen from a nearby tree. I managed to keep my balance, but in that momentary anticipation of contact with the cement, my hand opened and several pieces of mail fluttered to the ground. Cursing quietly, I got down on my hands and knees and worked to gather the scattered mail. But among the fallen envelopes, I noticed that one—addressed to Dolly Harvey—had become unsealed, the folded letter jutting out from the corner. The address was written in lovely looped cursive, and below the address was an intricate rose, colored red.

I glanced around and, seeing that nobody was around, extracted the piece of paper from the envelope. Why did I do that? Did I expect to find a passionate letter from a secret lover? A lurid blackmail message from an aggrieved enemy? It's hard to say. Sometimes we do things for no reason at all. When I unfolded the piece of white printer paper, however, I was disappointed to find that it was blank. I flipped it over. Nothing. No promises of love. No angry threats. No writing at all. "Huh," I said out loud. Then I placed the piece of paper back in the envelope.

I don't know why this bothered me. It should have been a brief peculiarity, quickly forgotten. But, for some reason, I ruminated on it. I delivered mail to a few more houses and then I stopped. I took another look around. The neighborhood was still empty, the only sound a single crow cawing from an electrical wire.

I reached into my mailbag, trying to find other envelopes that were sloppily sealed, other envelopes that I could peer inside. It didn't take me long to find two such envelopes. One was addressed to Michael Ruiz. Another to Melissa Blackburn. Like the letter to Dolly, both addresses were handwritten, but it was clear that they were written by different hands (one was full of masculine block letters, while the other was barely legible). With trembling fingers—what was I so anxious about?—I opened the first envelope and then the second.

Two more blank pieces of paper.

I was mystified by this turn of events. For a few minutes, I tried rationalizing. Maybe the sender had been in a rush and had accidentally put the wrong piece of paper inside. Maybe the sender had been mailing a check, folded neatly inside the paper, and it had slipped out. Maybe. But in all three envelopes? By three different senders?

Naturally, my curiosity was piqued. I wanted to open up the rest of the mail to see if there were more blank papers. But before I had a chance to do so, a young woman wearing a flower dress turned the corner and smiled at me. I didn't recognize her, but she recognized me, saying, "Hello, Mr. Davies. Beautiful day, isn't it?"

"It is," I said. "It's always beautiful in Bethlam. No place I'd rather be." I smiled and tipped my sun helmet before continuing on my route. I arrived at the Goldsmiths' house and placed two envelopes inside their mailbox. Then I went to the Boardmans' house and the Myers' house and the Sundbergs' house, all the while glancing furtively at windows and behind my shoulder, listening for footsteps on the concrete, worried that I was being watched.

For the rest of my route, I didn't open any more envelopes.

But I couldn't stop feeling that sense of dread.

———

I lived with my lovely wife, Iris, in a small, two-bedroom, one-bathroom home on Sixth and Mapleton. I clicked open the front gate and walked down the path that led to my porch. My neighbor, Mr. Downing, an old man with still-thick white hair and ruddy, red cheeks, paused from pruning his shrubs to wave at me and say, "Why, hello there, Hank! Beautiful afternoon, isn't it?"

"Yes," I agreed. "Beautiful. Nowhere I'd rather be."

I pushed open the front door and stepped inside. Our house was nothing fancy, but it was quaint and full of character. Oriental rugs covered hardwood floors scratched with age. Thick white drapes hid windows in need of a cleaning. Each nook and cranny, each crack in the wall, each piece of furniture represented a different memory from my life with Iris.

That's where I carried her across the threshold . . . That's where we first made love . . . That's where she dropped the bottle of champagne, the glass shattering everywhere . . . That's where I carried the platter of turkey on Thanksgiving . . .

From down the hallway, I could hear the faint echo of a laugh track. I removed my sun helmet and placed it inside my empty mailbag, which I left by the door. Then I wandered toward the living room. The television was on, but nobody was there to watch it. It was an old rerun of *M*A*S*H*. For whatever reason, Iris loved the show, and it was often on. In this episode, Hawkeye, full of angst, was talking to Father Mulcahy. "War isn't hell," he was saying. "War is war, and hell is hell. And of the two, war is a lot worse." I watched for a few minutes and then turned it off. TV always depressed me. Especially *M*A*S*H*.

I walked slowly through the house, peering in each room, searching for Iris. After a long day of delivering mail, this was the part of the day I most looked forward to: seeing her face, squeezing her hand, hearing her laugh. There were occasions, however, where I had the unfortunate feeling that those smiles and laughter were only obligations of marital duty.

I made my way to the back of the house, the wood creaking beneath my white walking shoes. When I reached our bedroom, I could hear Iris's voice coming from the behind the door. For some reason, instead of immediately opening the door, I pressed my ear against it. Her voice was soft, muffled. Still, I could make out bits and pieces of what she was saying: "Has your hair lost its shine? Is it missing its bounce? . . . Why settle for ordinary when you can have luxurious? . . . Made from nature's own ingredients like chamomile and shea butter . . . Skip the ordinary. Find the Luster. Because you're worth it."

I knew what was happening. She was pretending. She did that from time to time. She dreamed of being an actress. Of starring in commercials or TV shows or movies. But not me. I didn't have those dreams. I was pretty darn happy with my life the way it was.

I twisted the handle and pushed open the door. Iris, my sweet Iris, was standing in front of the mirror, holding a bottle of shampoo. The shampoo wasn't called Luster, though. It was my dandruff shampoo, Selsun Blue.

When she realized I was in the room, her face reddened in embarrassment, and she placed her hand to her chest. "Oh, darling," she said. "You startled me."

"I'm sorry. I should have knocked." And then: "Just so you know, I think you'd make a great spokeswoman. For shampoo or tampons or wine or anything. I'd buy the damn world from you."

She touched my shoulder, tenderly. "Oh, you're too sweet. It'll never happen, but a girl can pretend, right? I've always wanted to be on TV, you know. Ever since I was a kid."

"Yes," I said. "And it will happen one day. Just wait and see."

Her smile faded away. "Anyway. Enough of that silliness." She came forward and kissed me on the cheek. Always on the cheek. Never on the lips. "How was your day? Did you get all the mail delivered?"

"Yes. I got all the mail delivered."

"And did anybody invite you into their house? Like that Mrs. Martin? You need to watch out for her."

Mrs. Martin was a lonely housewife who lived on Seventh and Pine. Iris had told me that she was known to be flirtatious and then some. But I'd never had a problem with her.

"No," I said. "Nobody invited me into their house."

"Well, that's good. Do you want to go downstairs and have a glass of chocolate milk? We can sit on the couch and listen to some music."

"Okay. That sounds fine. Yes, let's go sit on the couch. Let's have some chocolate milk. There's something else I wanted to talk to you about. Something strange that happened on my mail route. I'll tell you about it just as soon as we sit down."

"Really? Something strange?"

"Yes. Strange."

"Right here in Bethlam?"

"Right here in Bethlam."

Iris's eyes narrowed to slits, and she gazed at me with concern. But then her face lightened, and her mouth spread into a smile. She placed her little hand in mine, and we walked out of the bedroom and back through the house, family pictures (but no children) on every wall.

Once in the living room, I sat down on the couch while Iris disappeared into the kitchen to get us the chocolate milk. (Dr. Hoover had advised me against drinking beer, so chocolate milk was my guilty pleasure.)

I removed my shoes and my socks and rubbed my feet, which were aching more than usual, blisters developing on the back of both heels.

Iris returned with the chocolate milk and sat down next to me. She tucked one foot beneath her opposite leg. She was wearing a blue dress that hung nice and low, giving me a peek at her cleavage. She must have noticed me staring because she quickly covered herself.

"I kept myself busy today," she said.

"Is that right?"

She flattened out her dress with her hand. "I cleaned the bathroom. Got it spick-and-span. Then I used a basket for tidying. You know, picking up items that were in the wrong place and putting them back where they should be. Then I reviewed the menu for the week and—" She stopped talking for a moment and covered her mouth with her hand. "But listen to me talking your ear off. You said something strange happened in your day?"

"Yes," I said. "Very strange."

"Well? What is it?"

I took a long drink of my chocolate milk. Iris looked at me with those doe eyes.

"It was during my route. I was over on Spruce Street."

"And?"

"And some letters fell from my bag."

Iris drank some of her chocolate milk, all the while watching me from the corner of her eye. She wiped her mouth clean with the back of her hand. "That doesn't sound like you," she said. "Usually, you're so well organized."

"Yeah, well. It's because I tripped over a branch. An accident. Anyway, one of the letters came loose from the envelope. I shouldn't have looked. I should have pushed the paper back inside. Instead, I took it out."

"Henry. You could—"

"And the thing is, the strange thing is, the paper inside had nothing on it. No handwriting at all. It was blank."

For a moment, just a moment, I saw a flicker of panic in Iris's eyes. But then, just as quickly, her expression softened. She fiddled with her wedding band. "Okay? So you found a blank piece of paper? So what?"

"Well, don't you think that's odd? That somebody would send a blank letter? What would be the point?"

"I'm sure there's an explanation. Maybe there was a check inside that you didn't see."

"I thought of that. I opened up more envelopes. Two of them. And there were the same blank papers. No checks."

Iris stared at me. Her mouth opened as if she were going to say something, but then it closed. She rose to her feet and walked to the window, pulled back the curtain. She gazed outside, her back toward me. The sun was beginning to set, and everything was turning orange and pink.

"You shouldn't be opening other people's mail," she said, her voice barely louder than a whisper. "It's against the law."

"I know. It was wrong. But what do you make of—"

She slowly turned back around toward me. Now her face was strained, her neck muscles twitching. "You took an oath when you got that job."

"An oath?"

"Yes. You promised to deliver the mail. Not to peek inside. I'm not sure you understand what an honor it is to work for the postal service. You know, it's been in existence longer than this country."

"But you're missing the point," I said. "You're missing the bigger picture."

She pointed at me. "No, mister, you're missing the bigger picture. You need to mind your own business, that's what you need to do. Just deliver the mail, and mind your own business. If you know what's good for you."

If you know what's good for you.

I didn't notice how hard I was squeezing the glass until it shattered in my hand. Chocolate milk, blood, and glass spread across the couch. Iris rushed over to where I was sitting. "Oh, darn! Look at what you've done!" she said.

But I didn't care about the mess. "What if all the envelopes were empty?" I said. "Every single one of them?"

"We need to get the couch cleaned. Chocolate milk stains are hard to remove. So are bloodstains."

I could feel my head begin to ache, the pain quickly spreading to my jaw. "What if they're playing a big trick on me?" I said. "What then?"

CHAPTER 2

That night, I slept by myself. I kept waking up and reaching for Iris, but she was never there. The sun finally woke me up for good. I opened my eyes and yawned. Iris stood at the foot of the bed, looking lovely in a white dress. Her hair was perfectly coiffed, her face perfectly rouged. In her hand, she held a small present wrapped in red paper. Behind her, a half dozen silver and purple balloons bobbed against the ceiling. Somehow, she had brought the balloons into the room while I slept. Whenever I became insecure about her love for me, she would surprise me, would remind me of her devotion. She was a wonderful wife in a wonderful town in a wonderful world.

"What's all this?" I said, stretching.

Her red lips spread into a wide grin, revealing perfectly straight teeth behind. "What do you think it all is, silly?"

"I don't know. I—"

"Why, it's your birthday! Did you forget?"

I thought for a moment. My birthday, my birthday. September 12th. Today. "I guess I did. Gee. I guess I did."

She sat down on the bed and kissed me on the cheek. "Thirty-three years old. Can you believe it? But still as handsome as ever. Tonight, we'll celebrate for real. Dinner. Presents. Your mom will join us. She's going to make her famous pasta. But until then—"

I sat up in bed and pulled back my hair with my hand. "Listen, darling. I appreciate it. I really do. But there's no need to make a big deal out of it. I'm a bit too old for pomp and circumstance, don't you think? I mean your birthday is what, a celebration for surviving another year?"

Iris stared at me for a moment, and then her lower lip started trembling, and her eyes began to fill with tears. She turned away so I wouldn't see her cry.

"What did I say? What—" And then I realized. "Oh, come on. You're not going to get emotional about that, are you?"

She turned back toward me. Mascara was leaking down her cheeks. "Emotional? What do you expect? It was a terrible accident. Awful. You could have died, you know? The blood. There was so much blood . . ."

"Stop it."

"For a few days there, I thought I was going to lose you."

I could feel my own emotions beginning to well inside of me. I squeezed my eyes shut, and I remembered. The rain falling in sheets. The man preaching through the static. The roses on the passenger seat. And then the lights of a semi coming over the ridge . . .

"So forgive me," Iris said, "if I do provide some pomp and circumstance. The fact that, as you say, you survived a year, is no small feat."

"I'm sorry," I said. "You're right. Of course you're right. You know, I shouldn't have almost died. Shouldn't have bled so much."

She managed to laugh through her tears. "Okay, wise guy," she said, handing me the present. "Go ahead and open it."

I took the present from her and then carefully removed the wrapping paper. Inside was a box and inside the box was a silver antique locket with intricate decorations.

I studied it for a few moments, not sure what to make of it.

"It's lovely," I said. "But I don't understand. What's the significance?"

"The locket was my grandmother's and then my mother's. Look inside."

I glanced at Iris and then back at the locket. I snapped it open. Inside was a small oval photograph of Iris and me. We were so young—what, eighteen or nineteen?—and were sitting on a Ferris wheel, the town of Bethlam glowing behind us.

"Do you remember this day?" she said.

"Yes," I said. "I remember." And I did. In fact, I remembered most everything—and with such vividness and detail that it was like it took place only yesterday. "A form of hyperthymesia," Dr. Hoover had once told me.

"We were at the county fair," I said.

"That's right. I still remember first seeing you. You looked so handsome in your white shirt and yellow tie. I was hanging with my friends by the Tilt-A-Whirl. Remember? And you were hanging with your friends by the high striker. I kept hoping that maybe you'd come over and talk to me. Just a word or two."

I nodded my head. "You were lovely. You're still lovely."

"And then you did come over. You walked with confidence. You did talk to me. You said, 'You look really pretty, Iris.' And right then, like magic, the band started playing. Ozzie Scanlon's band. I don't remember what they played. Do you?"

"I remember. They played 'Twilight Time.'"

"That's right. 'Twilight Time.' By The Platters." She hummed a verse and then stopped. "You took my hand and asked me if I wanted to go on the Ferris wheel."

"And you said 'yes.'"

Iris laughed and wiped more tears from her cheek. "And inside neither of us said a word, hardly. We were both so nervous. And then the Ferris wheel got stuck right when we reached the top."

"The wind caused us to rock back and forth."

"Do you remember how you held me? Do you remember how we kissed?"

"I remember."

She touched my cheek with the back of her hand. "I'm glad you remember. Aren't we lucky to have each other? Aren't we lucky to have Bethlam?"

"Yes," I said. "Lucky."

So why was I feeling so anxious?

———

I didn't figure anybody other than my wife and mother would remember my birthday, but somehow every person in Bethlam seemed to know. On the way to work, a pair of men wearing matching white shirts and black ties nodded at me and said, "Happy birthday, Mr. Davies." A fat woman wearing an apron and carrying a birdcage did the same. And once I arrived at work, Ms. Yeats and Ms. Keaton were waiting in the lobby, holding a cupcake with a single candle. They performed a badly off-key rendition of "Happy Birthday," and I blew out the candle. My only wish was to be left alone.

Meanwhile, my boss, Frank Temeer, had kindly organized my mail for me. When I entered his office, he removed his ever-present cigar, the mouth end now soggy, and patted me on the shoulder. "You're a good man," he said. "A good worker. But know this: I'll only organize your mail once a year. Only on your birthday. Understood?" And then he laughed.

I grinned. "Yes, sir. Understood."

"And a birthday gift for you." He opened his desk and pulled out a matching cigar and handed it to me. "Smuggled from Havana," he said. I placed the cigar in my mouth, and he flicked a match and pressed the flame against the end.

"Got any big plans to celebrate?" he asked. "I seem to remember that last year you and Iris went bowling. Isn't that right? And you damn near bowled a perfect game."

"Not quite. Two twelve."

"Close enough. My high score is one twenty-six. Two twelve is very impressive."

"No bowling this year. Just going to hang out at the house. Take it easy."

"That's fine. Your birthday is a very important day. Just remember this, Hank. You could have very easily died."

"Yes," I said. "That's what they say."

———

That morning, I hurried through my route, stopping every so often to talk with a man walking his dog or a woman pushing her baby carriage. "Happy birthday," they all said. "Happy birthday to you!"

I wondered how they all knew. Had they known last year? I couldn't recall. I couldn't recall turning thirty-two or thirty-one or thirty. No, that was wrong. I'd gone bowling last year. That was what Mr. Temeer had reminded me of. I'd scored 212. I remembered. I remembered.

I wondered about the mail I was carrying. Was every single envelope filled with a blank piece of paper? On a few occasions, I glanced around and, not seeing anybody watching me, removed an envelope from my bag. But as soon as I was about to unseal it, somebody would peer out their window or appear on the sidewalk. I thought about what my wife had said: *You shouldn't be opening other people's mail. It's against the law . . . You took an oath when you got that job . . . You promised to deliver the mail. Not to peek inside.*

And so, by the time my route was finished, all the mail had been delivered, and I hadn't peeked into a single envelope.

————

That night, as promised, my mother came over to celebrate my birthday. She was still remarkably spry and fit for somebody her age, somebody who was pushing sixty. She wore a red velour jogging suit, her gray hair recently dyed blond. She entered bearing gifts—a lot of gifts—as well as all the ingredients for her special pasta sauce. She gave Iris a long hug, called her "baby." The two of them were very close. In fact, there were times when I suspected that she loved Iris more than me. Not that I was resentful. Iris was easy to love. Me, maybe not as much.

Then she greeted me, placing both of her hands on my cheeks, as if to frame my face. I could smell her perfume: Chanel No. 5. "Oh, my sweet little boy," she said. "I promise I won't cry. But is it possible that you're all grown up?"

"It's possible," I said.

A big smile, full of what might have been joy. "But you'll always be my little boy. Even when you're my age, and I'm withering away. Still, my little boy."

"Yes, Mama."

"And what question am I going to ask next?"

"You're going to ask when we're going to have children."

And now I couldn't help but think about my father and how we used to play catch in the front yard, used to shoot baskets in the net-less hoop over Mr. McGregor's garage, used to go fishing in Holiday Lake, used to drive across town to the Dairy Queen for a vanilla cone. I missed him. And I knew my mother missed him too.

"And? Your answer?"

I glanced at Iris and then back at my mother. "Ask my wife," I said grinning. "She knows better than me."

Iris looked down, but she couldn't hide her reddening face. That was the thing about Iris. Whatever emotion she felt—anger, sadness, joy, shame—she wore for the world to see.

"Oh, Nina," she said (that was my mom's name). "Of course we want to have kids. And when the time is right, we will. Truth be told, I long for those days when I hear the little voices echoing against the walls, when I hear the patter of children's feet on the hardwood floor. And I can tell you this: Without question, without dispute, you'll make the world's number one grandma."

Now it was my mother's turn to show her emotions. She placed her hand against her chest, her eyelashes fluttering. "You think so?"

"I know so."

They hugged again. Both were sobbing tears of joy. And, truthfully, the whole scene would have been incredibly touching if it hadn't seemed like a scene straight from an afternoon soap opera.

———

My mother and wife cooked dinner and listened to Frank Sinatra—the same music my father used to listen to. I sat in the living room, watching the news. They were showing a feature story about a woman who collected

Barbie dolls. She had eighty-seven of them, to be exact, and they were on display on her mantel and table and cabinets and everywhere else in the house. She was grabbing the dolls one by one and discussing in alarming detail the history, social context, and personal meaning of each one. "I got my first one back in 1963," she said. "When I was only four. Who would have known that Barbie number one would turn into a lifetime pursuit?"

"And what does your husband think of your hobby?" the reporter asked off camera. "I mean, your entire house is filled with dolls. Does he get any say in the decorations?"

"Oh, he's very supportive. He understands that I don't collect them to try and impress or set some silly *Guinness Book* record. I only collect them to remember."

"Remember what?"

"My childhood. The way things used to be." Her expression changed to one of longing, and the tone of her voice changed to one of despondency. "It's so sad," she said, "the way the past disappears. And all that we're left with is souvenirs."

I didn't notice my mother standing behind me, watching.

"But what's wrong with souvenirs?" my mother said. "How else could we remember? How else could we be human?"

———

Soon, dinner was ready, and Iris called us to the table. At my place was a heaping bowl of pasta and, next to that, several presents wrapped in silver foil.

"You can open them while you eat," my mother said.

"Don't you think I'm a little old for this?"

"Yes, you most certainly are. But you've got a mother who likes traditions, and spoiling you has always been one of those traditions. Although, truth be told, I didn't buy you anything this year. Not a single thing."

"Then what's beneath the wrapping paper?"

My mother smiled, her teeth coated with lipstick. "Only memories," she said.

Memories. I was tiring of memories. Ever since the accident . . .

She had me open them in order. Each gift was a memento from the past, and each one had a note attached. The first gift was a brown baby bottle. And the note: *It seems like just yesterday you were a baby, tugging on your ear and sucking down formula. Boy, you were a big eater even then!* Gift number two was a Matchbox car (a red Corvette). And the note: *I can still picture you on your hands and knees pushing this car up and down the hallway, making zooming noises with your mouth.* Next, my old battered baseball glove. *You and your father used to toss the baseball for hour after hour. Big grins on your faces. Endless summer days.* And then an old Hardy Boys book: *The House on the Cliff.* And her note: *You de-voured these books. Every single one of them. You wanted to be a detective when you grew up. I'm proud of you for becoming a mail carrier instead.* And the last present, a rusted car key with an Oldsmobile insignia. And the note: *And there you were at sixteen years old, scaring your mother by making a beeline for my rusted Oldsmobile Cutlass.*

My mother: "I hope you like the presents. I gave them to you so you won't forget who you were."

"I won't forget, Mama," I said, my voice trembling. "Of course I won't forget."

———

After dinner and cake, Iris took care of the dishes and then excused her-self to her room. "I'm sorry," she said. "I just haven't been sleeping well. I can't help but feel worried about Hank all the time."

My mother smiled, said, "I understand." She gave her a long hug and whispered something in her ear. Iris kissed me on the forehead before leaving.

When she was out of earshot, my mother said, "She's a beautiful girl, that Iris. You did good, darling."

"I think so."

"We both did good." And even though she didn't say anything else, I could tell that she was thinking of Dad. I glanced down at my wrist, where I had a date tattooed in small red numbers: 10/23/11. The day he died.

We spent the rest of the evening laughing and talking about the old days. Nearing eleven o'clock, my mother finally gave one of those long sighs and rose to her feet. "Well, I suppose I should be going. Suppose I should let you get some sleep."

I nodded. "I suppose so."

We hugged, and my mother wiped tears from her cheek. "I love you so much, Henry. I don't think I've told you that enough. My only hope for you has always been that you'd be a good person. And you've become that. After the accident, I wasn't sure it . . . well, I worried that . . ." She forced a smile. "It doesn't matter. Good night, sweetheart."

"Good night, Mama."

I walked her out the door. I watched as she got in her car and drove away. The sky was dark and the moon was full.

———

It took me a long time to fall asleep that night, and when I did, my dreams were nonsensical and terrifying. Most of them I forgot upon waking, but one stayed with me. In the dream, I was running through a forest, and everything was silent. No sound of footsteps on the forest floor; no sound of my breathing; no sound of the wind through the thrashing branches. The rain was falling in sheets, and my hair was soaking wet. The air smelled like bubble gum and champagne. Up ahead, I could see a woman in a white dress, her silhouette illuminated by a string of lights wrapped around her body. She kept glancing back, her expression one of terror. And then she disappeared into the shadows of the trees. My running slowed to a jog and then a walk. Still no sounds, despite feeling the leaves crunching beneath my feet. I walked for what seemed to be forever until I came to an old stone well, surrounded by towering and angry trees. I circled around the well, and the rain stopped and so did the wind. I knew I had to look inside, but I was frightened of doing so. I touched the stone edge that surrounded the well, and it was cold to the touch. I leaned forward and peered down. All was darkness. But then there was a horrendous shriek that echoed against the walls. I stumbled away from the well and fell to the ground.

I woke up, body covered in sweat.

I looked next to me. Iris was sound asleep, her back turned to me, her shoulders rising and falling with every breath she took. Sighing deeply, I got out of bed and headed to the bathroom to pee. Then I went to the kitchen, flicked on the light, and poured myself a glass of water. I drank the water quickly and went to turn off the light.

And that's when I saw a face pressing against the window.

CHAPTER 3

I didn't scream. I didn't drop my glass, causing it to shatter. Instead, I just stood in the darkness, staring at the woman, visible from the moon and the streetlights. The moment was strange, but for some reason, I wasn't frightened at all. The woman looked to be in her twenties. She was Black, and her hair was wild. She wore maybe a half dozen silver bracelets on her wrist and a pair of thick collar necklaces around her neck.

She was wide-eyed and mouthing something that I couldn't decipher. I know it sounds crazy, I know it does, and maybe it was because my mind was still hazy from the nightmare or damaged from the accident, but instead of turning around and calling the cops, I reached out and unsnapped the latch. Then I pulled open the window.

The wind was blowing cold, the branches from a nearby tree swaying in slow motion. "Who are you?" I said. "What do you want?"

She pulled at her hair and then leaned forward so her face pressed against the screen. She was panting heavily, as if she'd been running, and when she spoke, I could smell gin on her breath. "My name is Veronica. Veronica Miller. You used to know me, but not anymore."

"Not anymore? I'm sorry, but—"

"I don't have time to tell you much," she said. "Your wife will be curious. She'll come to look for you."

"How do you know about my wife?"

"Here's what you need to know. Here's the most important thing. You can't trust them. They mean you harm. Do you understand? They mean you harm."

I glanced behind me to see if Iris was there. She wasn't. I turned back to the woman. "Who means me harm?"

"Your wife. Your mother. Dr. Hoover. Everybody."

"But why should—"

"I don't have time to talk. They'll find me. They'll find you. Here's what you need to do. Peel back the wallpaper. The truth is on the wall. Do you hear me? The truth is on the wall."

"The wallpaper? But why would—"

"My address is 328 Maple Street. When you want to talk. Don't forget. And until then . . . be careful. Otherwise . . ."

She didn't finish her thought.

Before I had the chance to ask any more questions, she was gone, disappeared into the darkness. I could hear her jewelry jangling for a few moments, and then it was quiet.

I stayed in the kitchen for a few minutes, taking deep breaths, scratching at my face, trying to make sense of what she'd just said. But no sense could be made. I left the kitchen and returned to the bedroom.

Not wanting to wake Iris, I quietly maneuvered under the covers, but Iris must have already been awake. She said, "Where were you, darling?"

I folded my hands behind my head and gnawed at my lower lip. "I went to the bathroom. And then to the kitchen for a glass of water."

She turned toward me, head resting on her open palm. "A glass of water? Is that all?"

"Yes," I said. "That's all."

"Funny. I thought I heard voices."

"No," I said. "I turned on the radio. Listened to a couple of songs."

She continued watching me. I thought of what the woman had said. *They mean you harm.* I closed my eyes, trying to fall back asleep. And I had just begun to drift away when Iris's voice caused me to snap awake. She said, "This time, you won't forget."

Outside, the flash of lightning, the groan of thunder. "Forget what?" I whispered.

But she didn't answer, and when I looked at her, her eyes were closed and she was snoring softly.

I lay there for a long time, thinking of the woman and what she'd said. From the light of the moon, I gazed at our quilt, blue-and-white diamonds folded over each other; and then at the ceiling, rust streaks across the eggshell white paint; and finally at the wall, the shadows of sycamore branches swaying slowly.

And then I noticed something. Where wall met ceiling, the wallpaper, blue flowers on a dull yellow background, was beginning to peel, and beneath the wallpaper I could see what looked like letters. My eyes narrowed to slits, and I leaned forward in bed. The longer I stared at the wilting wallpaper, the surer I was that there was something written beneath. *The truth*, she'd said, *is on the wall*.

————

Over the next few days, Iris never left me alone, not for more than a few minutes, so there was no chance for me to return to the wallpaper, to yank it down and see what was beneath. Even if I was in the bathroom for more than a few minutes, Iris would knock on the door and ask if I was all right, ask if I needed Dr. Hoover to check up on me. At nighttime, I would try to stay awake until she fell asleep, but as soon as I tried maneuvering out of bed, her eyes would fly open, and she would say, "Darling, is everything okay? Did you have another bad dream?"

(I'd been having nightmares ever since the accident. Almost every single night.)

"Yes. Another one."

"Then come back to bed. I'll hold you tight. I'll squeeze away your nightmares."

And so I returned to bed. And she squeezed me tight.

But the nightmares remained. The nightmares got worse.

———

And then, one morning, on my day off, my big break.

We had just finished breakfast when I noticed that Iris's eyes were filling with tears. I asked her what was wrong. "My father," she said, "is not doing well. His angina is getting really bad."

"I . . . I'm sorry to hear that."

It occurred to me that I didn't even know her father had heart issues, but I wasn't about to admit that.

"I'm going to need to go visit him this afternoon."

"That's kind of you," I said.

"Only I hate to leave you alone. Considering everything."

I shook my head. "It's not a problem. I'm a big boy. I can take care of myself. So you don't want me to come with you then?"

She answered quickly. "Absolutely not. I know how you hate being in that creepy old house. There's too much bad history there. No, you stay here. I'll eat dinner with my father, check up on him, but, if all goes according to plan, I should be home by ten."

"Okay," I said. "It's nice of you to take care of your sick father. I'll manage by myself."

We hugged. "Thank you, darling. I'm going to make dinner for you in the Crock-Pot. Pork chops. All you have to do is take them out of the pot. I'll prepare a salad for you, as well. You need to eat your greens. That's what Dr. Hoover said. But"—and now she whispered—"I've also left a piece of cake for you."

"You treat me too well, Iris."

———

Iris left shortly before four o'clock. As she walked out the door, she reminded me that Dr. Hoover was available if I ran into any difficulties.

I told her that I wouldn't be having any difficulties, that I was fine, absolutely fine. After she left and got into her car, I stood in front of the window, as still as an idol, gazing at the cloudless sky, making sure she didn't return.

Once I was satisfied that she was really gone, I closed the blinds on the windows. For some time, I paced around the house, trying to get up the nerve to go to the bedroom. What was I so terrified about?

Finally, after an hour or more, I entered the bedroom and stared at the wallpaper, which was still wilted at the corner. In the afternoon sunlight, the wallpaper seemed a duller blue and yellow, sickly even. I took a deep breath, grabbed Iris's wooden chair, and placed it against the wall. From outside, I could hear the sound of a piano, the same note being played over and over again. I could hear a dog howling. I could hear a child screaming. I stood on the chair, reached toward the corner of the wallpaper, and gave it a tug. It gave easily. I continued unpeeling the wallpaper, an inch at a time, careful not to tear it. Then I stopped. The breath was sucked from my lungs. Stapled to the top corner of the wall was a piece of lined paper, ripped from a notebook. On the paper was handwriting so tiny to be barely legible. The writing started at the top and went all the way to the bottom. "The truth," I muttered to the emptiness. Feeling a coldness rise up inside of me, I continued pulling back the wallpaper, and I saw another page and then another and another still. I heard more shrieking, but this wasn't from the kid outside; this was from inside my skull. My hands were trembling and were barely under my control. For ten, twenty minutes, I pulled back the wallpaper until it toppled completely to the ground. I took several steps back. I rubbed my eyes, mumbled, "Jesus."

The entire wall was covered with lined paper, and each piece was filled from top to bottom with the same minuscule, maniacal scrawl. Each of the pages had a single number at the bottom, like a book. There were exactly a hundred pages in all, each of them secured by a pair of staples.

The sun had faded and the room had darkened. I began the painstaking work of removing each of the pages, while from outside, that single piano note played over and over again.

Once my task was finally completed, I sat cross-legged in the middle of the room with the stack of papers directly in front of me. Shoulders heaving, heart pounding, I picked up the first page and began reading.

It was the strangest thing.

The handwriting wasn't mine. But I worried that the words might have been.

PART 2

WALTER "WALLY" DALEY

CHAPTER 4

Mailbag slung over my shoulder, sun helmet tipped back on my head, I walked slowly down the empty and sun-bleached streets of Bethlam, Nevada, and I couldn't help but feel uneasy, couldn't help thinking *those* thoughts. All around me were rows and rows of pretty houses with pretty lawns and pretty decorations, but still, there was something menacing about it all, as if the town's caretakers were busy gathering and hiding secrets, burying them beneath the red dirt.

Every day, the same mailboxes outside the same houses. The Browns, the McCabes, the Thompsons, the Ellisons. Sometimes a little boy would appear in the distance bouncing a red ball and laughing, and sometimes a couple would pass, walking hand in hand and smiling, and sometimes an old model Ford would drive down the street, windows cracked, radio playing the faint melody of another time. But most of the time, Bethlam, Nevada, was quiet. Most of the time it was empty.

I'd been delivering mail on this same route for a few months more than five years. Had it really been that long? In a lot of ways, the five years all seemed like one long day. I guess that's what happens when we live a life of routines. Each day becomes inextricable from the others. Five years becomes no different from ten, no different from twenty, no different than a lifetime.

But on this day, something different *did* happen. Something strange and unusual and unsettling.

I was walking down Spruce Street, humming some nameless melody, thinking about days gone by, when I stumbled over a branch that had fallen from a nearby tree. I managed to keep my balance, but in that momentary anticipation of contact with the cement, my hand opened and several pieces of mail fluttered to the ground. Cursing gently, I got down on my hands and knees and worked to gather the scattered mail. But among the fallen envelopes, I noticed that one—addressed to Dolly Harvey—had become unsealed, the folded letter jutting out from the corner. The address was written in lovely looped cursive, and below the address was an intricate rose, colored red.

I glanced around and, seeing that nobody was around, began to extract the piece of paper from the envelope. But I never got the paper out. Because that's when I heard somebody screaming.

It was coming from just up the block. Not a scream of delight. Not a scream of surprise. A scream of terror. For several moments, I didn't move; it was as if I were completely paralyzed. Eventually, I managed to pull a leg forward. And then another. I glanced around. The world, as always, was empty.

Better to ignore the sound, I thought. After all, it's a mailman's job to deliver mail, not to patrol the neighborhood. And, besides, I had never been known for my courage. But after a short respite, the shrieking continued, and it somehow sounded even more desperate, even more blood-curdling. Maybe it was instinct, maybe something else, but the next thing I knew, I was walking—and then running—toward the direction of the sound.

When I arrived at the corner of Elm and Third, I saw what the commotion was about. A woman—fifties, heavyset, blond bouffant, wearing an apron—was pacing back and forth across the porch of her house. In her left hand she held a Barbie doll. In her right hand, a paring knife. She was ranting and raving, screaming and screeching. Occasionally, she'd stop and place the knife to her throat, threatening to kill herself. "I've paid the price!" she said. A man (her husband?) stood just inside the doorframe of the house, his arms crossed, a bemused expression on his ragged face. I could see that she'd already nicked herself, a spot of red on her throat, another on the stainless steel.

Several people from neighboring houses had filtered onto yards and sidewalks to see what was happening. In an act of shyness or cowardice, I ducked behind a nearby bush and hid. I could see and hear what was happening, but none of them could see or hear me.

One of the neighbors—a heavily tanned man wearing khaki shorts and a polo shirt—called out, "Easy now, Mrs. Gordon. Put down the knife. Don't do anything stupid."

A moment later, Larry Hartwick, a man that I knew, a man with whom I'd attended barbecues, said, "We understand that you're frustrated. Hell, life is frustrating. But there's no need to do anything rash. No need to hurt yourself. You've got a lot to live for. We all do."

"Please," her husband said with saccharine sincerity. "Catherine. You know how much I love you. Please."

But Catherine Gordon kept pacing back and forth, occasionally letting loose with another shriek, occasionally pressing the knife against her throat. Her eyes were like fish in a tank, darting from one side to the other. Her pacing went on for several more minutes, but then, suddenly, she stopped. Her body seemed to relax. The Barbie doll dropped from her hand, but the knife remained. She turned toward her husband for a long moment and then back to her neighbors. Her eyes squeezed shut and her jaw fell slack. It was as if she were in a play. The porch was her stage, the neighbors her audience. They waited with bated breath for her monologue. When she finally spoke, I had to strain to hear her. "It's this town," she said. "This goddamn town."

Her eyes fluttered back open. She didn't say anything else. The monologue was short.

"Yes," a young woman in a flower dress said. "We understand. Of course we do. There are certain pressures that come with living here."

Mr. Gordon took a step forward. Was he going to try and grab the knife from her hand? No. He stuffed his hands in his pockets. He was nothing but a bystander.

Catherine Gordon continued talking. "I'm not sure what's real. Not sure what's fake. Sometimes I wonder if I'm the only one who really exists. If you're all just figments of my imagination."

"It can feel that way," the young woman said. "To all of us."

And now the neighbors, without any kind of observable signal, started moving slowly forward en masse. Mrs. Gordon didn't seem fazed, or maybe she didn't notice. She gripped the knife tighter. Her husband remained where he was.

"What you should know," she said, "is that I've been doing some investigating on my own. And I've figured some things out."

"Yes?" said the man wearing the polo shirt. "And what have you figured out?"

Mrs. Gordon laughed, and it was a desperate laugh. "All sorts of stuff. About my brain. About my husband. About you."

Larry Hartwick said, "What about your brain, Mrs. Gordon? What about your husband? What about me?"

"You think I'm going to tell you? No, no, no. I'm not stupid. I'm not—"

"Now, Mrs. Gordon—"

Her voice was getting louder and more frantic. "It's been going on for some time. Years maybe. Decades perhaps. The purposeful manipulation of my brain. Microchips being placed beneath my skin. The very water I'm drinking—poisoned." She turned toward her husband. "And him. Not even my real husband. A fraud." Another desperate laugh. She again faced her audience. "But he's only an agent. Only my caretaker. Dr. Zagorsky is the one who's behind this. He's behind all of this."

The neighbors continued moving closer. "Poor, poor woman," one of them said. "You're not well. We can help you. If you'd just give us a chance."

"No. Nobody can help me. It's too late for all that."

"Darling," Mr. Gordon said. "Put the knife down. Please."

For a second it looked like she might. Her fingers seemed to relax. She began to sob. "It's not fair," she said. "None of this is fair."

What happened next was confusing. The mad woman jerked the knife upward, sliced the flesh of her throat. A long pause, and she dropped the knife, fell to her knees, the Barbie doll directly in front of her. She placed her hand to her throat, and blood began soaking through her fingers. Soon her whole arm was covered in blood. "Oh, Lord," she said. "Look what you've done. You killed me! Each and every one of you."

I should have rushed to her side. I should have. But I couldn't convince my body to move, so I remained where I was. There was a commotion of screams and moans and chatter. And then, moments later, the neighbors were upon her. A large man, his stomach hanging below his belt, the sweat bubbling on his forehead, got to her first. He placed his hands beneath the crazy woman and picked her up like she was some rag doll. "Don't let her die!" somebody shouted. "She's too important to the cause!"

The fat man carried her in his arms, moving off the porch and toward the sidewalk. The way she was bleeding, the breath rattling in her throat, I feared that she didn't have much time left. A few of the neighbors followed the fat man. Two others comforted Mr. Gordon. They spoke to him for a minute or two, but I couldn't hear what they were saying. He was shaking his head, muttering under his breath. He seemed more annoyed than terrified. After a few minutes, he picked up the doll and went back inside. Wasn't he concerned about his wife? Didn't he want to accompany her?

The fat man holding Mrs. Gordon staggered down the sidewalk and across the street. A minute or two and he disappeared around a bend, gone from view. There were no sirens, no kaleidoscope flashes from emergency vehicles. I turned my attention to the rest of the neighbors. They were murmuring to each other and shaking their heads, and then, after a few minutes, they returned to the tombs from which they'd come.

As for me, I could barely breathe.

I waited a long time, until everybody was gone, before finally coming out of my hiding place. I wiped off my pants and my shirt. I readjusted my mailbag, my sun helmet.

And then, not sure what else to do, I continued with my route, a sense of uneasiness rising as if I'd lost something very important—or maybe had never had it in the first place.

CHAPTER 5

An hour later, I arrived home.

I lived with my father, my poor father, in a modest, three-bedroom, one-bath bungalow over on Sixth and Mapleton. I'd lived there my whole life. My parents had bought the house for $2,900 back in the early 1960s. How did they get it so cheap? Well, from what they told me, the town of Bethlam had originally been built as a community for the scientists and engineers who were in charge of testing nuclear weapons in the Nevada desert. A company town, really. For a while, it even became something of a tourist destination: people from as far away as Los Angeles came to view the beautiful mushroom clouds, and the town once even held a pageant to crown "Miss Atomic Bomb." Once the testing ended—and the radiation pollution was cleaned up—the government offered up the now vacant houses for cheap. My parents got the hell out of Detroit and moved west.

Bethlam was still a small town, population barely five hundred. Surrounded by red dirt and yucca and sagebrush, it really was in the middle of nowhere. But that isolation wasn't necessarily a bad thing. It forced us to do things the right way. "The safest town in Nye County," my mother had been fond of saying. And she'd been right. Other than a few kids getting drunk and maybe spray-painting the walls of the high school, or the occasional domestic dispute, there was no crime in Bethlam, certainly no violent crime. In fact, there hadn't been a murder in more than a decade, and even that had been done by an outsider, a man named Clyde Ellison, who had killed a waitress after a long night of drinking.

A white picket fence surrounded our neatly trimmed front lawn. On the porch there was a swing, and that was where I'd snuck my first kiss with Amy Harper, a sweet girl with red pigtails and freckles. I wondered what had become of Amy Harper. By now, she was probably married with kids. That's what happens with people. But not me. I lived with my father. Helped him with his illness.

I clicked open the front gate and walked down the path. My neighbor, Mr. Downing, paused from pruning his shrubs to wave at me and say, "Why, hello there, Wally! Beautiful afternoon, isn't it?"

I thought of the woman, Mrs. Gordon, pressing the knife against her own throat, thought of her grasping at the wound, blood seeping through her fingers. And then I thought of her fat neighbor scurrying away with her body.

"Yes," I agreed. "Beautiful."

I pushed open the front door and stepped inside. From down the hallway, I could hear the faint echo of a laugh track. I removed my sun helmet and placed it inside my mailbag, which I left by the door. Then I wandered toward the living room. The television was on, but nobody was there to watch it. It was an old rerun of *M*A*S*H*. For whatever reason, my father loved the show, and it was often on. In this episode, Hawkeye was angry that he was getting liver and fish for the eleventh straight day. "Fish! Liver! Day after day! I've eaten a river of liver and an ocean of fish!" I watched for a few minutes and then turned it off. TV always depressed me. Especially *M*A*S*H*.

Sighing deeply, I started walking slowly through the house, peering in each room, searching for my father, worried that he'd wandered off somewhere like he'd done a few weeks back (he'd ended up by the high school, meandering across the baseball field, mumbling about Mickey Mantle and Don Drysdale and Willie Mays). I made my way to the back of the house, the wood creaking beneath my white shoes. When I reached my father's bedroom, I could hear his voice coming from behind the door. "Now, Beula," he was saying. "You know how I feel about ballet.

I can't stand it. All those anorexic girls prancing on their toes. All those fruitcakes with extra padding on their crotches. Now rock 'n' roll music, that's what I like. Give me some Elvis Presley. Give me some Buddy Holly. Give me some Big Bopper."

I felt that old familiar dread. I twisted the handle and pushed open the door. As usual, my father was sitting on his bed. He was still in his pajamas. I could see his skinny, hairless calves, the varicose veins resembling rivers on a map. I felt bad that I hadn't been more forceful in getting him dressed, but I had my own life to worry about. His gray hair was disheveled, and his face was unshaven. On his lap was an old copy of *Life* magazine with a smiling Dick Cavett on the cover. "Dick Cavett: Offstage with the brightest face on screen." He'd looked through that magazine a thousand times at least. There was nothing significant inside, at least not that I could tell. But darn it, if he didn't love that magazine. In his right hand, he was gripping a soup spoon. He must have used it when he ate lunch and forgot to stick it in the sink. When he saw me, he grinned that moronic grin and said, "Hello, sir. Can I help you?"

It was the same routine. When this had first started, I thought it was all an act. Sure, he'd been becoming more and more forgetful and mixed up, but the idea that he'd forget who his own son was—*that* I had a hard time believing. Dr. Hoover, however, assured me that it was no act and that it was good that I was around to help him. "You're lucky," Dr. Hoover had said one morning after evaluating the old man. "He doesn't seem to be struggling all that profoundly. He doesn't get angry. Doesn't get depressed. He just doesn't remember. It's not the worst thing to live in a haze, you know?"

Maybe he was right.

"Dad," I said, forcing a grin. "It's me. Wally. Wally Daley. Your son. Don't you remember me?"

"Wally?" he said, although his eyes didn't reveal recognition.

"Yes. How are you feeling?"

He nodded his head. "I'm feeling just fine. I was having a conversation with my wife, Beula. She wants me to go see *The Nutcracker*. I told her that I don't like ballet. I don't like it at all."

"Easy, Dad," I said.

I sat down on the edge of the bed and stared at the walls, all lined with photographs. Souvenirs of a different time. There I was, as a child, riding a horse in Colorado. And there was my mother in the passenger seat of our old Chrysler, a red scarf in her hair. My mother. My gaze shifted to my wrist, at the date that was tattooed there in red ink: 10/23/11. The day she died. I waited for the feeling of unease to pass . . .

"The good news," I said, "is that Christmas, and therefore *The Nutcracker*, isn't for another six months. So you've got some time."

"Yeah, well. The goddamn Rat King scares me. What do you think, son? Does the Rat King scare you?"

"A little. Yes."

After that, neither of us talked for a while. He opened his favorite magazine and flipped through the pages. He stopped at a review for a movie called *I Never Sang for My Father*. He said, "They gave it four stars. Could be a movie the two of us could go to, huh? What do you say? A father/son evening? Grab some dinner at Lucille's?"

I sighed and shook my head. "I don't think that movie is playing anymore. Not since 1970. And Lucille's shut down nearly a decade ago."

He looked disappointed. He closed the magazine. "That's too bad. Maybe another time."

"Yes. Maybe another time."

He began to rise out of his chair, but it seemed to be too much effort for him, so he sat down again. "And how was your day, son? What did you say you do for a living?"

"My day was fine. I'm a postal worker."

"That's a fine job. Necessary in these times. You know, my son was a postal worker."

His brain was scrambled. "That's interesting."

"And did you get all the mail delivered?"

"Yes," I said. "I did." I was going to tell him about the woman, about Mrs. Gordon, but I decided not to. What was the point? He'd been a dentist, my father. Now I had to remind him to brush his teeth. I rose to my feet and began straightening up his room. Throwing away wrappers from the lollipops that he was so fond of. Picking up dirty clothes off the floor. Making his bed.

When I was done, I looked at him and smiled. "Okay, Dad. I'm going to work on dinner. I suppose we'll have breaded chicken tonight. Canned pears. I figure we'll eat in about an hour. How does that sound?"

He nodded his head. "That sounds good. A postal worker, huh?"

"Yes." I started toward the door. But then my father called out.

"Son?" he said.

I turned around. "Yes?"

"Tell me about Beula. Tell me about my wife."

He asked these questions a lot. Dr. Hoover thought it was a good thing. A way of reassuring him.

I leaned against the wall. "What do you want to know?"

"I . . . I want to know what her laugh sounded like."

"Her laugh?"

"Yes." And for a moment, my father sounded almost lucid.

What you should know is that I had the opposite problem of my father. I remembered most everything—and with such vividness and detail that it was like it took place only yesterday. "*A form of hyperthymesia*," Dr. Hoover had once told me.

I squeezed my eyes shut and got to visualizing her. Then I opened my eyes and nodded my head. "Her laughter was slow, like a meandering river. Her laughter was warm, like a mountain campfire."

"That's good, son," he said. "Tell me more."

"Sure, Dad. It seemed that she was always laughing. Not because she thought the world was particularly amusing. But because she thought the world was good."

"Tell me more. Did she love you? Is that what happened? Did your mother love you?"

I could feel the tears welling in my eyes. A memory formed of her standing in the kitchen, humming a tune, while I sat on my father's lap at the table. He was doing a crossword puzzle; she was baking. I could smell cinnamon rolls from the oven. I remembered her walking across the kitchen and kissing my father on the head, me on the cheek. And then I remembered her saying, "I love the both of you. More than it's possible to love anybody."

"Yes," I said, nodding my head. "She loved me. She loved the both of us."

A dreamy look came over my father's face. "Thank you, son," he said. "Thank you for telling me about Beula."

I wiped the tears from my eyes. "You're welcome, Dad. Dinner will be in about an hour."

I looked at my tattoo again, felt those competing forces of love and regret. Then I left his room.

———

I walked slowly toward the living room, my thoughts drifting away from my past and toward the trauma of what I'd seen that afternoon. Even though it had only been a couple of hours earlier, it almost seemed like a dream. I turned on the television. I wanted to see if there was anything on the news about Mrs. Gordon. I wanted to see if she'd survived. I flipped through the local stations. Channel two was showing a rerun of *I Love Lucy*. Channel four was showing *Wheel of Fortune*. Channel seven was showing the news. I sat down on the couch. There was a story about a girl competing in the Special Olympics. And then the weather forecast. And then the sports scores. Nothing about an attempted suicide. Nothing at all.

Maybe I'd missed it. Maybe it would be in the newspapers tomorrow.

I flipped off the television. I went into the kitchen and turned on the oven, an old aqua Frigidaire. I grabbed a package of chicken breasts from the refrigerator and a box of breadcrumbs from the cabinet. Then I went to the counter and worked on wetting and coating the chicken. Above the sink, a large window overlooked our front lawn. When they'd built the houses, I guess they'd envisioned a mother being able to watch her children play in the front yard while she cooked dinner. I didn't have any children. But I did have neighbors. And I could see a couple of them—Mr. and Mrs. Gibson—standing on the sidewalk, staring right at me. As soon as I made eye contact with them, they quickly looked away. I'd been noticing that a lot lately. Neighbors watching my house. For what? There was noth-ing to see. I was just a postal worker taking care of his amnesiac father.

I finished prepping the chicken. I laid the pieces on a baking sheet and placed the sheet in the oven. Then I poured myself a glass of choc-olate milk, added a single ice cube, and sat at the kitchen table. I kept reliving the scene from Elm and Third. Remembering her slicing through her own flesh. Remembering her catching the blood in her hand. But also remembering the things she'd said.

It's been going on for some time . . . The purposeful manipulation of my brain. Microchips being placed beneath my skin. The very water I'm drinking . . . Nobody can help me . . . It's too late for all that.

And then I remembered the name she'd mentioned. Zagorsky. I said it out loud. Where had I heard that name before?

I drank more chocolate milk. I glanced out the window. Another person watching me. A tall woman with a pixie cut. As soon as I rose from my seat, she scurried away.

"Fuckers," I mumbled. Then I sat back down.

Where had the fat man been carrying Mrs. Gordon away to? Why not just call an ambulance? And then another detail I remembered. A man pleading not to let her die. Shouting, *She's too important to the cause!*

It was all so strange.

I finished my chocolate milk and returned to the oven. As I opened it to check the chicken, I heard footsteps behind me. I turned around. My father stood in the entrance of the kitchen, looking confused. "Where's Beula?" he said. "I hope she doesn't miss dinner again."

I nodded. "Don't worry, Dad. She'll be home before you know it."

CHAPTER 6

The next day was a Sunday, so I decided to take my father to church. Neither of us were particularly religious, but we used to get all dressed up and go with Mom every Sunday, and Dr. Hoover said it was a good idea to continue these traditions. He said, "The more of those old routines you can stick with, the better it will be for your father's mental health. Hearing familiar prayers. Seeing familiar faces. Those kinds of things can only help."

And, if I'm being completely honest, those routines helped me as well. Grounded me in some way.

Of course, getting him out of the house was never an easy task. But, with a Herculean effort, I was able to get him fed (oatmeal and berries), dressed (no suit, but ironed pants and shirt), teeth brushed, and hair combed. Answering his question about where we were going at least a half dozen times, I was finally able to drag him out of the house. We walked through the neighborhoods toward Main Street, the sun rising above the hazy silhouette of the distant Sierra Nevada Mountains. For most of the walk, my father was quiet, but occasionally he would speak and, often, it was without context. He talked about Steve McQueen and Bobby Kennedy and the cost of eggs and my childhood dog, a corgi named Champ.

And the whole time he spoke, my head throbbed. These headaches had been occurring more and more frequently. I gritted my teeth and closed my eyes. When I opened them, I could see the church up ahead.

"I don't feel so good," I whispered. "Something's wrong with me."

"Champ was a good dog," my father said. "Except when he shit on the floor. He did that a lot."

———

By the time we arrived at the church, the pain in my skull had begun to dissipate. My old man was on his best behavior, nodding and smiling at the churchgoers, all dressed in their nicest Sunday clothes. Some of them came and talked to us, said it was a beautiful morning and they were so glad that we were here, but I couldn't help noticing how they regarded us with a sort of curious condescension.

And then there was this one woman. Her face was pale, and she wore a pastel-colored dress and costume pearls. I was sure that I recognized her, but I couldn't quite figure out from where. Had I seen her outside of Mrs. Gordon's house? Was she one of the witnesses to that blood-slicked porch? She shook my hand daintily and smiled. She had lipstick smeared on one of her front teeth. "Why, hello, Mr. Daley," she said to my father. "And hello, Wally. How is everything going?"

"Things are going fine," I said.

My father stared at her, eyes narrowing into the shape of coin slots. "Do I know you?"

"Why certainly! I'm Joyce. I used to play bridge with Beula."

An image flashed in my head. Of my mother and Joyce sitting at the dining room table, drinking wine and playing cards. And the smell of chocolate cake. And the sound of Frank Sinatra singing about it being a very good year. I remembered.

"Yes," my dad said. "Bridge with Beula. Of course."

"And how are you handling things, Wally? You must miss your mother something terrible."

Despite the fact I knew she was being disingenuous, I answered with full sincerity. "I do," I said, falling back into my nostalgic state. "When I was a child, she used to read me stories in bed. Sometimes she'd fall asleep right there next to me. On cold days, when the snow would fall, she'd make hot chocolate with marshmallows in it."

"Snow? Here in Bethlam?"

"And in the autumn, the leaves would fall, and they'd crunch beneath my feet. My father would rake the leaves into a pile. And then my mother and I would jump into the leaves and laugh and laugh."

The woman, Joyce, smiled, and now there was lipstick on her other front tooth, as well. "That's wonderful, Wally. And what else can you tell me?"

"She bought me a dog when I was eight. We named him Champ."

"Yes. Champ. I remember him. A corgi. What a wonderful little dog. What a wonderful mother. What a wonderful childhood!" She winked at my father, and I swear to God that he winked back.

The service was about to start, and people were milling into the church, a little wooden structure with an oversized cross on the steeple. And it was then that a large man came to where Joyce was standing and put his arm around her. It must have been her husband.

"Well, hello there, Wally," he said. "Hi, Mr. Daley."

It took me a moment to place him, but then I did. The man who'd carried Mrs. Gordon's body from her house. And his wife—she *had* been there, too. I remembered the agonized expression on Mrs. Gordon's face, the blood seeping through her fingers.

"Mrs. Gordon," I said under my breath.

"Excuse me?"

"Mrs. Gordon. How is she?"

But he only shook his head. "I'm not sure I know what you're talking about."

"Catherine Gordon. Your neighbor."

Joyce looked at her husband and then back at me. "Yes. Of course. Catherine is fine. Why do you ask?"

I could feel another crack of pain in my skull. "Well . . . it's only be-cause . . . yesterday. She didn't seem to be doing well. She had a knife.

She slit her own throat. I saw her do it. Witnessed it with my own eyes. And you, sir, were the one who carried her away."

For a long moment, there was silence. Neither Joyce nor her husband responded to my accusation. It was my father who finally spoke.

"I remember raking those leaves," he said. "I remember you jumping in them. I remember those fireplaces. I remember those hot chocolates."

Another long pause. Joyce and her husband were both looking me up and down, as if I were some science project. "Well," Joyce said, nodding at the people filing through the door. "I guess it's time to go inside."

"Yes," her husband said. "I guess it is. Very nice talking to the both of you."

It was as if they hadn't heard a word I'd said.

———

The service was long. The service was boring. The pastor—a white-haired and white-bearded fellow who looked like God himself—read from the Old and New Testament both. He delivered a sermon about loving thy poor and thy stranger. He even sang, though his voice was ragged and flat. And throughout the service not a single mention of poor Catherine Gordon. Not a single mention of the scourge of suicide. Even when he asked people to call out names of those who needed support and prayer, not a single mention of Catherine.

My father enjoyed the service, though. That is, he at least kept his shit-eating grin. When the pastor said, "The Lord be with you," my father responded with the rest of the congregation: "And also with you."

When the pastor said, "Lift up your hearts," my father said, "We lift them to the Lord."

And then Holy Communion, which my father took, eyes squeezed shut in pleasure, and which I refused, owing to my general cynicism or nihilism.

By the time the service was over, I was good and agitated, wiping the sweat from my brow and the red from my eyes. I just wanted to get the hell out of there, so I grabbed my father by the arm and led him toward the heavy door in the back. Joyce and her husband watched us leave, and so did the pastor.

I wondered about Mrs. Gordon and if the blood had dried on their collective hands yet.

———

My father and I stopped at Sweeney's for ice cream and then headed home with our cones in our hands. We'd only made it about two blocks when my father's ice cream fell off the cone and landed on the pavement. He stopped walking and stared at the quickly melting ice cream in bewilderment. I stood next to him, nodding my head. Pretty soon, a bunch of ants were swimming in the vanilla goo. "There's nothing we can do," I said.

"Nope," he said. "That ice cream's gone. I'm never getting it back."

And he sounded so sad, as if this was an existential crisis.

I offered him the rest of mine, but he said he didn't like chocolate, never had.

When we arrived home, the old man was exhausted. I walked him into his room and helped him out of his church clothes and into his pajamas. He lay on the bed and crossed his hands on his chest. He looked at me, blinking, and he looked so old and frail and pathetic. "I thank you, son," he said, and I was relieved he still knew who I was. "What time will Beula be home, do you think?"

I nodded my head slowly. "Not until later. Not until much later."

Ten seconds later, he was asleep.

CHAPTER 7

Over the next several days, I did my best to go about my daily routines because routines were comforting. In the morning, after showering and shaving, I would get dressed in my postal uniform—those white tennis shoes, khaki shorts, baby-blue shirt, white sun helmet—and then I would go downstairs and make a hot breakfast—bacon, eggs, toast, coffee—for Dad and me. We would sit there eating, and he would ramble about Beula and Dean Martin and Mickey Mantle. At 8:27 (or thereabouts), I would begin my walk toward the post office, a single-story white stucco building with an American flag pasted to the side. There, my boss, Mr. Temeer, eyebrows like caterpillars, lips like cased sausages, would be waiting for me with three cartons of mail, always three cartons, which I would sort by name and address and then place in my bag. I would wave goodbye to Mr. Temeer and Ms. Yeats (postal clerk) and Ms. Keaton (processing clerk) and begin my route, walking down the cracked sidewalks, humming some forgotten tune, sticking piles of mail and magazines in each mailbox. During the hours of my route, I saw several people doing yard work or walking down the sidewalks. Most of them I didn't know, but they all seemed to know me, crooked smiles on their faces, crooked thoughts in their brains. I also noticed people inside their houses, watching me from the gaps in the heavy curtains. That's what they were doing, wasn't it? Watching me? And I couldn't for the life of me figure out why.

I was just an ordinary man living an ordinary life. Nothing to see here. Nothing of interest.

And each time I would arrive at Third and Elm I would stop for a moment and stare at the Gordons' house, and the blinds were always closed, and there was never any sign of life, and I would feel that throbbing at the base of my skull. Then I'd look at my own hands and think of what Mrs. Gordon had said: *I'm not sure what's real. Not sure what's fake. Sometimes I wonder if I'm the only one who really exists.* And I couldn't help but shiver.

Move ahead to Thursday, late in the afternoon, as the cruel Nevada sun blistered my pale skin. Once again, I found myself frozen on the sidewalk, staring at the house in question. That was when, out of the corner of my eye, I saw Larry Hartwick exit from the house next door. Larry was the fellow I'd attended that barbecue with (we'd talked about lawn fertilizers), and he'd also been one of the witnesses to Catherine's madness. I was sure of it. When he spotted me, he nodded and quickly walked across the lawn. He stuck out his smooth, beefy hand, but I didn't shake it. "Hey there, Wally," he said in a voice just cheerful enough to make me distressed. "How's life?"

I shrugged. "Oh, about the same as always. Can't complain, I guess."

"And how's your father doing? I heard he's been having some difficulties."

I didn't want to talk to Larry, but I didn't feel like I could leave. "He's okay," I said. "He's doing better at remembering. It'll just take some time, the doctor said."

A big smile. Big white teeth. "That's great to hear. Wonderful. And, not that you asked, but things are going pretty dang well for us, too. You remember my wife, Darlene? Sure you do. She always liked you. Well, she's teaching kindergarten now. It's a lot of work, but she absolutely loves it. Meanwhile, our own kids are growing like weeds. Billy is eight. Can you believe it? Collects baseball cards. Just got a Rod Carew rookie. Sara is six. A budding ballerina. Ask her to do a plié one of these days. In any case, I hope we can catch up at the next barbecue. I can almost smell the burgers now. I like mine with onions and jalapeños. Ketchup and mustard both."

"That would be swell," I said.

His smile faded, and there was a long pause where neither of us spoke. Larry took a peek in both directions and then leaned in nice and close to where I could smell the salami and cheese on his breath. "Been a lot of strange rumors floating around," he whispered.

"What kind of rumors?" I said.

"About Mr. and Mrs. Gordon."

"I wouldn't know."

"About Mrs. Gordon being dead."

"Dead? That's strange."

He laughed. "Isn't it? Pure silliness. Can you imagine? Why, they're in their house right now. Mr. and Mrs. Gordon both."

I didn't believe him. "Is that right?"

"Sure. Do you want to see for yourself?"

I looked at the house and then back at him. I could feel the faint remains of my headache. "Yes," I said, without really thinking. "I'd like that. I'd like to talk to Catherine Gordon."

I think I caught him by surprise. He stammered at bit. "W . . . well, that would be just splendid. Why don't we go and knock on their door?"

"Yes," I said. "Why don't we?"

And so there we were, and everything was calm and still and antiseptic, the opposite of the chaotic scene that had taken place a few days previous. Still, sweat was dribbling from my forehead into my eyes, causing them to sting. I took a deep breath and started across the yellowed lawn toward the front porch. A moment later, I could hear Larry's shoes crunching behind me.

I climbed up the wooden steps and across the porch. I was about to knock on the door when I stopped, my hand dropping to my side. "What's the matter?" Larry said.

I shook my head. "Nothing's the matter." Then I faced him: "Don't tell me what I saw. She slit her own throat. I saw it with my own two eyes." His mouth curled into a slight smile, and he shrugged his shoulders patronizingly. I turned back to the door, took a deep breath, and knocked.

Time passed. Nothing. I took a step back. Then I could hear footsteps echoing from inside. The door opened a crack and I saw the center strip of a face. "Yes?" the man said.

It was Larry who did the talking from behind me. "Doug! Good to see you. The fellow who knocked on your door is named Walter Daley, but you can call him Wally. He wants to talk to you. Wants to talk to your wife. You remember me telling you about Wally, don't you?"

He nodded. "Sure, I do." A pause, and then the door opened wide, giving me a view of the same man who I'd seen the other day on the porch, the same man who'd stood there as his wife ranted and raved, stood there as she sliced through her own soft flesh. But now Doug Gordon smiled a wry smile and put out his hand. "Wally," he said, regarding me with more amusement than resentment. "Good to meet you. Strange times. Of course you can talk to me. Of course you can talk to Catherine. She's in the shower right now, so it'll be a few minutes."

I stood there in silence. I didn't know what to say. What could I say?

"Just to be clear," Larry said. "Your wife is healthy. She's not dead." He was mocking me.

Doug chuckled. "Not dead in the slightest. Why don't you two come in? I'll get you some lemonade. Some cookies. Fresh out of the oven. I'm not supposed to eat them. I'm supposed to be watching my weight."

Larry and I followed Doug Gordon into his house. Inside the living room, the floors were green-and-white linoleum, the walls were Scandi-navian brown, and the furniture was laminated plywood. On the coffee table was a poodle-shaped lamp and an abstract atomic sculpture. And then there were the cabinets, all stuffed full with Barbie dolls—mainly blond, but a handful of brunettes and redheads as well. They all looked to be old. Thirty, forty years at least.

Doug Gordon saw me staring at the dolls.

"They're Catherine's," he said. "She's always collected them. And they help her remember."

"Remember what?" I said.

But he didn't answer. Instead, he glared at me and said, "And how long have you lived here? In Bethlam, I mean."

"My whole life," I said automatically.

"And how long have you been a mailman?"

"For as long as I can remember."

Larry Hartwick stretched his arms above his head. "Well, I guess I'll be getting back home. Give you some time to get caught up. It'll be a great relief to our friend, Wally, to see Catherine without a nasty grin on her throat. A very big relief, indeed."

Doug patted Larry on the shoulder. "Sure," he said. "Get on home to that lovely wife of yours. Tell Karen hi."

Karen? Hadn't her name been Darlene? Didn't she teach kindergarten?

"Will do. I'll be seeing you."

"Not if I see you first."

Larry looked me up and down before nodding his head and walking across the living room toward the front door. "Goodbye, Wally," he said. "You're doing just fine." And then he was gone.

Now it was just Doug Gordon and me. Where was his wife? Still in the shower?

"But, please," he said. "Sit down. Take a load off."

"Your wife. I—"

"Sit down," he said, this time more firmly.

And so I did.

On the walls, I noticed several photographs of Doug and Catherine, most of them taken when they were young, most all of them taken in exotic or adventurous locales: Paris, the Grand Canyon, the Tetons, Venice. That was something I'd never been able to do: travel. Maybe one day I'd leave Bethlam. Maybe one day I'd leave Nevada.

I sat down on a love seat, which was covered with plastic. Gordon remained standing. I wondered why they kept the plastic on. Easier to clean, I decided. And then the thought darkened: easier to clean the blood.

"As I mentioned," Doug said, nodding his head briskly, "Catherine is taking a shower. That's why she's not in the living room. That's why she's not here talking to you."

"I understand."

"In the shower," he reiterated. "Not dead. Healthy as a horse, in fact. An alive horse, not a dead horse. I'll go get the cookies. I'll go get the lemonade."

He left the room, and for just a moment, I considered racing through the house looking for Catherine, but Doug returned less than a minute later, a tray trembling in his hands. On it was a single glass of lemonade and two cookies. He placed the tray on the table and then handed me the glass of lemonade and one of the cookies. He sat down on the couch and ate slowly, the crumbs falling on his lap. I didn't eat my cookie. Didn't drink my lemonade.

Everything seemed like a dream. Minutes passed. Still, Catherine Gordon didn't appear. He'd said she was in the shower.

Maybe she was in the morgue.

"About your wife. I—"

But then there were footsteps, and a long shadow stretched across the floor. Catherine Gordon appeared in the doorway. The same Catherine Gordon that I'd seen committing, or at least attempting to commit suicide. She wore blue jeans and a brown turtleneck, and her curly hair was wet from the shower. I grinned bitterly. Of course, she was wearing a turtleneck. To hide her wound or, as Larry Hartwick had put it, the nasty grin on her throat.

Doug rose to his feet. I did the same.

"Good afternoon," she said. Her voice was slow and flat, her eyes empty.

"Hello, sweetheart," Doug said. "How was your shower?"

Her eyes rolled back in her head as if she were thinking things over. "Lukewarm, so now I'm cold."

I took a sip of lemonade. It was sour, not enough sugar. Doug said, "Darling, I'd like you to meet Wally Daley."

She looked at me. Blinked once. Blinked twice. "Hello, Wally Daley."

"Hello," I said. "It's nice to meet you."

"Wally delivers mail," Doug said. "He delivers our mail."

"Yes," I said. "For as long as I can remember."

"That's nice," Catherine said. "Doug is the one who goes and gets

the mail from the mailbox. Sometimes there's a letter from our daughter. Her name is Martha."

Doug cleared his throat. "Wally was very concerned about you. He
was worried that you'd hurt yourself. Killed yourself even. Did you hurt
yourself, Catherine?"

Her mouth opened, but no words came out. I studied her face. She
had bags beneath her eyes and lines on her cheeks, but I could tell that
she'd been a beauty once upon a time.

"Catherine? Did you hurt yourself?"

This time she shook her head. This time she said, "No. I didn't hurt
myself."

I wanted to get a look beneath her turtleneck, but I thought it would
be rude to ask. So I didn't.

And then, seemingly out of nowhere, she said, "Doug and I have a
lovely marriage. He's never raised his voice or a hand in anger."

Doug Gordon: "Would you like more lemonade, Wally?"

"No," I said. And then, under my breath, "I saw you hurt yourself. I
was here."

She took a step forward and then another. "Bethlam," she said, "is
a wonderful place. The people are wonderful and so is the weather. My
daughter grew up here. Her name is Martha. She left several years ago.
Moved to Illinois. She married a boy named Isaac. Isaac is a nice boy. He
works in a bank, just like my husband."

"I helped get him the job, in fact," Doug said.

"You pressed the knife to your throat," I said. "There was blood everywhere. Your husband stood on the porch and watched. He didn't try
to help you. And then the fat man, the one I saw at church on Sunday,
carried you away. I saw it with my own two eyes. I know what I saw. I'm
not crazy."

I rose to my feet. I didn't know what I was going to do. Gordon might
have taken it as a threat. "Mr. Daley," he said, his voice rising. "I think it's
time you should go."

"I'm not crazy."

"Your father is waiting for you."

I shook my head. A shard of pain. "Something's happening in Beth-lam," I said. "Something strange and wicked and frightening."

"It's got nothing to do with Bethlam," Doug said. "Don't you get it?"

"Bethlam," Catherine said, "is a wonderful place."

Without another word, I picked up my mailbag from the floor and marched across the living room to the front door.

As I was leaving, I noticed another Barbie doll, this one lying face down in the corner of the room. And I could swear there was a spot of blood in its hair.

CHAPTER 8

Over the next several weeks, my sense of unease became more acute due to a series of oddities. On their own, none of these incidents were particularly significant. But taken together, they showed a pattern of maleficence.

Oddity #1:

After work one day, I was standing outside Sweeney's, debating whether or not to buy some jelly beans, when a wild-haired blond boy, dressed in overalls and running ahead of his mother, stopped and stared at me for a few moments before pointing at me with derision. "I know you," he said in a husky voice. "You're one of them. One of the scrubbed." Before I could respond, before he could say anything else, his mother, a smartly dressed and attractive woman, swooped in and hurried him away, apologizing profusely as they disappeared around the corner. I'd never seen them before. I never saw them again.

Oddity #2:

Back in the residential neighborhoods, this time during my route. I had just stuffed envelopes and a magazine into a mailbox when I looked up at the house and saw an impossibly thin man hunched over what looked like a cage full of mice. It was such a surreal sight—I couldn't help but stare. The strange man looked as if he were injecting one of the little bastards with some type of a long needle. I was confused. As soon as we made eye contact, he wagged his finger and then hurried to the window and shut the blinds.

Oddity #3:

This was the day I went to the pet shop. You see, I had been in the market for new goldfish for a while. That's because Dr. Hoover thought having my father watch them swim might relax him.

Polly's Pets was located on Main Street within a humble strip of businesses. There was a diner, a hardware store, and a hair salon. There was a dentist, a grocery, and a gas station. And then there was the pet shop. The name, Polly's Pets, was painted on the window in yellow, along with amateurish renderings of a cat, a rabbit, and a parrot. No dog for some reason.

Inside, I had expected the loud squawking and barking and meowing of a mass of animals, but that wasn't the case. In fact, there couldn't have been more than six or seven pets in the shop. In addition to the fish, there was a Boston terrier puppy, a single parrot, a few lizards, and a rabbit. And that was about it. If a kid wanted a pet in this town, there wasn't much to choose from.

A man, his nose sharp and crooked, his long gray hair tied into a ponytail, stood behind a counter, reading a book. When he saw me, the man came quickly from behind the counter and shook my hand. He was a cheerful enough fellow, asking me if I was in the market for a companion, and when I told him yes, but only goldfish, he smiled and said those were the best companions of all. He found me two—red ryukins—that he guaranteed would live more than a few days and stuck them in a plastic bag.

And then the odd thing. As I handed him the money for the fish, his shirt pulled up in the front, and I noticed something: the black handle of a handgun. The pet shop owner noticed me noticing. He smiled again and said, "Oh, this. I'm just being extra careful is all. You never know when somebody will get desperate and try stealing some cash. Or worse, try stealing a parrot."

I nodded and left the shop. At first, I didn't think much of it. But as the days went on, I began noticing more and more people carrying guns. Salesclerks in the grocery store had them in holsters under red vests. Waitresses at the local diner, the handles bulging behind their aprons. Even

Pam Haley, the librarian. And it seemed that whenever I approached them or made a sudden move, their hands would edge toward those weapons.

I couldn't help but feel anxious. Why did the town need to be armed?

Oddity #4:

Back home after a long day at work, I heard voices and laughter coming from down the hallway. But as I took one step on the hardwood floor, and then another one, the laughter ceased. I peered inside my father's room and saw him sitting on the edge of the bed, wearing his usual filthy pajamas. And standing in front of him, a white doctor's coat fitted tightly over a white dress shirt, a black medical bag near his two-toned Italian shoes, blond hair perfectly coiffed, eyes too blue to be real, was Dr. Hoover. It was a real disappointment to see him. He spun around, smiled, and gave me an awkward salute. "Well, hello there, Wally. We were wondering where you were." His skin looked fake. No pores. No blemishes. Not a hint of facial hair.

"Just delivering mail is all."

"But you're a little late. Usually you arrive home at 3:36. Right now it's nearly ten past four."

"I stopped at Lucille's for a slice of pie."

"Is that right?"

"That's right."

"In the future," and his voice was infuriatingly kind, "you should let your father know when you're going to be late. He was confused."

"Really? I thought I heard you guys laughing when I walked in here. Seems like he's doing just fine."

My father leaned forward. The corners of his mouth were caked with spittle. "The reason I was laughing," he said, "was because the doctor told a joke."

Dr. Hoover smiled that bleach-white smile. "Yes. Your father is telling you the truth. I did tell him a joke."

"I like jokes," I said. "Tell me the joke."

I could see the wheels spinning. He hadn't told a joke, and now he had to make one up. But he came through. "Two psychologists pass each other in the hallway. The first one nods at the second one, says, 'Hello.

How are you?' The second one forces a smile and says, 'Fine.' When the first one is comfortably out of earshot, he says out loud, 'Jesus Christ. I wonder what *that* was all about?'"

My father laughed. I didn't.

"It's a good one," my father said. And then he looked at me as if for the first time. "And who are you?"

I shook my head and sat down on the chair. I didn't have time for this. Not today.

"Anyway," Dr. Hoover said, "I was just about to run some tests."

"What kind of tests?"

"Oh, you know. Routine stuff."

"Routine stuff," I said. "Sure. Can I ask you a question?"

"Of course, Wally."

"How come you make all of these home visits? I mean, I'm sure Dad is flattered that he's so important, but—"

"But he is. Important, I mean. You're both important. Someday, you'll understand."

It was an awfully strange thing to say . . .

Dr. Hoover leaned down and touched my father's face with the back of his palm before reaching into his medical bag and pulling out a bunch of doctor's equipment: a stethoscope, a sphygmomanometer, an ophthalmoscope, and so forth.

"If it's all right with you," he said to my father, "I'm going to take your vitals."

My father didn't look at him; instead, his gaze remained focused on me. "My son, right?"

I nodded my head. "Yes. Your son."

"We used to play catch together. In the backyard. You were much younger then. You had freckles on your face."

"Yes."

"Tell me about it. Tell me about playing catch."

But I didn't feel much like talking. "Not today," I said. "Maybe tomorrow."

Dr. Hoover checked my father's pulse and his blood pressure, his heart and his eyes. "Looks good," he said. "Everything looks good." And then, after a few minutes, he turned back to me. "You know, Wally, it would be really good for your dad."

"What would? What would be good for my dad?"

"Talking about the past. Playing catch, for example."

"But I'm tired of the past. I'm tired of everything."

Dr. Hoover pulled out a notebook and scribbled down some numbers and phrases. He mumbled some words that I had never heard, words that must have been medical jargon.

"In our times together, I've noticed that you have a remarkable memory. A form of—"

"Hyperthymesia. Yes, you've told me many times before."

"And the more you can share those memories with your father—"

"We used to play catch," my father said, and his eyes were bulging, like he'd recalled something astonishing.

"Yes," I said. "We used to play catch."

Dr. Hoover put down his notebook. "As I said, his vitals are in good shape—"

Father: "Son. Wally. Tell me about playing catch. When you had freckles. Please."

Fuck.

Dr. Hoover nodded his head and winked. "Come on, Wally. Don't let him down."

The way Dr. Hoover called me "Wally" made me feel strange. As if it were a name that he'd made up for shits and giggles.

"I don't know, I—"

"It's important," Dr. Hoover said.

I looked at my father, his lower jaw hanging as if unhinged, his tongue lolling around his mouth.

I sighed deeply, just to show them that I wasn't thrilled about this. "Okay," I said. "Fine. We used to play catch in the backyard. You used an old JCPenney first baseman's glove that must have been thirty years old. Remember? The webbing was torn at the bottom, so sometimes the ball would go straight through. My glove was a cheap MacGregor. A

Pete Rose model. It was so broken in that the leather was floppy. But I loved that glove. I could catch anything. You used to throw me grounders and pop-ups. Our fence had ivy wrapped around the metal. Just like Wrigley Field, you would say. We'd use that fence as the outfield wall. You used to do a fake broadcast. As you would throw the ball up in the air, you would make the sound of the crack of the bat. Shout out in your deepest voice, 'There's a high fly ball to DEEP center field. Back goes Wally Daley. Back, back, back. He's at the wall. He leaps and . . . he makes the catch! I don't believe it! An unbelievable catch.' And, to me, it felt like it was really happening. Felt like I was really playing center field for the Cubs. Felt like I'd really just won the game. I was just a boy, and I had freckles."

I looked at my father, and there were tears in his eyes and his lower lip was trembling. And then I looked at Dr. Hoover, and goddamnit, if his eyes weren't filled with salt water as well . . .

After a few moments, the doctor spoke. "That was very good, Wally." *Wally.*

I kept going. The memories came fast and free. "But baseball wasn't always easy. I remember the first time I tried out for the A level of Little League. I was so nervous. I'd never played on a team before. Just played catch with you out back. So there I was in my oversized cleats and stirrups and baseball pants and Ryne Sandberg jersey. The other kids seemed more relaxed, laughing with each other. When the tryouts started, each of us was assigned a number that they stapled to our shirts. We ran to right field and took turns fielding fly balls. I did okay with that, although I did misjudge one that sailed over my head. After that, we ran to shortstop, and the coach hit us ground balls and watched our throws across the diamond. My fielding was good, although my arm was weak. 'Put some mustard on it, number twenty-two!' he shouted. And then it was time to hit. We lined up at the batting cage. The first four kids hit a bunch of line drives. One of them hit a few balls over the fence. Then it was my turn. The coach's name was Ron and he had a mustache that curled at the corners, like Rollie Fingers. The first pitch he threw me was outside, but I swung, and I heard the ball slap against the catcher's mitt. Another pitch, and again I swung, and again there was the sound of cowhide against leather. And so it went. Pitch after pitch. Swing and miss after swing and miss. The coach was a nice guy and wanted me to have some success. He moved closer, threw slower. But it made no difference. I couldn't hit the damn ball.

"After practice, I didn't even wait for the coach to tell me that I hadn't made the team. I knew. You were there to pick me up. You patted me on the head. Said, 'How did it go, son?' I didn't answer. Instead, I just burst into tears. There was nothing I could do. You pulled me close, hugged me. You whispered in my ear. 'I love you, pal. It's okay. Do you hear me? It's okay. It took guts for you to try out. It took guts for you to fail. And you know what I'm going to do? I'm going to take you out to the ball fields every single day. And I'm going to throw you pitch after pitch after pitch. It won't take long. Next time those coaches see you, they'll wonder what's gotten into you.' And that's what you did. That's how we spent the summer. Every single day. Pitch after pitch after pitch. And the next year, I tried out for the same team. And the same coach with the same Rollie Fingers mustache threw me batting practice. And his head whipped around when I hit the first line drive. And then again when I hit the second. Line drive after line drive. Gap to gap. I was eleven then. You taught me well, Dad."

The memory was done. It felt good to talk about the past. By now, my father was sobbing like a baby. Maybe Dr. Hoover was right. Maybe sharing my memories would help him remember his. Then he did something that surprised me. He rose to his feet. He opened his arms. He wanted me to hug him. For the longest time, it hadn't felt as if he were my father. It felt as if he were a stranger living under the same roof. But now, for just a moment, I had him back. I don't know if he really remembered or if he was just touched by the narrative, but it didn't really matter. I walked across the room and pulled him close. He was trembling like a leaf. And all the time, Dr. Hoover was saying, "That's good, Wally. That's very good."

———

Later, I went to my room. Dr. Hoover said that he wanted to run a few more tests, talk a little bit more to my father. I lay on my bed and stared at all the happy childhood photographs on the wall, all the childhood trinkets on my chest of drawers (baseball trophies, old report cards, letters from my mother, Matchbox cars). I closed my eyes and started to drift away.

But I was startled awake by the sound of Dr. Hoover and my father, once again, laughing.

CHAPTER 9

It was a Saturday morning, a few days after Dr. Hoover had made his home visit, and, per tradition, my father was taking his weekly bath. These baths tended to be lengthy: anywhere from thirty to sixty minutes. Sometimes I would stand outside the bathroom door and listen to him try to unscramble memories, listen to him sing Sinatra. His voice wasn't bad, a baritone. *"When I was seventeen / It was a very good year / It was a very good year for small town girls / And soft summer nights."* On this particular morning, after listening to him sing and babble for a bit, I decided to be productive and work on cleaning his room. It had been weeks, and things had gotten out of control. Not to say I was a clean freak, but this was too much for even me.

I started by picking up all the dirty silverware and empty cans of Hormel Chili and Campbell's Soup: his typical lunch when I was at work. Next, I gathered all of his dirty clothes and placed them in the hamper. I stripped and remade his bed, which I hadn't done in forever. Finally, I organized his desk, which was covered with old photographs and souvenirs and letters. One of the letters was from my mom—I could recognize the handwriting. She must have written it when she and Dad first started dating.

> *Dear Harold,*
> *I miss you something awful. It's hard to believe that it's*

only been a week since we were together. It seems like so much more. This summer will be long, but I promise that I will write to you every day. You don't even have to write back. After all, I know you're not much for letters! Anyway, there's nothing much to say. Camp begins tomorrow morning. I can't believe I agreed to be a counselor. I'll want to strangle the kids by the end of the summer. At least Emma is here with me. She'll make things bearable. She snuck some weed into her backpack. So I've got that to look forward to. I want you to know something else. I love you. It's hard for me to say in person because I'm shy. But I'll say it in each letter. I love you. I feel so lucky that I'm your girlfriend. I hope we're together forever. I know we will be.

Love, Beula.

I couldn't help but get a little choked up reading the letter. I thought about time and how it moves so quickly. How one day you're young and in love, and then, in the blink of an eye, it's all gone. Ah, hell, what was the point in thinking that way? At least they had all those years together. At least they experienced all that love. But not me. Not that I didn't long for it. I just hadn't been very lucky. And now that I spent my evenings caring for my father, love seemed further away than ever. Ah, hell, what was the point in feeling sorry for myself?

I refolded the letter and placed it back on the desk, back with the rest of the souvenirs. I was just finishing up stacking everything in a neat pile when I noticed a section of wood on the desk that was shallower than the rest of the panels. When I pressed on the wood, a hidden panel popped open. Curiosity piqued, I stuck my hand inside and pulled out an unsealed envelope as well as several DVDs in plastic cases.

I probably should have just put the stuff away. It wasn't my right to snoop, even if my father was in the throes of dementia. But I was only human. Shaking my head and sighing, I peeled the envelope open. My eyes narrowed as I studied the contents: a check from the United States Treasury for $10,000. But it wasn't made out to my father. It was made out to Hal Barker. I stared at the check for a few moments, trying to make some sense of things. I'd never heard the name Hal Barker before. Who was he? A friend of my father's? And why would my father be in possession of his money? Hands trembling, I placed the check back in the envelope, placed the envelope back in the secret drawer.

I stared at the DVDs. And still I was curious. I left the room, bringing the discs with me.

I walked down the hallway and stopped at the bathroom door. I figured my father still had another ten or fifteen minutes to soak. I knocked on the door. "You doing okay there, Dad?" I said. "Your bathwater still warm?"

"Oh, I'm doing wonderful, just wonderful," came his muffled response. "It's all about the Federal-Aid Highway Act. Eisenhower's greatest achievement. Don't you think?"

"Yes," I said. "Either that or ending the Korean War."

I continued toward the living room. The DVD player was in an old wooden cabinet beneath the television. I turned on the machine, pressed "eject," and placed one of the DVDs inside. At first the disc just spun, and the player whirred loudly. But then it quieted, and a grainy image appeared on the screen. Fade in to a creepy looking old house, obscured by an abundance of fog from a fog machine. The music was analog synthesizer, the same few notes over and over again. And then the title of the film appeared, in dripping red letters: *The Blood House*. The DVD must have been copied from some old VHS tape, and the quality was ragged. The title dripped off the screen (neat effect) and was replaced by a list of actors and producers and a director, none of whom I'd heard of. The music got louder, more jangly, and the camera swept away from the house and toward the street where a police car was parked, its lights flashing. The door to the vehicle opened, and a mustached officer stepped outside. He spoke into his police radio, saying, "Officer Clyburn here. At 1400 Juniper Avenue. Report of domestic abuse. Over." On the other end, a single word: "Roger."

It didn't take long for me to realize that this was a sleazy horror movie from the '80s or early '90s. The music. The set design. The sound. I kept watching. I don't know why. The officer walked slowly, cautiously, up the walkway, stopping for a moment to bend down and pick up a man's dress shoe from the ground. He studied it for a moment before tossing it aside. He walked up the wooden steps, and the camera cut to a picture of his own shoes, giving us the sound of the wood creaking loudly. Cut back to the officer knocking on the door, saying, "Hello? Ms. Harper? It's the police. We got a call that—"

The door creaked open (so much creaking), and an old woman stood in the doorway, the low-budget makeup and a poorly constructed gray wig not hiding the fact that the actress was probably in her late thirties. "Hello, officer," she said, a creepy smile spreading across her face. "What seems to be the problem?"

Officer Clyburn: "We received a phone call. A neighbor reported somebody screaming."

She laughed. "Well, that's just silly. It's just little old me here. I've only been drinking tea and knitting a sweater." She opened the door a little wider and pointed to the couch, where there was a hot cup of tea and some yarn.

The officer leaned forward, said, "Mind if I take a look?"

The "old" woman hesitated but then said, "Certainly. Come on in."

Bad idea. She moved backward and opened the door fully. The officer's radio was crackling, and he stepped gingerly inside. He glanced around, looking for anything out of the ordinary. "You live by yourself, do you, Ms. Harper?"

She nodded her head. "That's right. Ever since my husband died last year. Such an awful death."

"Yes," Officer Clyburn said. "I heard about that. My condolences."

Ah, good. A backstory.

"Sometimes I get lonely," she said. "Sometimes I long for company. Which is why it's nice that you're here. Would you like to have a seat? I could make you some coffee."

"No," the officer said. "That's kind, but it won't be necessary."

The acting was not good. They read their lines with too much gusto. Their facial expressions were overdone.

The officer poked around the house for a little bit longer. He didn't seem to have much of a plan here. He hadn't been trained properly. Eventually, he turned and walked toward the front door, said, "Well, everything looks okay here. Wonder what screaming they heard?"

"Why, I don't know, Officer."

He tipped his cap. "In any case, if anything comes up, please don't hesitate to call."

"Oh, I won't, Officer. You sure you don't want to stay?"

"Yes, I'm sure."

But he'd just opened the door when there was muted moaning, and then a slurred, "Help me."

Officer Clyburn turned around. "What was that?"

"What was what, Officer?"

With renewed urgency, he walked through the living room and toward the back of the house. The moaning got louder. The cheesy horror synthesizer started playing again, and it was louder than before.

"Hello?" the officer said. "Is somebody here?"

He reached the back of the house where a bedroom door was closed. The old woman, Ms. Harper, said, "It's best if you don't open that door, Officer."

He looked at her and then back at the door. A hesitation and then he twisted (another creak!) the handle and slooooooowly pulled the door open.

I'd never liked horror movies, so out of habit, I covered my eyes. But then I peeked through my fingers, watched the rest of the scene. The officer stepped into the room, and there he saw a man on the bed, only his arms and legs were stumps, and the mattress was covered with blood.

"What is this?" the officer said, and it was a stupid question.

"Help me!" cried out the armless, legless man.

The old woman laughed. He should have known she was evil! "Officer, I'd like you to meet Mr. Bennett. Mr. Bennett is a neighbor of mine. Mr. Bennett came to check up on me. A poor old widow. But then he wanted to leave. I didn't want him to leave. So . . ."

"Help me!" Mr. Bennett moaned.

The officer took a step forward, and then another one, and then the old woman took an axe (where the hell had she found an axe?) and raised it high over her head. The camera focused in on the glint of the metal and then showed it coming down hard and burying into the officer's skull. He spun around in confusion, brains and blood oozing from his head—a pathetically low-budget special effect—before falling to the ground.

The old woman (nay, the youngish woman with the wig and fake wrinkles) wiped the blood or ketchup or whatever from her face and grinned. "And to think he might have taken you away from me. I'll never let that happen. Never, ever, ever."

"Noooo!" shouted the man on the bed. "Noooo!"

Fade to black. End of the first scene of *The Blood House*.

I grabbed the remote control. Hit rewind. Replayed the scene with the woman and her limbless slave. When there was a close-up of his agonized face, I paused the DVD. I got onto my hands and knees and moved nice and close to the television. I stared at that image for a long time, having a hard time believing what I was seeing. It was true that he was much younger, it was true that his hair was a different color, but the longer I studied his face, the more convinced I became.

The actor who played Mr. Bennett was my father.

CHAPTER 10

The movie was loud enough that I didn't hear the old man enter the living room, didn't hear him rustling behind me. But then I saw movement out of the corner of my eye, and I spun around. My father stood in the corner of the room, a frayed towel around his waist, leaving his hairless, concave chest exposed.

He nodded at the television. "What's that?" he said. "What are you watching?" He sounded lucid, not the voice of the dotty old man I'd grown accustomed to.

I turned off the video and stared at a clump of dust and hair on the floor. I answered my father truthfully because there was no time to fabricate a story. "I'm watching an old horror movie. It's called *The Blood House*."

One of those long pauses before he spoke again: "*The Blood House*. That sounds gruesome. And how do you like it?"

"It's hard to say. I just started watching. I was cleaning your room, and I found it in your desk. I was curious."

"In my desk? But why were you looking in my desk?"

It's crucial to point out how different his tone had become: to me, he sounded articulate, threatening.

"I shouldn't have," I said. "I'm sorry. In any case, the movie is a strange one. Not high quality. A B movie, if that. You could call it pure shlock."

"I'm sure you could."

I didn't mention the most startling fact of all: that he was in the movie, that he played the role of the tortured man. I also didn't mention the US Treasury check made out to Hal Barker. I was afraid of what would happen if I confronted him.

A quick pivot on my part: "Anyway. Enough of that. Let's talk about dinner. I was thinking of making meatloaf tonight. What do you think of meatloaf?"

He nodded his head slowly, and, as if suddenly remembering the role he was supposed to play, began speaking slower and with a doltish drawl. The idiot father returned to service. "I like meatloaf," he said. "I like it very much. Beula used to serve it with corn and mashed potatoes. She'd get mad at me for putting on ketchup. Do we have any ketchup?"

"Yes," I said. "We have ketchup."

A dumb grin spread across his face. "Well, that's wonderful to hear. Now remind me of one thing that I've been wondering about ever since we started talking. Who are you? What's your name?"

———

Over the next week, when I wasn't delivering mail, and when the old man was sleeping or in the bathtub, I watched more of the DVDs. I'd returned the check, but I kept the DVDs hidden in my room, in the front pocket of an old suitcase. I figured that the old man, in the throes of his dementia, wouldn't miss them, but I didn't want to risk him accidentally finding them. All of them were low-budget, certainly straight to VHS if they had even been released at all, but not all of them were horror. In fact, there was only one other horror movie, a brutally gory one called The Devil's Skin. Otherwise, there was a low-budget action movie (Die Before Midnight), a sleazy teen comedy (Big Mama's Boys), and a cheesy holiday movie (The Magic of Christmas). In every single movie, my father appeared, always playing a fairly inconsequential role. In The Devil's Skin, for example, he played a taxicab driver who appears for about two minutes before getting decapitated by barbed wire. In Die Before Midnight, he played a grocery store stocker who ducks behind a tower of canned soups at the beginning of a ten-minute gunfight. At the end of the poorly directed scene, he peers out from behind the cans, lifts his radio to his mouth, and says his all-too-predictable line: "Clean up in aisle two." In *Big Mama's Boys*, he played the brother of a teenage girl who is lucky enough to walk in on her and her friends having a topless pillow fight, breasts bouncing every-where. And in *The Magic of Christmas*, perhaps his biggest role, he played a successful lawyer and the love interest of Sally, a greeting card writer. Unfortunately, his unbridled love of money and material goods aren't the values Sally was looking for, so she returns to the loving arms of Lance, a veterinarian who understands the true magic of Christmas.

Each time I watched the credits, my father's name never appeared. But each time, another name appeared that I did recognize:

Hal Barker.

———

Move forward a few weeks to early July. It had been a hot one that day, triple digits, and it was still steamy at night. I lay in bed with the window open, the fan whirring, and a bag of ice resting on my forehead. Still, I couldn't sleep. I kept staring out my bedroom window at the rosebushes, il-luminated by the nearly full moon, but instead of focusing on the lovely and delicate petals, I kept thinking about the slugs and maggots and worms that oozed beneath the dirt. It was a tough night. When I'd close my eyes, I was greeted by more disturbing images: Catherine Gordon slicing her throat, the blood seeping through her fingers; my father in *The Blood House*, each of his limbs chopped off. And then the worst one of all: An image of a young man who looked an awful lot like me, sobbing and screaming, all the while pounding his fists against a floor slicked with blood.

It was past midnight when I finally drifted off to sleep, but I was awoken by somebody pounding on the front door. At first, I thought it was part of my dream and kept my eyes squeezed shut, but the knock-ing continued, and I became alert. My face was wet from sweat and the now-melted bag of ice.

Cursing under my breath, I sat up in bed and then pushed my legs over the side. I grabbed my jeans and T-shirt that were in a pile on the floor and fumbled to get them on. The loud knocking continued.

In hindsight, I should have called the police right away—after all, it was dangerous opening the door in the middle of the night—but I was curious, maybe a little disoriented, so I stumbled through the hallways and living room toward the front door. Despite the pounding on the door, my father remained asleep. I stood in front of the door and asked who it was, but his voice was muffled and hard to understand. I pulled the door open a crack.

A man stood on the front porch, swaying back and forth like a toy punching bag. He wore jeans, a ragged flannel shirt, and a thick red beard. He could have been thirty; he could have been fifty. His face was half lit by the streetlights and half hidden by the shadows, giving him a menacing appearance.

"What do you want?" I said. "Who are you?"

His upper lip lifted into a snarl, and he slurred, "Who am I? Better question is who the fuck are you? And why don't you get the hell out of my house?"

I should have shut the door and locked it. I should have. But I didn't. Instead, I engaged with him. Instead, I opened the door wider and said, "Your house? What do you mean? What are you talking about?"

He was drunk. That much was obvious. I could smell the whiskey he was drenched in. He didn't answer my questions. Instead, he came barreling through the door, pushing right past me and into the living room.

For some reason, I wasn't terrified of the stranger. For some reason, I was calm. "Come on now," I said. "Get out of here. Or I'll be forced to call the police. Do you hear me? Get out."

His head was jerking all around, and he was wild-eyed. "What did you do with my furniture? What did you do with my moose head? It was right up there on the wall. Above that ugly-ass couch."

"You're drunk," I said. "You're confused. You need to get out. Please." I was pleading, not commanding.

He looked at me or, more accurately, right through me. Then he stumbled across the floor, slumped down on the couch, and placed his head in his hands. "I need some water," he mumbled. "Get me some water."

I shook my head. "I'm not getting you water. You're not a guest in my house."

A bitter cackle. "Correction. *My* house. This is my house. And I do need water. I'm not feeling well. Not feeling well at all."

It was all wrong. Everything. I stood there like an idiot, and then I nodded my head. "Fine. I'll get you some water. But then you need to leave. Do you understand?"

Not surprisingly, he didn't commit to my negotiation. I went into the kitchen and pulled down a glass and poured him some water. When I returned to the living room, my father was also there, wearing his filthy pajamas, his hair sticking in a thousand and one directions. He didn't address the intruder; instead, he looked at me. "Who is this? Is this a friend of yours? Is this a friend of Beula's?"

I shook my head. "No. No friend. He came knocking on our door in the middle of the night. Busted right on through. He claims that this is his house."

At this, my father's body straightened, and his jaw jutted. He took a quick step forward and for a brief moment, I thought he might attack the stranger. But instead, he stopped, took a deep breath, and began speaking.

"Wrong, young man, wrong!" he said. "This house is not yours. This house is mine and Beula's and Wally's—ours alone. Bought and paid for with blood, tears, and sweat. A place of laughter and hugs and tears. A place of family dinners and puzzles and late-night snacks. It was in this very house that Wally learned how to walk. It was in this very house where he said his first words, where he dreamed his first dreams. No, this house is not yours. This house is ours." He thumped his chest, and I couldn't help but feel proud of the crazy ol' badger.

The intruder gazed at my father for a few moments and then stared at the floor in front of him. I was still holding his glass of water, and it started shaking in my hand. I handed it to him, but he didn't drink. He leaned forward so his head was near his knees, and I thought he was going to vomit. But he didn't. Instead, after a few moments, he lifted up his head, narrowed his bloodshot eyes, and said a single word:

"Bullshit."

CHAPTER 11

I'd had enough. I finally left the room and called the police and told them about the intruder. They asked for more information. Was he armed? Was I in danger? "I don't know about any of that. I just know that he's drunk. I just know that he's crazy."

"Don't panic," the operator said. "We'll have somebody over shortly."

When I returned, my father was sitting on the floor, cross-legged. He mumbled something about Beula and Joan Crawford and Russian Blue cats, and then leaned forward and closed his eyes. Within a minute, he looked to be asleep, lips puffing with each breath.

The bearded man glowered at me. He must have heard the conversation. "Yeah, I'm drunk," he said, "but I ain't crazy."

I sat down in the chair opposite him, and I could feel my head beginning to ache again. It was the same old story. I gritted my teeth and massaged my temples. It did no good. "Maybe you're not crazy," I said. "Maybe you're just confused. Maybe that's the problem. Thinking this is your house."

He laughed a deep boisterous laugh. "No, no. I ain't confused, neither. This *is* my house. Lived here for nearly a quarter of a century. I can promise you that."

"That's impossible," I said. "I've lived here my whole life. My parents bought the home after—"

"What you've got to understand is that I never wanted to leave. And I wouldn't have if the men in suits hadn't come to town."

"The men in suits?"

"There were only a few of us left. On account of the economy. On account of the recession. That's when they came to town in their fancy cars and their fancy suits. Offered each and every one of us money to leave."

I humored the stranger. "Offered you money? But why? I don't understand."

"They said that they represented the interests of the government. They cited something called eminent domain. Have you heard of eminent domain?"

"No, I—"

"They said that if I didn't take the money, they'd force me out of the house anyway. In the end, I didn't have much of a choice. And so I left. Moved into a little apartment down in Stanton. But now . . . circumstances have changed. I've returned. I'll give them back the cash if that's what they want. I want my house back. I want my life back."

His story wasn't making sense. Not any sense at all.

I said, "I've been in this house ever since I was a baby. Never lived anywhere else."

"Not true," he said, his voice getting louder. "Not true." He drank his water quickly, some of it spilling onto his flannel shirt.

The strange circumstances were piling up like dirt on a potter's field.

"You ever heard of Catherine Gordon?" I asked for some reason. "You heard of Hal Barker?"

But he only shook his head, didn't bother answering.

"You want to know the truth?" he said. "The truth is my daughter don't love me no more. Because I hit her. It was an accident, you see. Just a momentary loss of temper. My ex-wife, Jolene, came and took her from me despite all of my pleading, despite all of my apologies. I cried real tears. But she showed no empathy. Eventually, it was just me. I had a hard time facing myself alone. I got to drinking. And that's when I decided to come back."

"I'm sorry they made you leave in the first place," I said. And then I repeated the line I'd heard so many times. "Bethlam is a wonderful place. The people are wonderful and so is the weather."

He shook his head. "Bethlam? This ain't Bethlam."

"What do you mean? I—"

From down the block there were muted sirens, and the intruder and I both looked at each other, expectantly. Another minute or two and there was a knocking on the front door. The man, the intruder, didn't budge. My father continued sleeping. I rose to my feet and hurried across the room.

I opened the door. A police officer, mid-fifties, ruddy cheeks, stood on the porch. He flashed a sideways grin and said, "Good evening. I understand that there's been a disturbance." I could hear static-filled police jargon through his radio.

I nodded my head. "Yes, sir. A man. An intruder. He walked right into the house. He's sitting there on the couch. He claims this house is his. Got some wild story about eminent domain, about men in suits. I can't make sense of it. But maybe you shouldn't arrest him. He's going through some hardships. That's the problem. I can't blame him. It's tough all over."

The officer sort of chuckled before entering the house, his left hand resting just above the edge of the holster. When he saw the man sitting on the couch, he nodded his head and said, "I figured it would be you."

The man looked up at the officer and sucked at his teeth. "Am I supposed to know you?"

"Maybe not. But I know you. Why, it wasn't more than two days ago that I arrested you for breaking into the Harrisons' house across town. Spouting the same nonsense. Claiming that the house was yours."

The man shook his head. "Lies. You're telling lies."

The officer looked at my father sleeping, and then at me. "His name is Al Denning. He's not well. Not well at all. I'm just sorry you had to deal with this." Then he looked back at Denning. "All right, buddy, time to leave this poor family alone. Time to get to your feet. Don't make this harder than it has to be."

"How'd you know my name?"

"Get to your feet."

He remained sitting. "I ain't standing up until you tear up the contract. Until I get my house back. Until I get my life back."

"Get up. There's no contract."

"The hell there isn't. On account of eminent domain. The paperwork is right in my car. I've lived in this house for nearly a quarter century. Until they came in their fancy cars."

"He's not well," the officer said again.

My headache was getting worse. I leaned against the wall, tried taking some deep breaths. The intruder stayed where he was. Meanwhile, the officer took another step forward. I could see his hand twitching next to his gun.

"Don't make me call for backup. That'll only put me in a worse mood."

"It's my house."

The officer reached for his weapon. The man, Denning, rose to his feet. I thought the officer was going to shoot him, but he didn't. Denning raised his hands in the air, giving himself up. "That's a good boy. Now turn around. I'm going to put these cuffs on you, nice and gentle."

Denning did as he was told. But as he was getting cuffed, he looked right at me and spoke. The booze must have worn off because he now sounded completely sober. "Here's what you should do. Go into the kitchen. Look at the wall next to the stove. You'll see some marks. My daughter's name is Kirsten. I shouldn't have hit her. It was a mistake. I'll never be able to live it down."

The cuffs were snapped on, hands behind his back. The officer grabbed his arm and guided him toward the front door.

"You'll see some marks," he said again.

The officer gave him a shove and then looked at me and said, "I hope you can get some rest, Mr. Daley. He won't be bothering you more tonight. He won't be bothering you ever again."

"Look," Denning said. "Right next to the stove. They stole my home. On account of eminent domain. This town ain't Bethlam. It's called Gilford. They're tricking you. They're tricking me. Don't you understand?"

The police officer opened the front door and shoved the man out. He tapped an invisible hat and shut the door behind him.

I slid down the wall until I was sitting cross-legged, just like my father.

At that moment, his eyes flew open wide. "The bad man," he said. "Is he gone?"

"Yes. He's gone."

"He could have hurt you. Could have hurt both of us."

"Maybe. I'm going to go look in the kitchen."

"The kitchen? Why the kitchen?"

"He said there were marks. He told me to look in the kitchen. By the stove."

I rose to my feet. My father reached for my arm, said, "Wait." I didn't.

I hurried to the kitchen, strode toward the stove. I studied the wall on both sides, searching for the mark that Denning had mentioned. I didn't see anything. Some paint peeled away. Some dirt near the baseboards. But no marks. And now my father was standing directly behind me.

"Tell me about playing catch," he said. "Tell me about the pretend broadcasts I used to recite."

I got down on my hands and knees, looked closer. Still nothing.

"Tell me about your mother's laugh. Tell me about the cinnamon rolls she would bake on Sunday morning."

Back to my feet. I placed my hands on the back of the oven and began pulling. I pulled until it was maybe a foot away from the wall. Then I walked around to the other side and did the same thing.

"Such a good memory you have. Help your old man out. My memory is disintegrating, like newspaper in the fireplace."

My eyes narrowed to slits. And that's when I saw them. The marks that Denning had been talking about. I had to get in nice and close to see them. There were four lines, marked in pencil, each an inch or two above the other. And next to each line there was a label, marking the age and height of Kirsten, the man's daughter. Kirsten—six years old; Kirsten—seven years old; Kirsten—eight years old; Kirsten—nine years old.

I squatted down on my haunches and nodded my head slowly.

And I wondered what the hell was happening in Bethlam, Nevada.

CHAPTER 12

Mailbag slung over my shoulder, sun helmet tipped back on my head, I walked slowly down the empty and sun-bleached streets of Bethlam, and I couldn't help but feel uneasy, couldn't help thinking those thoughts.

There seemed to be more townsfolk out on the streets today than usual. Every few minutes, a man or a couple or a family would pass by, and they would all smile at me and say good morning and isn't it a lovely day. I agreed that it was. Yes, every day was lovely in Bethlam (except on those rare occasions when ladies stood on their porches and cut their own throats). Every night was peaceful in Bethlam (except on those rare occasions when strangers broke into your house and claimed it was theirs). Something I noticed today, although maybe it had always been this way: Each time a person passed and talked to me, they kept eye contact for several moments too long. It was as if they were studying me. As if I were some mental patient.

And maybe I was.

And then I remembered the child who'd approached me. The one who had looked straight into my face and said, *You're one of them. One of the scrubbed.* What did that mean? Nothing, it meant nothing. I was becoming paranoid. Mental health was hereditary. Who was to say my father's delusions and dementia hadn't been passed down to the likes of me?

The thoughts were troubling. I couldn't stand them anymore and got to yanking at my hair, tearing at my skin. "Go away," I muttered through gritted teeth. "Leave me alone." It was no good. I was overreacting. I took a deep breath. Then I forced a smile. "Relax." I started humming songs from my childhood to make the thoughts go away. "99 Luftballons," "Against All Odds," "Missing You." I reached Maple and Third. The anxiety was waning. The humming had helped. But not for long.

"Do you want to see my paintings?" At first, I thought the voice was part of my own ruminations. But then I looked up and saw a Black woman, mid-thirties, thin. She wore several silver bracelets on her wrist, and they jangled when she moved her arm.

"Excuse me?" I said.

"My paintings," she said. "I think you'd like to see them."

For some reason, I felt a coldness rise up inside of me. The way she spoke. The way she looked at me.

"I'm sorry. I've got to continue my route. I've got to—"

She took a few steps forward. Despite the ridiculousness of the situation, I could see a flicker of intelligence in her eyes. Her mouth remained frozen in a grin, but she was somehow able to whisper without moving her lips as if she were a ventriloquist. "I've got some things to tell you. Some things to show you. My name is Veronica Miller. Come inside. Let me tell you what I know. But you have to pretend. You have to want to look at my paintings." I opened my mouth, but no words came out. I managed to nod my head slowly. In a louder voice, with a phony Southern accent, she said, "You know, it was Mrs. Cain who taught me how to paint. Back when I was in third grade. She was my art teacher. She told me that I had a lot of talent even back then. Teachers can really make a difference, don't you think?"

I glanced around. Several neighbors were milling around the sidewalks glancing furtively at Veronica, glancing furtively at me. Waiting to see what we'd do. I nodded my head. "Okay," I said. "I'll come inside. I'll see your paintings."

I followed her onto the porch and inside the house. She shut the door behind me.

The living room looked like something time had forgotten. It had that same 1950s style as Catherine Gordon's house. A mustard-colored couch and a love seat—both sealed in protective plastic—rested on a green shag carpet. An old grandfather clock leaned against the wall, the pendulum unmoving. Flower-pattern wallpaper covered the walls. And just as she'd promised, there were paintings, a half dozen or so hanging on the walls, and another, half finished, on an easel. Actually, when I first saw them, I thought they were photographs, the details so exact. But when I looked closer, I could see evidence of brushstrokes. There was a portrait of a man, another of a butterfly, one of Coca-Cola bottle, and, the strangest one, a single finger, detached, but not bloody.

As I studied the paintings, still amazed that they weren't photographs, Veronica stood in front of the plastic-sealed couch, biting her lower lip nervously.

"Do you like them?" she asked.

"Amazing. Absolutely amazing. I can barely draw a stick figure."

She laughed nervously. "Well, we all have our own talents. I'm sure you're good at something else."

"Maybe," I said. "But I can't think of what."

"Would you like some coffee?" she said, still with that same phony accent. "Some pie?"

I placed my mailbag on the floor. "No pie," I said. "I just want you to tell me what this is all about."

She flattened out her dress and nodded her head for several seconds. Her face took on a dreamy expression. She took my hand in hers. It was odd. Everything was odd.

"When I was four years old," she said, "my mother bought me a stuffed rabbit. I loved that rabbit. I used to play with her beneath the kitchen table while my mom cooked. I remember hearing my mom whistle, the pitter-pat of her shoes on the floor. I remember the smell of cinnamon rolls baking in the oven. I remember the warmth of that kitchen."

It was all fascinating, but I was getting frustrated. I was wasting my time. I reached for my mailbag, preparing to leave, and now Veronica Miller's eyes narrowed to slits. In the same ventriloquist whisper that she'd used outside, she said, "They're watching us. They're listening. But there's a place in the house where they can't see. A place where they can't hear." She smiled again and returned to telling her stories. "I kept that rabbit for a long time. When I was in junior high school, I was too nervous to go to the school dance all by myself. So I brought her with me. She gave me confidence. I recently painted that rabbit. From memory. My memory is very good. Can I show you?"

"Yes," I said.

I followed her through the living room and down a long hallway until we came to a small door covered over with paint. She bent down and tugged on a handle until the door cracked open. I peeked over her shoulder and saw a staircase that led into darkness. "My most prized painting," she said, and began walking slowly down the steps.

I followed her, and the door shut closed behind me. It was pitch-black, and I felt like a blind man waving my hands in front of me. "Wait just a moment," she said. "I'll get us some light." I stopped where I was, and a light flashed on. It was just a single bulb hanging from the ceiling, and it weaved back and forth, causing strange shadows to appear on the wall. The area belowground was small, probably no more than ten feet by ten feet. There was no painting of a stuffed rabbit, only an old, rattling furnace and a busted wooden chair.

Veronica waved me forward, and I continued down the stairs. "We don't have much time," she said, "to speak freely."

"Why not?"

"Because people will be arriving soon. That's what always happens. Neighbors, bringing over a pie or asking to borrow a hammer. And if not them," her expression darkened, "my husband."

"I'm not sure I understand."

"They saw you enter the house. But now we're out of view of the cameras. Out of range of the bugs. It was an oversight on their part. Of course, after today, I'm sure they'll fix that problem."

"Cameras? Bugs?"

"That's right. In every room. I'll bet they're in your house too."

"That's crazy."

"Yes. It is. And in the back of your neck. A microchip."

I reached around and touched the back of my neck, felt the jagged scar above the skin. But that wasn't a microchip. That scar was from when I was a child. I had been on a rope swing, swinging over a creek, and had run into a low-hanging branch. I'd needed twelve stitches. It wasn't a microchip.

"But why would they be surveilling us?" I asked. "And why wouldn't they want us talking to each other?"

She smiled, and she sure looked sane to me. Despite the things she'd said. Despite the things she would say. "Because we both know that something is going on in this town. Something strange. And they don't want us finding the truth."

I shook my head quickly. "It seems paranoid. It seems—"

"Come on, Walter. Think about it. You're just as mistrustful as me, isn't that true? Just as worried? So maybe we're not paranoid. Maybe we're onto something."

"I don't know. I—"

"And what about Catherine Gordon?"

"She went crazy. She sliced her throat with a knife. But then I went to her house. I knocked on the door and—"

"—and she was fine. And she wore a turtleneck hiding the scar. I know all about it. I've been there as well. I've tried talking to her. It's no use. But here's the thing. I know some things. I know the truth about why she went crazy. About why she tried killing herself."

I leaned forward. "Why?"

She nodded her head and licked her lips. "Let me show you." Moving past me, she stepped over the busted chair and walked across the room toward the furnace. She got down on her knees, reached beneath the metal box, and pulled out a Phillips screwdriver. Then, without comment, she placed the screwdriver flush against a screw on the lower panel and began twisting. A minute and the screw popped out. Then she did the same thing at the other three corners. The metal panel fell to the concrete floor.

She placed her entire arm through a tear in the filter. Eyes focused on me, lips pursed in concentration, she reached around for several seconds until she found what she was looking for. Slowly, she removed her arm from the furnace, and I could see that she was gripping a tattered leather-bound journal.

My skin started itching all over. "What is it?"

"It's a journal. A diary."

"A diary? Your diary?"

She shook her head. "Catherine Gordon's. She brought it to me the night before she attempted suicide. It will help you understand. About this town. About the doctors. And maybe about you."

"About me? What do I—"

But she only shook her head. "There's no time for me to explain. My husband will be here soon. Take the journal. Put it in your mailbag. That way he won't see. That way *they* won't see."

None of this made any sense. I was filled with dread and was having a hard time breathing. I was about to ask her more questions when I noticed that she was gazing up the staircase toward the main floor. And then I heard the footsteps.

"Veronica?" a voice called out. "Are you down there?"

Veronica looked at me. "It's him," she hissed.

The footsteps were getting louder. "I'm down in the basement!" Veronica called out. "I'm showing the mailman my secret paintings."

His voice got louder. "The mailman? Now that's interesting. I'll come down. I'll—"

"No!" she shouted. "Just wait. We'll be up in a minute."

For the next panicked minute, I helped Veronica return the metal plate to the furnace, although there wasn't time to screw it in properly. I stuffed the journal in my mailbag. Then I followed her up the staircase.

"Here we come," she said, turning off the light.

When we reached the top of the stairs, I came face-to-face with Brian Miller. He was tall with a ruddy face and thick black hair slicked straight back. He was handsome, straight out of central casting.

He looked at me suspiciously, which was understandable. Then he looked back at Veronica. "And this is the mailman?"

She nodded. "Yes. His name is Wally."

I stuck out my hand and smiled. "Wally Daley," I said. "She wanted to show me her paintings. So I agreed. Maybe I should have said no."

He paused for a moment before shaking my hand. "Brian Miller," he said. "Pleasure."

After that, for a long while, he didn't say a word. Nobody did. I could feel the tension. It seemed like we were in trouble, but I didn't know what for. Then Brian nodded toward the staircase. He looked back at Veronica, his eyes narrowing to slits. "And what did I tell you about going down there?"

"You told me not to."

He shook his head. "Not until we get somebody to fix those live wires and that jagged cement. And not until we check for asbestos." He turned toward me. "The door to the basement was painted over, so for the longest time we didn't even know the basement existed. Veronica only found it by accident."

He grinned and placed his arm around his wife. I noticed that she flinched.

I nodded my head at him. "Well, I suppose I should be going. I need to finish my route."

"It was awfully nice for you to stop by," Brian said. "To take a look at Veronica's paintings. She's very talented, isn't she?"

"Yes, sir. She is."

And the whole time he kept glancing at my mailbag, and I wondered if he knew that I was hiding the diary inside.

"Feel free to stop by anytime," he said, and smiled that same broad, yet forced, smile.

"Thank you," I said. "I will."

Brian watched carefully as Veronica walked me to the door. And I had just opened it and stepped outside, when she leaned in toward me and whispered, "Read the journal. Every page. Something strange is happening. And I'm afraid of what might happen next."

CHAPTER 13

When I got home, Dr. Hoover was sitting on the front porch waiting for me. His legs were crossed, his doctor's bag was at his feet, and a pair of headphones were on his ears. When he saw me, he removed the headphones and smiled.

"Hello, Wally," he said. "Did you have a good day at work?"

"Yes," I said. "I delivered mail."

"Certainly, you did." He nodded at the mailbag. "And what's inside of the bag? Something that you're hiding?"

"No," I said and gripped the bag tighter.

Just like with Brian Miller, I thought he would ask to search it. But he only laughed as if it were a big joke.

I stared into his eyes, the sclera slightly yellowed, and shivered. I didn't like doctors, never had, and I especially didn't like Dr. Hoover. He was supposed to be here for my father, but I couldn't help but think that he was here for me too, studying me, watching every twitch, noticing every stumble. He meant me harm; I was sure of it.

"I suppose you weren't expecting me to be here," he said.

I shook my head and clenched my fists. "No. I suppose I wasn't. Did you already see my father?"

"Yes. I saw him. He's doing fine. Resting now. His mind is working better and better. More and more memories. You've really helped with that. Every time you recall one of your memories, it helps him recall one of his."

"That's good. I'm happy to hear that. I love my father. I always have."

"Yes. Such a wonderful childhood you had."

From off in the distance, I could hear the sound of a wounded dog yelping, could hear the sound of children laughing. The laughter sounded sinister somehow.

"So why are you here?" I asked. "What do you need?"

But he answered with a non sequitur. "For the last hour, I've been listening to opera. I've been listening to Ambroise Thomas. Do you like Ambroise Thomas?"

"I don't know Ambroise Thomas."

"Of course not. Opera is not for most people. It takes too much patience. It forces you to close your eyes and imagine. That's difficult."

"I suppose."

"Sound and smell. That's what causes the most powerful memories. I want you to recall. You, as a small boy. And what was the song you listened to? What was the song you listened to over and over again?"

My stomach tightened. He was scratching at the surface, but I felt as if my skin was peeling off in chunks. "I don't recall. I mean, if I—"

"Oh, but I can read your mind. I know that you used to sit in the living room and listen to the Peter, Paul and Mary version of 'Puff, the Magic Dragon' over and over again. On your parents' record player. A Garrard 301 turntable. Isn't that right, Wally?"

I didn't answer him, but he was right. I didn't know how he knew, but he was right. As I stood there, I recalled, I recalled. "*Puff, the magic dragon lived by the sea / And frolicked in the autumn mist in a land called Honah Lee.*" When I listened to the song, I would close my eyes and imagine that friendly dragon in that autumn mist. And I pretended that I was Little Jackie Paper, Puff's friend, and that we would travel on a boat with a billowed sail, me keeping a lookout, perched on Puff's gigantic tail . . .

"And your favorite superhero was Spider-Man. You dressed up as him three Halloweens in a row. You were quite the web-slinger yourself! Using those imaginary webs to climb up beds and chairs and dressers."

Again, he was right. And not only Spider-Man but also . . .

". . . the Incredible Hulk. You would tear off your shirt. You would pound the walls with your fists. You would throw toys across the room. You would groan and growl. Your parents didn't like it when you turned into the Hulk, did they?"

"No," I said, my voice trembling. "They didn't."

Dr. Hoover smiled, but there was no kindness in that smile. "Aren't memories wonderful? Don't they make you appreciate the present more? I have my own childhood memories. Maybe one day I will share them. Maybe one day I can be the patient and you can be the doctor. But for now, would it be okay if we went inside? That way the neighbors won't listen. There are so many nosy neighbors. It's human nature, you know?"

I nodded my head slowly, that sense of dread spreading. "Yes. Let's go inside."

He uncrossed his legs, stretched his arms, and rose to his feet. He walked inside first, and I followed after him. The journal was in my mailbag. The journal would have to wait.

From my father's room, I could hear the muted voice of Frank Sinatra. I could hear my father singing along.

"He always loved Frank, didn't he?" Dr. Hoover said.

"Yes. He loved the song 'My Way' the most. He used to sing it in the kitchen. When he was cooking pasta. And Mom would laugh and say, 'He sounds just like Frank, doesn't he?' And I would laugh too."

I sat down on the couch. Instead of sitting in the chair across the room, Dr. Hoover sat down right next to me. He massaged my shoulder and then touched my face. I wanted to get the hell out of there. But I stayed. There was nowhere to go.

"The opera I mentioned," he said, "is called *Mignon*. It's about a young woman who was captured by Gypsies when she was just a child. Eventually, she gets rescued by a handsome—and rich—young man. She longs to remember who she really was before she was captured. At some point, due to many circumstances that I won't go into, she falls into a coma. Her lover takes her to a beautiful castle that he's planning on buying.

Miraculously, she immediately begins recovering. When she awakens, her surroundings trigger something inside of her. She remembers! She remembers everything! It turns out that the castle he has taken her to is the castle of her childhood, the place she lived before being kidnapped by those Gypsies. You see, she was a princess, and now she will get to resume the life she should have lived. It's a lovely opera. And it has a happy ending. I only like operas with happy endings. Which is why I deplore Puccini."

"I like happy endings too," I said. "But I don't believe in them. Because our ending is always death."

Frank Sinatra still sang, but my father was quiet. Maybe he'd fallen asleep. Frank's voice was muted by the door. Music sounded better that way. Distant. Mysterious.

Dr. Hoover touched my knee. I flinched. "But enough of opera," he said. "Enough of happy endings. I understand that you recently made a discovery."

I didn't know what he was talking about. I inched away from him on the couch. "Discovery?"

"Yes. In your father's room."

My back tightened and my eye twitched. I felt ashamed, as if I had been caught doing something very naughty. "You're talking about the DVDs?"

He nodded his head. "It must have been a surprise to see your father in all those old movies."

"Yes. A big surprise. He looked young. But I recognized him. He's got a distinctive look, you see. His cleft chin. His widow's peak."

"And until then, until you found the DVDs, you didn't know that he was an actor, correct?"

"No," I said. "I didn't know."

Dr. Hoover laughed, and his laughter was a bit manic. "Well, of course you wouldn't have known. Nobody did. Not even your mother."

"No?"

"It has long been a secret."

"But why? Why would he keep something like that a secret?"

Dr. Hoover didn't answer me, not right away. His hands fell limp in his lap, and he nodded toward the wall, a look of disgust on his face. He said, "Every few years they come. And it looks like this is the year." I twisted around and saw what he was referring to: a dark gray miller moth frozen against the wall. "During the day," he continued, "it's not so bad. But at nighttime. Oh, boy. Fluttering everywhere. Enough to drive a man crazy." Without saying another word, he bent down and untied his shoe, removed it. He walked across the room to where the moth was and studied it for a moment. Then he raised his arm, and for a moment, he looked like a warrior holding a spear. In one violent motion, he slammed the shoe against the wall. The moth dropped to the floor, its legs twitching for a moment before it was still. On the bare wall above a portrait of my parents, there was now a grayish-black spot, a thick layer of dust.

He bent down and put his shoe back on, whistling while he tied it. Then he returned to the couch. "Now then," he said. "We were talking about your father. About his secret."

"And I wanted to know why he—"

Laughter. "Did you watch the films?"

"Yes. At least a portion of them."

"Then you should understand. These were no masterpieces, were they?"

"No."

"'Pure shlock,' you called them."

"How did you know that I—"

"It's why he used a stage name. Hal Barker. The name fits the roles, don't you think? A bit sleazy. A bit carnival-like."

"Yes. I suppose."

Dr. Hoover flicked a piece of lint off his pant leg. "But, please. Have some empathy for your father. Like all of us, he dreamed of making it big. Of being the next Paul Newman or Robert Redford. But dreams die hard. That's the way it is in this life. Maybe the next one will be better. Don't you think, Wally?"

Frank Sinatra had stopped singing. Now it was Tony Bennett. "Rags to Riches."

For some reason, I decided to confide in Dr. Hoover. I can't explain why. He scared me. I didn't trust him. But I felt compelled. He had some sort of power over me, maybe.

"I found a check," I said. "From the US Treasury."

He raised his eyebrows. "A check?"

"That's right. And it was made out to Hal Barker. I can't figure it out. If Hal Barker was his stage name like you say, then why did he have a check made out in that name?"

Dr. Hoover crossed his legs and furrowed his brow. He looked away, but I might have caught a glimpse of panic on his smoothly shaved face.

"That is strange," he said to the wall.

"Yes. I thought so."

"Very strange." He turned back to me, and his expression was light again. "Although I'm sure there's a simple explanation. Something to do with tax returns or something. Perhaps he filed under that name? Who knows? The film industry is a funny racket. It doesn't really matter."

"No. I suppose it doesn't."

"But if you wouldn't mind my asking: how much was the check for?"

"I'd rather not say."

That cruel smile. "I understand."

Dr. Hoover sighed deeply and then rose to his feet. He straightened out his pants with his hand and then looked at me in his typical condescending way. "I've been meaning to ask you," he said. "That tattoo on your arm. 10/23/11. What does that signify?"

"It was the day my mother died."

Dr. Hoover arched his eyebrows. "2011? Has it been that long?"

"Yes," I said. "It's been that long."

He nodded his head for a long time before saying, "*For pain must enter into its glorified life of memory before it can turn into compassion.*"

"What does that mean?"

"It's from *Middlemarch*. By George Eliot."

"I don't know it. I never read it."

"Well, if you ever do, and you want to discuss it, or want to discuss anything, you know where to find me."

"Not really. You always show up here. I don't even know where your office is."

He stood there a moment, not saying a word. I felt the sudden urge to attack him, to place my thumbs in his eyes and press. I sat on my hands to suppress the urge.

"My office is around. Here, there, and everywhere. If you need me, you'll find me. So until then." He stuck out his hand for me to shake, but I didn't reciprocate. My hands remained buried under my legs. He shrugged. "Goodbye, Wally."

"Goodbye, Dr. Hoover."

He turned around and left. After that, I didn't see him for several days, and by that time, I had learned some of the nefarious secrets about Bethlam, Nevada.

And all because of Catherine Gordon's journal.

PART 3

CATHERINE GORDON

CHAPTER 14

I'm writing these words while sitting at an old wooden desk in Martha's room. It's drafty in here, but my handwriting is shaky, not because of the cold but because of my nerves. The only sound comes from the old furnace rattling and creaking in the basement, and the only light comes from the old Emeralite lamp, which sometimes flickers off, leaving me in the darkness. I tap on the lamp a few times, and then the light flashes back on. It only adds to my nervousness.

I come to her room in the hope that they can't see or hear me. I don't know who "they" are. Not exactly. Faceless men, hiding in the shadows, lurking on lawns, crawling through my brain. Sometimes I peek out the front window, and I can see them, odd shapes floating through the darkness. They want me to know that they are out there, want me to feel fear in their presence. I should ignore them, but it's difficult. I'm coming apart at the seams.

Doug is sleeping. He's a sound sleeper, and I can hear him snoring through the thin wall. So now I can take deep breaths. Now I can write.

It was Veronica, the artist, who convinced me to write it all down. And when I'm done, I'll give it all to her for safekeeping. Before they take me away.

I call it Martha's room, but she moved away many years ago. It's really more of a guest room, although I don't recall us ever having

guests stay here. When I was a child, the room was mine, and I still remember the way it looked back then. I remember every detail, every
nook and cranny. I have a good memory for some things. For other
things, I'm in a constant fog. Back then, the desk was new and shiny
and in addition to remnants of my schoolwork (multiplication tables,
cursive sheets, connect-the-dots), it was filled with leather-bound jour-
nals, art sketchbooks, and various trinkets (a shiny rock, a shark's
tooth, a glass tiger). The walls were covered with blue-and-yellow floral
wallpaper that bubbled in some places, and the carpet was yellow and
always freshly vacuumed. There were dozens of books, mainly Nancy
Drew mysteries (*The Secret of the Old Clock, The Hidden Staircase,
The Secret of Red Gate Farm, The Message in the Hollow Oak*), neatly
stacked on the shelves. There were stuffed animals—a penguin, a bear,
a horse—on my four-poster bed. And, of course, there were the Barbie
dolls. So many Barbie dolls.

I can also remember the way the room looked, the way it had been
transformed when Martha was a child and called it her bedroom. By
that point, the wallpaper had been torn and scraped away, and the wall
above her bed was decorated with a mural of her getting pulled by four-
teen Siberian huskies through the thick Alaskan snow. Martha always
loved the idea of Alaska—the wilderness, the freedom, the snow—and
she also loved dogs. She loved dogs so much. We wanted her to be happy,
so we tried getting her a dog, not once, not twice, but three times, and
each time it failed miserably. There was the Australian shepherd that
bit her on the cheek, the Yorkshire terrier that wouldn't stop barking,
and the beagle that got sick four weeks after we bought her. So the best
we could do was the mural. It really was lovely, and she adored the artwork for most of her childhood. When she entered high school, however,
she was suddenly embarrassed by it and made me paint it over. That's
the way kids are. What else? She had the same bookcases, but instead
of Nancy Drew novels, they were filled with nonfiction books about animals and faraway places. The wooden desk, no longer shiny, beginning
to chip, was scattered with glass figurines, photos of her friends, concert
tickets, and handwritten notes. I don't know where all those souvenirs

went. Maybe she brought them with her to Illinois. Maybe she threw them away. In the end, it doesn't matter.

But even though my daughter's souvenirs were discarded, all my dolls and artwork and letters remain. Dr. Hoover says it helps to have artifacts because otherwise, the memories might fade away. And when they're gone, they're gone forever, ice melted in a stream.

So now it's time to tell you my story. But where to start? I guess I'll start in the place that makes the most sense. When I first opened my eyes.

CHAPTER 15

"You've been in an accident."

The words sounded muted, blurry, as if I were underwater. When I opened my eyes, they stung, and it took several seconds before they finally focused, before I could see that I was lying on a hospital bed, an IV hanging from my wrist. There was whiteness everywhere, from the walls and the ceiling and the floor, to the jacket of the man who was speaking. He was a doctor, that was easy to see. Above his humorless face was a disheveled shock of red hair.

"An accident?" I said, my lips dry and my voice raspy from disuse. "What kind of an accident?"

"A car accident. Do you remember?"

I stared at the man, trying to place him. Then it came to me. I'd seen him in my dreams. Dreams more vivid than real life.

"No," I said. "I don't think so. I don't think I remember."

"That's okay. It's normal. There's no need to recall. It won't do any good."

"I'd like to know what happened though."

"Of course," he said, and then he told me what he knew. It was a hit-and-run. They never caught the guy who did it. The car flipped on its side. I suffered a traumatic head injury. No need to go into the medical details, but I had been in a coma for nearly a week. It was only over the last few days that I'd begun recovering. Had opened my eyes. Responded to questions. I didn't remember any of it. "There is still some worry about neurological problems," he said. "Still some worries about cognitive deficits."

It took a moment for all of that to sink in. And then another thought. Was I alone in the car?

The doctor shook his head no. "Your husband was the one driving."

I felt a stab of pain in my gut. "My husband? Is he okay?"

"Yes. Other than a broken collarbone and some cuts and bruises, he made it out fine."

A tremendous sense of relief washed over me. "Good," I said. "That's good."

The doctor grabbed a clipboard from the table. He removed a pen from his jacket. "I'd like you to do something for me, Catherine. I want you to tell me about your husband. Anything at all. You see, sometimes memory can be affected by such a trauma."

The back of my skull was aching. I squeezed my eyes shut. "His name is Doug Gordon," I said.

"Yes. What else?"

"He has brown hair that is beginning to gray. Most days, he wears a shirt and tie. That's because he works at the bank. He doesn't smoke. He doesn't drink. He's never tried drugs. Sometimes he hums, which annoys me. He's allergic to shellfish. We have a happy life together."

I opened my eyes. The doctor seemed very interested in all of this. He jotted down everything that I said. "And how long have you been married?"

"Twenty-seven years," I said, "this August."

"And children?"

"A daughter. Her name is Martha. She lives in Illinois now and teaches kindergarten. She married a boy named Isaac. Isaac is very kind. He's also a teacher."

Another question: "And how did you meet your husband?"

I answered quickly. "At Larry Hartwick's barbecue. I was there with my sister. He kept staring at me. And then he approached me, introduced himself. I thought he was very handsome. We were married less than a year later. But I don't want to talk anymore. My head is aching."

The doctor gazed into my face. I wondered how I looked. Probably hideous. "I understand. Just know that I'm very pleased with your progress. Soon your husband will come visit you. Soon you will be able to go home."

"I'd like to sleep now."

"Of course. But before you sleep, I'd like to give you some pills. They will help with the pain."

He handed me two large, yellow pills and a glass of water. I swallowed them down one by one. And as soon as I did so, an image flashed in my head. Of Martha when she was just a child. She was in a red plastic sled, and I was pulling her through the snow toward October Hill. And the whole time, she was saying, "Faster, Mommy, faster," and I was laughing and laughing, my cheeks numb from the cold. It was a good memory.

"Be careful not to touch the back of your head," the doctor said. "There's an incision. It will heal soon. But we don't want to pull the stitches out too quickly."

I nodded, promised to leave it alone. As he started for the door, I called out. "Doctor? What's your name?"

He turned around and wiped some perspiration from his forehead. "Dr. Zagorsky," he said. "And I promise that you are in very good hands. The best hands you could be in."

———

My husband didn't visit me, at least not for the next couple of days. I asked about him many times, and they told me that they wanted to make sure that my brain was healing before he arrived. Seeing him could create a lot of emotions, and they didn't want there to be any setbacks.

Those days were mostly filled with tests. Usually, it was just Dr. Zagorsky, but sometimes there was an equally dour nurse present. Her name was Shelley. A few of the tests were physical—checking my heartrate, my reflexes, my strength. Pulling blood to evaluate my kidneys, liver, and thyroid. But most of them were cognitive. To test my short-term memory, for example, the doctor would read five words and ask me to repeat them immediately, and then again after some time had passed. To assess my concentration, he would read a list of digits and ask me to repeat them in reverse order. He had me identify animals. He had me tell time (digital and analog). He told me I was doing very well. I wasn't sure if I believed him.

He also spent a lot of time asking me about my memories. He wanted me to provide as many details as possible. The sights. The smells. The sounds. The tastes.

"Do you remember teaching Martha how to swim?"

"Yes," I said. "I remember."

"Tell me."

"It was at the lake by October Hill."

"That's right."

"Late summer."

"Yes."

"I had a terrible sunburn."

"And?"

"Doug held her. She was only about five at the time. I stood in the lake, just a few feet away. She reached out and grabbed my arm. I took a step back. She glided back to Doug. Each time I took another step back until she actually had to swim on her own. She learned quickly. We called her our little fish. She was a good swimmer."

Dr. Zagorsky didn't write any notes, but Nurse Shelley did. The doctor's eyes were gray and piercing. For just a moment, I had the strange notion that he was God or the devil or both.

"And now I'd like you to smell something."

"Smell something?"

"Yes. When you had your accident, you damaged your olfactory bulb, which is directly connected to the amygdala and hippocampus. For most people, the olfactory bulb is our smell center and can trigger a detailed memory. But when it's damaged, the triggers don't always come."

"I don't understand. I—"

He handed me a yellow-and-red piece of cloth. "I'd like you to press this against your face. I'd like you to breathe deeply. And then I'd like you to tell me if you remember anything."

I stared at the piece of cloth for a good long while. Then I pressed it against my face. I closed my eyes. I inhaled. It smelled like rain. It smelled like gardenia. It smelled like happiness.

Like happiness . . .

Nighttime. I was running through the neighborhood, streetlights drenching the houses in a mystical orange glow. The air was filled with sound: the faraway ringing of a church bell, the laughter of children, the mournful strings of a violin. The rain fell, and my white dress was getting soaked, but I didn't care because I was happy, I remember, I remember. A young man was running behind me, and he wore his military uniform. He was so handsome. His hand was extended outward, and he was laughing. A Russian Blue cat appeared in a stream of light and then disappeared behind a bush. The black poplar trees scratched away the moon, and then the rain stopped, and the young man held me and spun me around and kissed me, and more violins were playing, a string quartet, and we fell into the wet lawn . . .

"And what was his name?"

"Marcus."

"And he was a soldier?"

"Yes. He was on his way to the war."

"And you loved him."

"Yes. I loved him."

"But you never told Doug about him."

"No. We've all had secret loves. And it's better if they stay that way. Secret, I mean."

———

It was on May 13th that my husband finally came to the hospital. I know that because it was my birthday. He showed up with five pink balloons and a dozen red roses. I'd been very lonely and was glad to see him. I sat up in bed and smiled, not speaking at all.

"Cathy, Cathy, Cathy," he said, and he was wiping tears from his cheeks. "I can't begin to tell you how happy I am to see that smile. The most beautiful smile in the world. Happy birthday, my love."

"Doug," I said. "I missed you so much. I've been here all by myself."

"I know, darling. I wanted to be here. But the doctor, he thought it best if I waited. But now, here I am. Oh, Cathy. I thought I might lose you! That's what I thought."

Doug sat on the edge of the bed and kissed my forehead. I said, "Does Martha know? About the accident, I mean."

He nodded his head. "Of course. She's been worried sick about you. But I've been giving her updates."

I thought of Martha, and a wave of gratitude fell over me. My Martha! I loved her so.

"We're going to get you out of here very soon," Doug said. "I will take a few days off from work. And then another doctor will come by to check up on you. His name is Dr. Hoover. You'll like him. He's very kind."

"He's going to come to the house?"

"Yes. It's a little extra cost, but I don't want to have to drag you to some medical facility, not if we don't have to. You should be able to stay home. I made sure it's nice and clean. And stay home you will! Maybe a walk now and then. But no driving. Not for another month, at least. Doctor's orders."

"Okay," I said. "I'm ready to come home, Doug. I'm ready."

He smoothed back my hair with his hand, and his skin felt so nice on mine. "Soon," he said. "Very soon."

———

It was the following morning that Dr. Zagorsky told me that I would be released. "Your husband will be here shortly. He'll drive you home. You've made wonderful strides, Catherine. I'm thrilled."

"I thank you, Doctor, for everything."

Nurse Shelley gathered all of my things into a hospital-issued duffel bag. Dr. Zagorsky explained all of the drugs I would be taking and all of the cognitive exercises I would be practicing. He also mentioned Dr. Hoover and how Dr. Hoover would help me. But when I was all ready to get dressed and wait for Doug, Dr. Zagorsky said, "There's something I want to discuss with you. This clinic is quite a ways from Bethlam. I worry about the long drive. I worry about the bright Nevada sun. I'd like to give you some medicine. To make the trip easier."

"I don't think that's necessary. I—"

But before I could say another word, he pulled out a long needle and stuck it in my arm. I cursed and kicked.

"I'm sorry, Catherine," the doctor said. "It will relax you. Make you tired."

The medicine seemed to work almost instantly. And it did relax me. It did make me tired. In fact, when I finally woke up, I was home in bed.

CHAPTER 16

For the first several days after arriving home, Doug took good care of me. He cooked meals. He folded laundry. He cleaned the house. Jobs that had always been mine.

Whenever we were together, he told stories. Stories about us. About when we met, when we got married, when I got pregnant. Stories about Martha. About when she learned to walk, learned to talk, learned to argue.

"We've had a good life," he said. "Don't you think?"

"Yes. A very good life."

And then there was Dr. Hoover. For the first week or two, he came to the house every single day, sometimes more than once. He was just like Dr. Zagorsky. Sometimes I got them mixed up. Despite the fact that he was very kind, despite the fact that he was very calm, I always felt anxious in his company.

Just like when I was in the hospital, he performed tests, physical and cognitive. He gave me lots of pills and always watched carefully to make sure I swallowed them. Other than the occasional headaches, I was feeling much better. My memories were becoming clearer and more intense. And after some prodding from Dr. Hoover, I was even able to recall bits and pieces of the accident itself.

It was late at night and we were driving home from Reno. That's where Doug's sister lives. Her name is Claire, and she has Irish-red hair and emerald-green eyes. I remember the song that was playing on the radio: "Have You Never Been Mellow" by Olivia Newton-John. I also remember the smells. In the back seat, there were some leftovers from dinner. Baked chicken and fruit salad. And then after the collision, the smell of gasoline and burning tires.

"And do you remember the broken glass? Do you remember the shattered screams? Do you remember the warped car horn?"

"No."

"You will, Catherine. You will."

Every time Dr. Hoover came to the house to perform his tests, ask about my memories, my husband would sit there quietly, just watching me. It made me nervous.

Dr. Hoover: "Tell me about the accident. Tell me about your first kiss. Tell me about the wedding. Tell me about when Martha lost her first tooth. Tell me about this Barbie doll. When did you get it?"

"I remember," I said. "I remember."

Doug: "We've had a good life. Don't you think?"

———

One afternoon, I was sitting in the living room, staring at the Barbie dolls, staring at the photographs that lined the walls. Photos of Doug and me and Martha. In every single one of them, we looked so happy. Doug sat down next to me and squeezed my hand. That wasn't like him. He's not a tender man. But he just sat there, holding my hand for what seemed like a very long time, and we were both quiet. Eventually, he looked at me, his blue eyes piercing and cold. He said, "I want you to listen to me, Catherine."

"Okay."

"I just don't know if what I'm doing is the right thing."

I didn't know what he was talking about. I figured maybe he was referring to something at work. I responded by saying, "Oh, Doug, I'm sure you're doing the right thing. You always do the right thing."

But he only shook his head. I could see that his lower lip was quivering and that his eyes were glistening with tears. "What they're doing to you . . . it's hard to watch."

My stomach tightened. What they were doing to me? I didn't understand. "What do you mean?" I asked.

"They're treating you like . . . like a lab rat."

"No," I said. "They just want me to get better. From the accident."

He turned away. "Yes. From the accident. Do you believe what they tell you?"

And that was all he said. I didn't know how to respond, so I didn't. We stayed together for a few more minutes, and then he rose to his feet. He went into his office and closed the door.

An hour later I got busy on dinner. Spaghetti with meatballs. Caesar salad. I was glad that I was back on my feet, glad that I was able to, once again, take care of domestic duties. When dinner was ready, I called out Doug's name and he appeared from his office. We ate and talked about normal things. He didn't mention the accident or me as the lab rat. A part of me was curious and wanted to press him further. But another part of me didn't want to know. Deep down, I knew that something was wrong with me, with him, with the town, but I was terrified of hearing him speak the words.

I wish I'd remained oblivious. I would have been happy, I think.

———

That night I had trouble sleeping, and when I did finally fall asleep, I had a horrifying nightmare. In my dream, I was sitting in the living room, and I was wearing a black dress and a black veil. Outside, the snow was falling, and the trees looked like skeletons, bones reaching toward the window. Everything had been quiet, but then I heard the sound of a crow. The cawing got louder and louder. Then there was another crow cawing and another and another. I shut my eyes and covered my ears with my hands. When I opened my eyes, the snow had stopped falling, and it was night. The crows were still screeching. I rose to my feet. The door creaked open without me touching it. I walked outside and toward the sound of the crows. Soon, I was in a forest, the pinewoods swaying menacingly. A crooked dirt path led to a muddy pond, and that's where I saw the crows. There must have been a hundred of them, at least. They were flapping their black wings excitedly, pecking each other until they bled. I noticed that, for some reason, I had an old flint gun in my hand. I raised it toward the sky and squeezed the trigger. The blast caused most of the crows to fly away, leaving just a few remaining.

Now I could see what they were pecking at. At first, I couldn't tell what it was, but as I moved closer, I saw that it was a doll, badly mangled—eye decals torn off, ear missing, face scratched grotesquely. I took a few steps backward. Some of the crows returned to the water. And I saw something else. Something floating in the pond. I dropped my flint gun and ran toward the edge of the water. It was a little girl, face down, arms spread like a miniature Christ. With my breath caught in my throat, I flipped her over, and, to my great horror, saw that it was Martha and that her face was just as mangled and grotesque as the doll . . .

I woke myself up with a shriek. I turned toward Doug, but he was still asleep, a thousand miles away. I curled up into a ball and started crying silently. I cried for a long time. I didn't fall asleep for the rest of the night.

I couldn't get the image of that decomposed face out of my mind.

CHAPTER 17

The next morning, I tried calling Martha. The dream had terrified me, and I wanted to hear her voice. She didn't pick up her phone, so I left a voicemail and told her to call me back. I didn't hear from her. I called again an hour later. Still no answer. Another voicemail. I felt anxious, and so I kept calling. She would be annoyed when she saw all of my phone calls. She would claim that I was being overbearing. But I couldn't help myself. She was my daughter.

It was on my fifth or sixth attempt that Doug startled me. He had been standing behind me, watching me, and I hadn't known he was there. "You need to stop," he said.

I spun around, the receiver dropping from my hand. "I . . . I didn't know you were there."

"She's not going to answer," he said.

"What do you mean by that?"

He placed his hand on my leg. "Martha loves you very much. But she's not going to answer that phone. You need to focus on what you can control."

"I don't understand."

"Dr. Hoover will be here soon. He wants to make sure you're progressing."

———

Dr. Hoover was indeed pleased with my progress. My brain was healing nicely. My neurological and cognitive functioning were proceeding as planned. The headaches had become less frequent. Of course, I didn't tell him about the dream. There was no point. He might have prescribed more pills. I was taking enough pills.

Eventually, Doug went back to work at the bank. He asked me over and over again if I felt okay about it. He felt guilty leaving me alone. I told him not to feel guilty, that I would be just fine in the house. If you want to know the truth of it, I was looking forward to him leaving, looking forward to getting some time on my own. True, Dr. Hoover still came by most days, but at least I had a few hours where I wasn't being smothered.

And then this happened.

It was maybe a week after Doug had returned to work. I was performing my daily tasks: cleaning the bathrooms, dusting the floorboards, folding the laundry, vacuuming the carpets. Everything looked lovely. Everything was in its place.

Once I had finished with the rest of the house, I ventured into his office. I didn't go in there very often, but I figured since I had time, I'd straighten it up. I was being a good wife. Now, I wish I hadn't gone in there. Sometimes it's better not to know.

I started by washing his windows, which had become foggy from grime, and vacuuming his carpet, which had become filthy with crumbs. Then I got to work on his desk. It was piled high with banking papers—dates and check numbers and deposit amounts.

When I finished his desk, I tackled his closet, which was an absolute mess. There were giveaway clothes piled messily in the corner, stacks of books pressed crookedly against the wall, and boxes of junk spread haphazardly from front to back.

I got down on my knees and began folding the clothes and organizing the books. One of the boxes was filled with toys and tiny shoes and baby clothes. Another box was filled with photographs that I'd never bothered placing in photo albums. I flipped through them quickly, and it was strange seeing me and Doug look so young, strange seeing my daughter as a toddler.

"Looking at the photographs is good for you," Dr. Hoover would say. "And even if the photographs are only an impetus for constructing a fictional narrative, that's okay. Because all of us create those fictional narratives. We just assume they're real."

But I did remember. And what I remembered was real. It didn't matter what Dr. Hoover said. Didn't matter what Doug said. I could differentiate reality from fiction. I knew who I was and what had happened to me. Although, to be fair, sometimes doubt crept in.

I stared at those photographs, and soon I was breathing deeply, and a feeling of profound sadness seemed to be moving inside of me. That happens whenever I think too much about the past. I don't know why. Other than the accident and that Saturday morning when I found my father after his heart attack, there was no real trauma in my past.

I gathered the photographs and dropped them in the box, and then I shoved the box into the corner. I decided I wouldn't look at them again. No matter what Dr. Hoover said.

But I had just risen to my feet when I noticed a manila folder in the corner of the room. It must have been hidden beneath one of the boxes. I bent down and picked it up. On the front, in voluminous Sharpie ink, was the name "Jane Desmond."

The envelope was sealed. I was curious, so I used a jagged fingernail to lift up the flap. I began breathing heavily, my sense of nostalgic sadness shifting to an unexplained dread.

I pulled out the documents.

The first thing I saw was a single photograph of a young girl. She had pigtails and a gap-toothed smile. There were also a bunch of official-looking documents. A birth certificate. School records. Doctor reports.

And finally, at the bottom, a coroner's report.

The report was dated from 1999, more than twenty years ago. Jane Desmond. Age: 6. Cause of death: drowning. Place: bathtub.

And then, at the bottom of the document, the coroner's decision: homicide.

I sat cross-legged in the closet for a long time. No matter how hard I squeezed my eyes shut and tried to think, I couldn't make sense of any

of it. Who was Jane Desmond? Who had killed her? And, most importantly, why did Doug have these documents in the first place?

———

Looking back, I should have kept my mouth shut, but I couldn't help
myself. That evening, as we sat at the dinner table eating lamb and mint
jelly and drinking pineapple juice, I asked him about Jane Desmond. He
winced noticeably, but then his body quieted, and he continued chewing
his lamb. He picked up the napkin from his lap and dabbed the corners
of his mouth. Then he looked me in the eyes and said, "Jane Desmond?
Never heard of her."

I used my fork to move the mint jelly back and forth across the
plate. "Are you sure?" I said. "Are you sure you've never heard of Jane
Desmond?"

He shook his head. "I'm sure. Who is she?"

"I don't know. I was cleaning up your office, and I found a folder
there with documents about her and pictures of her. She was just a girl.
She had pigtails."

His chewing slowed. He picked up his glass of juice and took a long
gulp. Then he said, "In my office? That's strange. I wonder how it got
there. It must be some kind of a mix-up."

He was lying. He knew Jane Desmond.

"Somebody drowned her," I said. "More than twenty years ago. I
wonder why somebody would do that? She was just a girl."

He took another piece of meat and placed it in his mouth. "I don't
know. It's hard to know why anybody does anything."

"Just a mix-up, then?"

"Just a mix-up." His lips curled into a faint smile.

"It's too bad," I said. "She was such a pretty girl too. Jane Desmond
was her name."

"Jane," he whispered.

I rose to my feet to clear the table, but Doug said, "Take a load off. I'll
take care of the dishes. Why don't you go lie down? But first, you need to

take your pills. We don't want any setbacks. You've made such progress already."

I nodded my head and smiled. "Yes. Tremendous progress. All thanks to Dr. Hoover and you."

Who was Jane Desmond?

"Not at all," he said and reached into his shirt pocket for my canister of pills. "You're the one who has done all the hard work." I placed my hand out and he shook two of them into my hand. "Swallow them down."

He watched me closely. I placed them in my mouth but then maneuvered them beneath my tongue. I only pretended to swallow. When he rose to his feet to clear the table, I spat them into my hand.

"I'll go upstairs now," I said. "To lie down."

"Yes," he said. "That's a good idea. I love you, Catherine Gordon. You're a wonderful mother. A wonderful wife."

I forced a smile. "And you're a wonderful father. A wonderful husband."

It was a very nice moment. I felt like I was going to vomit.

I went upstairs to the bedroom and lay down on the bed, resting my hands behind my head. Pretty soon, my mind began wandering like it was bound to do. I couldn't help but wonder if Doug had had something to do with Jane's death. The way he'd responded only added to my suspicion. Maybe, I thought, I should go to the police station with the documents. Maybe they would help get to the bottom of it. But, no. Doug would find out. He would get mad. He had never hit me before. But if I betrayed his trust, he might do that and worse.

I rolled onto my side and stared at the yellow wallpaper that was beginning to peel from the wall. I thought of a story I had read when I was a child:

"There are things in that paper which nobody knows but me, or ever will. Behind that outside pattern the dim shapes get clearer every day."

Soon I fell asleep. I had the same dream as the night before, only this time instead of Martha, the crows were pecking at the bare flesh of Jane Desmond.

CHAPTER 18

As the days moved on, I became more and more suspicious of my husband. Even though we had been married for twenty-four years, there were times when it seemed like twenty-four hours, times when it seemed that I didn't know him at all. I would stare at his thick and hairy hands and imagine them holding that poor girl underwater while she violently slapped the porcelain tub.

Then I would feel ashamed. I was being ridiculous. My husband wasn't capable of doing something like that. But whether I was being unreasonable or not, whenever I was in his presence, I felt a mixture of revulsion and fear.

In bed, he would place his hand on my breast and try kissing me, and I would push him away. "I'm still not ready," I would say. "Not until I'm fully healed."

But it had nothing to do with my brain. It had everything to do with my heart.

Whenever Doug was gone, whenever he was at work, I would study those documents. From the school records, I learned that Jane attended New Vista Elementary School in Topeka, Kansas, (a long way from Bethlam, Nevada) and that she had been diagnosed with autism. From the birth certificate, I learned that she was born on February 6, 1993, to Travis and Lucinda Desmond. And from the doctor's report,

I discovered that she had suffered a dislocated shoulder just weeks before her death.

I spent hours staring at the school photo, at that gap-toothed smile, wondering who could have done such an awful thing to such an innocent girl. Doug? Logically, I knew that he couldn't have had anything to do with it. After all, the homicide happened several years after Doug and I were married. Not only that, we'd never lived in Topeka. In fact, I didn't think we'd ever *been* to Topeka.

Still, I couldn't help creating narratives about young Jane and my husband. And the narratives were dark and twisted.

In one of the narratives, I convinced myself that he'd been secretly married to Lucinda Desmond from Topeka, Kansas, and had fathered the child. Frustrated by his daughter's autism or angered at his wife's infidelity, he had drowned the girl in a fit of rage . . .

I would have looked up the case online, found out who Lucinda and Travis Desmond were, but Dr. Hoover had barred me from owning a phone or having access to the internet, claiming that it would sabotage my recovery.

So my only resources were those documents.

Until one day, they vanished.

———

I had taken to hiding the manila folder beneath the dresser. Ever since I'd revealed the discovery to Doug, I'd been worried that he would demand I give him the documents back, but that hadn't happened. In fact, he'd acted indifferent and unconcerned and had made no further inquiries.

But one morning, while he was at work, I reached beneath the dresser, and the folder was gone. I slid my hand back and forth. Nothing. I located a flashlight and peered between the shadows. I was convinced that Doug had found the folder and shredded the documents inside.

What did he have to hide?

I obsessed over confronting him about the folder, but I worried that he would become enraged at the accusation. Finally, I got up the courage.

We were sitting in the living room. He was sipping on coffee, and I was holding a mug of Earl Grey tea. Doug's legs were crossed, and he was reading a book: *Chaplin: His Life and Art.* I kept trying to find the right moment to speak. From the hallway, I could hear the pendulum of the grandfather clock swinging back and forth.

"Darling?" I said, my voice meek. "Remember when I asked you about that girl? Jane Desmond?"

He didn't look up from his book. "Jane who?"

"Desmond. The one who'd been drowned."

He furrowed his brow. "It doesn't ring a bell."

"There were documents and photographs. I stored them beneath the dresser for safekeeping. Inside a folder. Did you take that folder?"

He shook his head. "I don't know what you're talking about, Catherine."

"This girl, Jane. She had pigtails. She was autistic. Somebody killed her. I don't know who took the folder. Are you sure it wasn't you?"

He rose from his chair and walked over to where I was sitting. He placed his hand gently on my shoulder.

"Catherine, darling. Listen to me. You never mentioned a girl named Jane. You never mentioned a drowning. I didn't find a folder with documents. Maybe you need to get more sleep. Maybe we need to adjust your dosages."

I felt panic swelling in my chest. "The folder was there! I swear! All sorts of documents inside. Her parents were named Travis and Lucinda. They lived in Topeka."

"Take a deep breath," Doug said. "It's okay. Your brain is healing. These things take time."

―――――

In the days that followed, I returned to the comfort of routine. Each morning, I would wake up at seven o'clock; Doug would wake up a half hour later. That gave me time to make breakfast. He would come downstairs at eight o'clock, dressed in his banker's suit, and would kiss me on the cheek and ask how I'd slept. Then he'd sit down at the kitchen table and read his newspaper and eat his scrambled eggs and bacon, drink his coffee. I normally didn't eat with him because my stomach never felt right in the morning. At eight thirty, he would rise from the table, take a final swig of coffee, and kiss me on the cheek again. Then he'd leave for work.

I'd clean his dishes and place them in the dishwasher and then, after watching my stories on television, would get busy on the rest of the house.

But I couldn't stop obsessing about my husband's possible connection to Jane Desmond. So one day, I deviated from my routine.

On this day, I left his dishes where they were. On this day, I didn't sweep the floor and vacuum the carpets.

On this day, I decided to check up on him at work. I don't know what, exactly, I expected to find. But I knew I'd find something.

In my closet was a yellow raincoat that I didn't remember ever wearing and a Nancy Drew–style cloche hat. I put both of them on and then looked at myself in the closet mirror. I looked like an amateur sleuth—I *was* an amateur sleuth—and I couldn't help but grin. I took another couple of steps forward to get a better look at my face. That was the hard part. Studying my features too closely. See, for some reason, I didn't always recognize myself. No, that's not quite right. I recognized myself, but it was a face I didn't trust, with secrets behind those blue eyes.

I stepped outside and stood on the front porch for a few minutes, gazing into the distance toward the Sierra Nevada Mountains. Not another town for twenty miles. Just us. In Bethlam, Nevada.

Eventually, I started walking. I walked through the neighborhoods, and the houses were all identical. A company town it had been. Back when they were testing nuclear weapons. But they'd cleaned up the air. They'd cleaned up the soil.

And why was everybody watching me? From their kitchen windows. From their front porches. Everybody smiling, but the smiles weren't real. I knew all of them. The Johnsons. The Hardys. The Martins. We'd gone to the same churches. Our kids had gone to the same schools, had performed in the same choir concerts and soccer games. We'd laughed together, eaten together, gossiped together.

But somehow, the memories weren't right.

I can't explain it.

I arrived at Main Street. A scattering of people meandered down the street, and they all glanced at me furtively.

I thought more about Bethlam, the company town, the town that I used to read about in school. It was here that the scientists had lived and nearby where they'd tested those nuclear bombs, preparing for some kind of a postapocalyptic world. Those scientists were all gone now. But not the town. Not Bethlam. And then I started thinking about a different kind of town, those replica towns our government had created in order to see the effects of the bomb. I'd seen pictures. They looked like typical Norman Rockwell towns, only instead of people sitting inside the houses, there were mannequins. And then, after the explosion, the faces turned to melted plastic. The images always scared me.

I walked slowly down Main Street, glancing at the businesses lining the street: Diner, Pet Shop, Grocery, Barber. I pressed my face against the glass of the diner. A man wearing a white apron stood behind the counter, staring straight ahead. Everything was in place—a counter, vinyl booths, a chalkboard with today's special—but there were no customers. Next, I went to the barber and saw a similar scene: a man with a flattop standing motionless behind the barber's chair, a comb in one hand and scissors in the other. Similarly empty. I whispered, "The world is dead. The world has always been dead."

I heard a mournful moan, and I spun around. Standing across the street from me was a Black woman, beautiful. She was staring right at me, her mouth ajar. With painful deliberation, her right arm raised from her side, and her index finger extended until she was pointing at me. I glanced around to see if it was possible that she was pointing at somebody else, but no. I was the only one around. She stayed like that for a long time, pointing at me. Then her lips moved, and I could tell she was speaking. I couldn't hear what she was saying. I took a step forward. She spoke again. Her voice was faint, but I was pretty sure I understood what she said: "I know who you are."

We both walked toward each other, but she'd just reached the street when a man wearing a blue raincoat and carrying an ice cream cone grabbed her arm and pulled her away. "Come on, darling," he said. "Let's not make a scene."

I stopped in my tracks and watched as the man forced her down the street. Every so often, she turned her head toward me, and each time she said those same words: "I know who you are."

Then she was gone, and I looked at my hands and saw the faint residue of dried blood.

What's done cannot be undone.

———

Bethlam Bank was located on Main and Third, in between the post office and the dentist. It was a windowless brick building. I seemed to recall Doug showing me the building, saying, "This is where I spend my days, darling," but I don't think I had ever gone inside. I'd never actually seen him work. For five minutes, ten, I stood there staring at the building, my arms folded over my chest. What was I doing there? What did I expect to find? The sun shone overhead, and sweat bubbled on my forehead and trickled into my eyes.

And then, like in a dream, I was walking toward the entrance, the air a hazy yellow, Main Street completely empty. I reached the front door and pushed, but it was locked. I pounded a few times on the door, but there was no answer.

Why would they be closed in the middle of the day?

Every morning, Doug kissed me on the cheek. Every morning, he read the paper and ate his breakfast. Every morning, he went to work at the bank. That's where he was. Of course, that's where he was.

I should have gone home. But my sense of discomfort was so acute that I felt compelled to enter the building. I walked around the block toward the alleyway. There were no cars, no trash cans, no people. I closed my eyes for a minute, listened. Absolute silence. I had the strange sensation that I was the last woman on earth, that everybody else was dead and gone. Or maybe I was one of those nuclear mannequins, ready to be smoldered by fire.

I walked down the alley slowly, hesitantly, until I came to the back of the building. There was a glass door with a faint cartoon painting of a bee holding an ice cream cone, as well as an outline of the name of the business that must had been there before the bank: *Freeze Bee.*

I pushed on the door; surprisingly, it was unlocked. I took a deep breath and stepped inside. Ahead of me was a long hallway, the floor black-and-white-checkered linoleum. As I walked, my flats echoed against the brick walls. My heart felt like a trapped bird, flapping against my rib cage. It seemed to take forever to reach the end of the hallway. When I finally did, there was another glass door. This one had the name of another business, long gone, written in rainbow script: *The Holiday Hotel.* I tried peering in, but the glass was foggy, and I couldn't see a thing. But this door was also unlocked, and so I entered.

Inside, there were no customers, no bank tellers, no bank counters. Everything was empty and abandoned. The carpet had been pulled up, and there was sawdust on the floor. Where was Doug? Where was the world?

I closed my eyes and my ears were full of an overwhelming silence. When I opened my eyes, I saw that a man was standing in front of me. I gasped. He had jet-black hair but a gray beard. He grabbed me by the arm, his fingers digging into the flesh. "What are you doing here, Mrs. Gordon?" he said.

How did he know my name? "I . . . I'm looking for my husband. This is where he works."

"You shouldn't be here. Not today. You should be in your house."

"Where is everybody?" I said.

The man with the beard shook his head. "You're just confused. From the accident. Let's take you back to your house. You're just confused."

He took a step forward, trying to move me, but I didn't budge.

"What's your name?" I asked. "Who are you?"

"My name is Dale," he said, and jerked at my arm. "I'm only here to help. We're all here to help."

"I don't need help. I just want to find out what is happening in Bethlam. I just want to find out what is happening in my brain."

"There will be time for all of that," he said, and this time he jerked harder. There was no use fighting.

We walked out of the empty bank and down the empty streets, and the whole time, he tried soothing me, saying things like, "Don't worry, everything will be okay," and "They're working on a permanent fix."

None of this felt right, so every so often, like a stubborn toddler, I would stop walking. Dale would sigh, say he understood my confusion, and then jerk me back into motion.

By the time we finally arrived at my house, the sun was high in a cloudless sky, and the man was asking me to tell him my earliest memory.

I just shook my head. "It's hard to say. I don't know what to think about my memories."

After he walked me to the front door, after he shut me inside, I remained at the kitchen window for some time. Dale, the man with the beard, remained on the sidewalk. And then another man joined him and they talked and laughed and laughed some more.

And I thought of the woman pointing at me and the words she said.

I know who you are.

CHAPTER 19

I decided that I wouldn't let on to Doug that I'd been outside of the house that day. I wouldn't let on that I'd been to the bank. Wouldn't let on that the bank was empty. I would be stealthy in my approach, playing the role of a good wife and a good housekeeper.

He got home at his usual time, the door banging open and his footsteps echoing on the hardwood floor. I was in the bedroom and quickly fixed my hair in the mirror and undid a button on my blouse. Then I hurried to the living room, a good wife excited to see her hardworking husband. When he saw me, he grinned a crooked grin before hanging his blazer on the coatrack. Hands clasped together at my chest, doing my best to look like Patmore's "Angel in the House," I approached him and gave him a quick peck on the lips.

"Welcome home, darling," I said. "How was your day?"

"It was just fine," he said, grinning again. "Working hard, hardly working. And what about you? Were you able to stay busy? Did Dr. Hoover stop by?"

"Oh, yes," I said. "There's always so much to do around the house. Sweeping. Dusting. Vacuuming. Watching my stories. Reading my romance novels. I kept very busy, indeed. But Dr. Hoover didn't stop by. Maybe he had other patients he needed to see. Maybe he wasn't feeling well himself. It's okay. I'm doing very well. I'm just about back to normal, I think."

Doug frowned. "Hmm. That's odd. He was supposed to check up on you. That was the plan. Oh, well. I'm glad you're doing well."

"In any case," I said, still trying to play it cool, "it was a beautiful day. Sun shining in a blank blue sky. Were you able to get outside the bank at all?"

No hesitation on his part. "Unfortunately, no. I was stuck inside. Too much work to do. Did some refinancing on a couple of mortgages. Opened a few accounts. But I won't bore you with the details."

"Oh, you wouldn't bore me," I said. "In fact, I'd love to come into the bank sometime. Just to pay you a visit. Just to see the kind of work you do."

He glanced at me sideways before sinking down into the couch. "Sure, darling. But enough talk about work. How about a drink?"

"Of course," I said.

Dr. Hoover had forbidden me from drinking alcohol, so it was just Doug who would be drinking. I went into the kitchen and poured him a beer. Meanwhile, all sorts of thoughts were racing through my mind, and none of them were all that good. I thought about the dead girl and the empty bank. I thought about Dr. Hoover and Dr. Zagorsky. I thought about the man with the white beard.

And that's when the phone rang. Doug rose to his feet and answered it.

For a brief moment, my hopes were raised that it was Martha, sweet Martha. I hadn't talked to her in such a long time; I could barely remember the sound of her voice. But, no. I could tell from the inflection of Doug's voice that it wasn't our daughter. I could tell it was a serious call. I stood at the edge of the living room, holding his beer, listening to his end of the conversation.

"I see . . . Is that right? . . . I wasn't aware of that fact . . . I'll have a conversation with her . . . No, I don't think it's necessary to report it . . . Yes, I'll make sure it doesn't happen again."

Report it? Report what?

He hung up the phone and stared straight ahead. I walked delicately across the floor and placed the beer on the coffee table. He looked at me for a beat and then at the beer. He picked up the glass, took a long swallow, and then placed the beer back on the coffee table.

"Who was that?" I asked, my voice trembling. "Somebody from work?"

He shook his head. "No. Nobody from work."

"Then who?"

His voice softened. "It doesn't really matter who." He pointed toward the seat next to him. "Have a seat, darling."

"I should probably start dinner. Otherwise—"

"Sit."

Something was definitely wrong. I sat down, flattening my dress with my hand. He took another drink, this time a much longer one, and wiped his mouth with the back of his hand.

"Well?" I said. "What is it?"

He didn't answer right away. Instead, he began chewing on his fingernails, something he did when he was anxious. Eventually, he looked up at me, his eyes jutting slightly. When he spoke, his voice was severe. "When I left for work, you promised that you would stay home."

I lied, as if from instinct. "But I did stay home. Of course I did."

He tapped the coffee table with his fist. "Don't lie to me, Catherine. Not now. You were spotted around town. Peeking in store windows. And then sneaking in the bank."

"No, I—"

He jerked his body toward mine, and for just a moment, I thought he would hit me. But he didn't. Instead, his voice changed to a tone of sympathy. "I'm not upset at you, darling. I understand you wanting to get out and about. But you have to listen to me. You must not go out by yourself. Not yet. Not until Dr. Hoover says it's okay."

"I don't understand," I said. "It's a safe town, Bethlam. The safest in Nevada. Why can't I go for walks? I don't want to be locked in the house forever."

"You won't be. Of course you won't be. But right now, it's not safe for you to leave the house by yourself. Because you're still not completely well. Your perceptions . . . they might be a little bit off."

"No. That's wrong. There's nothing wrong with my perceptions."

He leaned toward me, words escaping from nearly gritted teeth. "Listen to me, Catherine. I'm only telling you this for your own good. Please trust me. If you leave the house, you'll be in danger."

Maybe. But not from the town, I thought. From him. He'd killed that girl. I knew he'd killed that girl. And he'd kill me next.

"I understand," I said, forcing a smile.

His body relaxed, and he touched my knee. I couldn't help it: I flinched.

"I'm sorry this is happening," he said. "I don't like it."

"Yes," I said. "I'm sorry too."

"What's important right now is that you keep your routines. That's what Dr. Hoover says. And I tend to agree with him."

"Yes. My routines." I rose to my feet. "Which is why I should make dinner."

He massaged the bridge of his nose, his jaw muscles flexing. Then he nodded his head. "It's a good idea. Besides, I'm awfully hungry."

———

As the days passed, I felt more and more like a prisoner. It wasn't that I was locked up in a cage or a padded room. Instead, it was because Doug was always watching me, always keeping tabs on me.

I'd find myself wandering through the hallways and Doug was always within earshot. I would go to the bathroom, and he would wait outside, and if I were there for more than four or five minutes, he would knock on the door and ask if I was okay. When I wanted to go to the bedroom and lie down, he always made sure to crack open the door.

Even at night, when I was sleeping, I felt like a prisoner. I'd wake up from a bad dream, open my eyes, and Doug would be on his side watching me, studying me.

Why does he have pictures of a dead child?

But he wasn't the only one keeping me prisoner. Now, when he left for work, I noticed that there were always men (and sometimes women) keeping watch outside my house. If I stepped outside, they would ask how I was doing (they were always very polite), and if it looked like I was about to go for a walk, they would encourage me to stay home. The "encouragement" felt more like a threat.

Meanwhile, Dr. Hoover came by more and more frequently. He ran more tests. He drew blood. He placed electrodes on my temple. It's because of the accident, he said.

The accident.

The accident.

It's because of the accident.

———

Move ahead two days, three at the most. I was all alone, sitting on the couch reading a *People* magazine, the Barbie dolls watching my every move, when I heard knocking on the front door. At first, I assumed that it was Dr. Hoover, and my stomach tightened in anticipation. I placed the magazine on the coffee table and rose to my feet. From the dining room, I could hear the pendulum of the grandfather clock swinging with a dull and monotonous clank; I thought of time gone by and shuddered.

When I opened the front door, nobody was there. But what was there, leaning against a potted plant, was an envelope. I bent down and picked it up. It was addressed to me. I looked around and, not seeing anybody, returned inside and shut the door. I sat down on the couch and studied the handwriting on the outside of the envelope; it was a lovely variation of Western calligraphy.

With great care, I unsealed the envelope. There were several pieces of paper inside, all with the same lovely handwriting. The pendulum kept swaying, kept clanking, and as I started to read the first page, I couldn't help but feel an overwhelming amount of foreboding.

CHAPTER 20

Dear Catherine,

My name is Veronica Miller. I live at 328 Maple Street, the blue-and-white house across the street from the transmission tower. I've lived in this very house, in this very town, for almost all my life. Bethlam is a wonderful town, a wonderful place to live. At least that's what they've always told me. At least that's what I always thought.

Let me explain. Not so many weeks ago, I was badly injured when an intruder entered my home. I don't remember the details, but I'm told that the intruder entered the house while I was making lunch. He hadn't expected me to be home. When I appeared in the living room, he panicked and hit me over the head with a blunt object, maybe the barrel of his gun. I lay unconscious for nearly an hour before my husband, Brian, returned from work and found me. Naturally, he rushed me to the hospital. I was in a coma for nearly a week. The doctor who treated me there was named Dr. Zagorsky.

The days following my awakening are hazy. My husband wasn't there. Dr. Zagorsky and his assistants performed all sorts of tests on me. Most of them were cognitive in nature, and a good many of them dealt with "testing" my memory, which was strange because I wasn't having any problems with my memory. Headaches, yes. Memory issues, no.

Anyway, I stayed in that hospital for several more days. My room was small with no windows. Each day, when the doctors and nurses were done testing me and giving me medication, they left the room, making sure to lock the door behind me. I asked about Brian, of course. I asked about my sister, Julia, and they told me the time would come for them to visit, but the time wasn't yet. I worried that I had been placed in an insane asylum, but nobody had told me.

As I mentioned, they always locked the door. But on one particular morning, a nurse got lazy. After giving me my morning meds, she was busy staring at her papers, and when she left the room, the door didn't click shut. I praised Jesus for my good fortune. I waited a few minutes, making sure she didn't return. Then I readied myself to explore.

My legs had atrophied from lying on the bed for so long, so it was rather arduous to walk. Still, I managed to lurch across the room. I pushed open the door, just a crack, and peered outside. The hallways were empty. Praying for courage, I left my room.

I'm not a writer, so my descriptions of the hospital will leave a lot to be desired. What I can say is that it didn't look like any hospital that I'd ever seen. Instead of normal hallways, both the floor and walls were made of concrete, and they curved like a mountain tunnel. Additionally, there were several catwalks dangling from the ceiling, and from those catwalks extended several metallic ladders that stretched toward panels in the ceiling. Just like in my room, there were no windows, and I could hear anguished cries echoing against those hardened walls. I know now that I was underground, and understanding the sordid history of Bethlam, I'm guessing that it was an old converted nuclear shelter.

I was a patient, not a prisoner, but still, I felt great trepidation walking through those hallways; I was terrified that they might discover me and, upon doing so, punish me. It sounds ridiculous, I know, but maybe not so ridiculous. Anyway, I inched along, my back pressed against the concrete walls, my weakened legs dragging along the concrete floor. Every ten or so feet, there was a door, but they all were closed, and when I pulled at the handle, they were all locked.

Frustrated and confused, I was ready to turn around when I heard the sound of voices and wheels on the concrete floor. I hid around the corner, back to the wall and waited, barely breathing for the fear they might hear me.

The voices and wheels got louder and louder. I peeked around the corner and saw something that my mind couldn't quite make sense of. Coming down the corridor was a procession of hospital stretchers, maybe ten or twelve in all, each one being pushed by matching nurses dressed in white, nursing caps on top of hair tied in buns. On each of the stretchers was a patient, or maybe a corpse, right arm hanging off the side. And what was so shocking was that each patient—again, I was unsure if they were living or dead—had an identical expression: eyes shut, mouth frozen in a silent scream. It took all the willpower I could muster not to scream myself. While remaining out of view, I did my best to study each face, to recall the details.

At some point, the procession stopped. The final stretcher, a nurse behind it, was just a few feet from where I stood. And then the nurse left her position. For just a moment, I thought she had spotted me and was going to approach me, but she quickly turned and walked in the direction of the front of the line. Now the patient was unguarded. I took a step forward to get a better look.

And that's when the patient, a woman, turned toward me and opened her eyes.

A shriek escaped from my mouth. Feeling lightheaded and nauseous, I scurried down the hallway, all the while wondering who those poor men and women were, wondering what were they doing to them.

I retraced my steps back toward my room, every so often glancing over my shoulder for signs of a nurse, but after a while, I realized that I had gotten turned around and was heading in the wrong direction. I heard a loud pounding, and when I looked above me, I saw that one of the panels in the ceiling had opened and a man dressed in black was crawling down one of the metallic ladders. I spun around and began to run, galloped is more like it, and I felt more and more panicked.

I wasn't sure which way I was going, wasn't sure which way was my room. Eventually, the hallway came to an end, and there was only a concrete wall. In frustration, I slapped the wall with my hand, leaving an almost immediate bruise on my palm. I heard footsteps, and when I spun around, I came face-to-face with a nurse that I didn't recognize, her gray hair strangled in a bun.

"And what are you doing out of your room?" she asked in a stern tone.

I answered quickly. "I . . . I wanted to get some fresh air. Wanted to go for a walk. But then I got turned around. I forgot where my room is."

The nurse glared at me for some time, obviously suspicious, but then she nodded her head. "I'll take you back to your room," she said.

And she did.

She helped me into my bed, and I squeezed my eyes shut, pretended to sleep. As soon as she left, I got out of bed and located a pad of paper and a pencil. I've always been a good artist. Over the next hour, I drew the faces of the patients as best as I could remember them. I folded them and placed them in the front pocket of my purse, which was beneath the chair.

I stayed in the hospital for another three days. I didn't leave my room again. Dr. Zagorsky and the nurses continued treatment. They performed more and more tests. They had me recite more and more memories. I never mentioned to them what I had seen.

Eventually, I was released from the hospital. However, I

didn't get to see the outside of the hospital. That's because Dr. Zagorsky filled my veins with some poison. When I finally gained my senses, I was home in bed.

―――

Over the next few weeks, my recovery from the assault continued. A new doctor, Dr. Hoover, checked up on me almost every day. And just like Dr. Zagorsky, he focused on my memories.

Whenever I was alone, whenever I knew Dr. Hoover wasn't going to be observing me, I studied my drawings. I began doubting my own perceptions. Had I really seen what I thought I'd seen? I wasn't so sure.

―――

And now, back to where I first saw you in Bethlam. I was walking down Main Street with my husband. He'd gone into the ice cream shop to get us two cones. As soon as I saw your face, I felt the air sucked out of my lungs. I took a step forward and then another. It couldn't be. And yet, I'd never been so sure of something in my whole life. You were one of the patients that I'd seen on the stretchers. You were the one who had turned to me and opened her eyes. I still have the picture of you. I studied it for so many hours. I would have approached you right then and there. I would have told you what I knew. But it was at that moment that my husband appeared in his blue raincoat. It was at that moment that he grabbed my arm, whisked me away.

A day passed, and then two. I did some research, asked around. I found out your name. I found out where you lived. I've been scared to approach you. But I wanted you to know. And so I wrote this letter.

I don't understand either.

VM

———

As I finished reading Veronica's letter, another piece of paper fluttered to the floor. Hands trembling, I bent down, picked it up, and smoothed it out on my lap. It was a pencil drawing, but the details were remarkable. The drawing was of a woman, her eyes shut, her mouth frozen in a silent scream. But most frightening of all? The woman was me. The woman was definitely me.

I stared at the drawing for several minutes, my temples beginning to ache. I refolded the papers and placed them back in the envelope. I tried to make sense of things, but I couldn't. What had they done to me at the hospital? And why couldn't I remember?

I sat on the couch for an hour or more, staring at the shadows on the wall. I thought I should cry, maybe, thought I should scream.

Instead, I just sat there.

And I wondered what was real and what was fake.

CHAPTER 21

I wanted to talk to Veronica in person, but I was too afraid to contact her. That's because I was convinced that they—whoever they were— were tracking my every move.

I know it sounds paranoid. God knows I do.

But just because you're paranoid doesn't mean they aren't after you.

Remember the incision in the back of my neck? The one I received at the clinic? The one that has turned into a jagged scar? I am convinced that they placed a pea-sized microchip beneath my skin. I am convinced that if Veronica touched the back of her neck, she would feel that same jagged scar. That way, they could tell if we left the house. That way, they could tell if we tried to escape . . .

———

A couple of evenings after receiving Veronica's letter, I overheard Doug talking on the phone. He didn't know that I was listening. He thought that I was sleeping. He was in Martha's room, and I had my ear pressed against the door. His voice was muffled, but I could hear much of what he was saying.

"Let's plan on Tuesday, midmorning . . . Things are crazy here . . . A real shit show . . . Only a couple more weeks on my contract . . . Tell Elizabeth that I miss her."

Doug must have moved away from the door because soon his voice became softer, and I couldn't make out the words. I tiptoed down the hallway and back to our bedroom. I got into bed, curled under the covers. When he entered the bedroom, an hour later, I was still awake.

———

The next day, Doug told me that he was going on a business trip.

"Where are you going?" I asked. "What kind of a business trip?"

He answered with vague statements. Corporate offices outside of Reno. Needed to work on consolidating workforces. It would be a quick trip. A single day and night. My friend Marie would stop by to keep me company.

"Marie? Yes, good. I haven't seen her for a while. She's a good friend. It'll be good to catch up. I'll miss you."

He kissed my cheek. "And I'll miss you, my little dumpling. But don't worry. It's only for a day."

I nodded my head. "Yes. Only for a day."

But I knew that he was lying. I knew there was no business trip. I knew he was going someplace secret. And I needed to find out where that was.

After dinner, I pretended that I was going to take a bath. Smuggled in my bathrobe was a paring knife, used hours earlier for slicing onions.

A microchip beneath my skin.

Dr. Zagorsky had inserted it while I was in the hospital.

What else had they done to me?

And that's when the patient, a woman, turned toward me and opened her eyes.

Once in the bathroom, I removed my shirt. I gazed at my flabby stomach, my saggy breasts. When had I gotten so old? Frowning, I pulled my hair away from the back of my neck. I gripped a hand mirror in one hand and the knife in the other. I angled the hand mirror so I could see the back of my head reflected in the bathroom mirror. I took a deep breath and then reached around so the tip of the knife was touching the skin on my neck, right below the jagged scar. I mumbled a prayer to the nobody in the sky, gritted my teeth, and pressed the point against the skin until it punctured. I gasped in pain. The blood leaked down my neck in two narrow streams. With my fingernails, I dug around, but I couldn't find the microchip. I cursed under my breath. Once again, I pressed the knife to skin and made another slit a few millimeters higher. More blood. More pain. But still no microchip. I wasn't crazy. The town was crazy. I heard my husband's voice from outside the bathroom. "Catherine? You doing okay in there?"

Always checking on me. Even when I was taking a bath.

Even when I was cutting out a microchip.

"I'm fine, Doug. Just relaxing in the warm water."

"Relaxing? Are you stressed? Is that the problem?"

"No, no. Not stressed. I'll be out shortly."

I might have panicked a bit. I began poking and peeling, stabbing and slicing. When I touched the back of my neck with my fingers, they quickly became wet with blood. I moaned in discomfort. Doug must have been standing just outside the door, perhaps with his ear pressed against the wood, because he said, "Catherine? You don't sound so good. You sound like you're in pain."

"No!" I shouted. "Don't come in. As I said, I'll be out shortly. I'm just washing off."

I continued digging into the flesh. It felt as if I was peeling off large swaths of skin, and that made me shudder. Finally, I felt something hard and slender. Carefully, I plucked it out. Then I moved my trembling and bloody hand in front of my face and stared at the implant, a tiny black transponder encased in silicate glass.

I felt a great sense of relief at my accomplishment. I placed the microchip on the back of the bathroom sink.

"Catherine?"

"I'm just drying off! Just dressing."

I grabbed a towel from the cabinet and pressed it against the back of my neck, hoping I could get the bleeding to stop, but when I removed the towel, it was soaked with fresh blood. I grabbed another towel, and then another. It took ten minutes, more, before the bleeding finally slowed and stopped, and the whole time Doug was outside the door, threatening to come in, saying that it was highly unusual for me to be in the bathroom for so long.

I opened the medicine cabinet and located a bandage, which I stuck on the wound. I'd just put back on my shirt when I heard Doug ramming against the door. Once, twice, three times, and the door slammed open. Doug stood in the doorway, his face red and angry, his eyes full of contempt.

"It's time to come out," he said. "Forty minutes you've been in there."

"Yes," I said. "I'm coming out. Can't you see? I just got dressed."

His eyes darted like fish in a bowl, first at me, then at the bathroom. I was terrified that he was going to spot the microchip on the sink. I was terrified that the blood would start pouring down my back and puddle on the floor.

Instead, his eyes focused on the towels, two of which were soaked with blood.

He took a step forward. "Did you hurt yourself?" he said.

I shook my head. "Menstruation," I said quickly.

His eyes narrowed into slits. "Menstruation? Aren't you too old for that?"

"No," I said. "Not too old."

For a moment, I thought he was going to hit me. I don't know why. But instead, he just nodded his head. "Get those towels cleaned," he said. "Let's have a cup of tea together."

And so I did. And we did. Have a cup of tea, I mean.

With the microchip in the palm of my hand.

CHAPTER 22

The next morning consisted of the same routines as always. I felt oddly calm. Seven o'clock wake-up time. I made his scrambled eggs. His bacon. His coffee. At eight o'clock, he came downstairs, dressed in his banker's suit. He kissed me on the cheek, and it took all my willpower not to wipe away the saliva residue. "How did you sleep?" he asked.

"Very well," I said. That was a lie. Everything was a lie.

He sat down at the kitchen table and read his newspaper and ate his breakfast.

"Are you excited about your business trip?" I asked, even though I knew that he wasn't going on a business trip.

He didn't look up. "No. Not excited. It will be mundane. But I will be back tomorrow evening. That's the good news."

"That is good news."

He flipped through the pages of the newspaper. The war was still raging. The war would always be raging.

"And what time will you leave?" I asked. "How long is the drive?"

He glanced at his watch. "I guess I'll be leaving at eight-thirty just like normal. It'll take me an hour to get there. My first meeting is at ten. That should give me enough time, don't you think?"

I nodded my head. "Let's see, if you leave at eight-thirty and it takes you an hour, you should arrive at nine-thirty. Yes, that should be plenty of time."

After that, we sat in silence for several minutes. I kept my eye on the clock. 8:22. 8:23. 8:24.

When the clock struck 8:25, I rose from the table and flattened out my apron. "Darling," I said. "I'm going to say goodbye now. I've got a headache, and so I'm going to lie down."

He looked up. Was he suspicious? Maybe. Probably. "Headache?"

"Nothing unusual. Just didn't sleep well last night."

"I'll make sure Dr. Hoover swings by today."

I shook my head. "That won't be necessary. You said Marie would be stopping by tonight, right?"

"That's right."

"Marie is a good friend. We used to dance together when we were children. We used to laugh so hard that the milk would come out our noses."

"You've told me about that. She is a good friend. A lifelong friend."

I kissed Doug on the forehead. "Have a good trip," I said. "I'll see you tomorrow. Please drive safely."

"Of course," he said. "I'll see you tomorrow. And Catherine?"

"Yes, Doug?"

"I love you. I love you very much."

"I love you too."

It was no business trip.

I walked out of the kitchen. When I was out of his view, I quickly hurried to the living room. I placed the still-bloody microchip in Malibu Barbie's aqua blue swimsuit. Then I returned to my bedroom. I pulled at the window. It was jammed. I quickly glanced behind me, checking if Doug was there. No. He was still in the kitchen, still finishing his coffee. I took a deep breath and yanked hard. The window opened a little. I banged at the bottom with the palm of my hand and it moved some more. Another yank upward. It was now open wide enough for me to fit through. To escape the house.

To hide in Doug's car.

I quickly grabbed a blanket off the bed and returned to the window. I placed one leg through. Then I ducked my head under. And finally,

the other leg. I toppled from the window and fell onto the flower bed—
roses, gardenias, lilies. My knee got scraped, but it was fine. I got to
my feet and dusted myself off. Then I pulled the window shut. I only
had another minute or two before Doug would be walking through
that front door.

Body hunched forward, blanket tucked beneath my arm, I scurried against the side of the house toward the front, where his car was
parked. I prayed that none of my neighbors would see me. The microchip indicated that I was still in the living room.

I reached the car and glanced around. No sign of Doug. No sign of
anybody. His car was a four-door sedan. He kept it unlocked because
there was no crime in Bethlam. I opened the back door and crawled
inside, closed the door softly behind me. I huddled behind the driver's
side seat, covered by the blanket, trying to make myself as small as
possible. If he found me hidden in the back seat of his car, I'd just tell
him that I couldn't bear the thought of being without him that night.
Surely, he'd understand. Surely.

I thought he'd come out right away. That's what I thought. But
I waited there for a minute, five, more, and nobody came out. I got
worried. Maybe he'd gone to my room to check on me before he left.
Maybe he'd heard me opening the window. Maybe he'd already called
Dr. Hoover. Or Dr. Zagorsky. I thought about ending the plan prema-
turely, opening the car door and returning to the house. Cutting my
losses. But then I heard the front door of the house open and close. I
couldn't see a thing buried beneath the blanket. I held my breath. Didn't
move a muscle. I could hear his footsteps on the pavement. He opened
the passenger-side door and dropped his briefcase on the seat. Then I
heard him walk around the car to the driver's side. The door opened.
He got inside. The door slammed shut.

Never had I been so scared. Never had I been so excited. I was
going to find out where he was really going on this trip. I was a detective. A detective! I regretted that I hadn't worn my yellow raincoat
and cloche hat.

Doug started the car and sighed deeply. Before shifting into drive, he muttered something under his breath. I can't be sure I heard right, but I think he said, "Goodbye you crazy fucking bitch."

The town. The town was crazy.

We drove, and I remained under the blanket, still as an idol, breathing as shallow as I could manage. Doug turned on the radio, and at first it was news about the war and the economic collapse and then it was a fire-and-brimstone preacher and then it was 80s music—Hall & Oates, Huey Lewis and the News, Whitney Houston. On one occasion, Doug slowed down the car, lowered the window, and spoke with some type of authorities at what seemed to be a checkpoint. A checkpoint for what? They asked him questions that I couldn't hear. Doug's responses were terse, usually single-word answers: "Yes." "No." "Absolutely."

It's hard to tell how long we drove. My head was filled with all sorts of unruly thoughts. Through my blanket, I could see the shadows shift on the ceiling. Doug turned off the radio and then turned it on again. He tapped on the steering wheel with his fingers. He muttered to himself. Sometimes he laughed. It didn't sound like my husband, even though I knew it was.

At some point, I could tell that we were no longer on the highway. The car was moving slower, and there were more stops. We must have been in another town. He honked his horn, said, "Asshole." A few minutes later, the car slowed and came to a stop. Doug turned off the engine. I heard him sigh deeply before pulling the keys out of the ignition and opening the door. He came around to the passenger-side door and opened that one too. He must have been grabbing his briefcase. Then he slammed it shut. I could hear his footsteps on the pavement outside. They got softer and softer until they were gone.

I waited a minute, breathless, before pulling the blanket away and sitting up. The sun shone bright, and I had to use my hand to shield my eyes. We were in a neighborhood, only it wasn't like Bethlam. It was poor and run-down, with metal fences that corralled rotting houses. Beat-up station wagons and pickup trucks were parked on the streets, most of them ten years past their intended expiration date. One of the cars had its hood open, and a man on crutches was bent over the engine while his two filthy children looked on. A mangy cat and a mangy dog fought near a gutter. One thing was obvious: It was a neighborhood of poverty.

My eyes focused on Doug, looking ridiculously out of place in his suit, walking toward one of those houses, a sad-luck pink bungalow with the numbers 3-2-8 leaning crookedly against the wall. My mind raced. Certainly, he didn't have business partners living in a neighborhood like this. But a mistress? That seemed more likely. I felt like I was going to be sick. He walked up the rotted porch toward the front door. He didn't knock. Instead, he simply opened the screen door and then the front door. He stepped inside.

I wasn't sure what to do, how to respond. I remained in the back seat of Doug's sedan for some time, unwanted thoughts ready to transform into violent actions.

I don't remember getting out of the car, but at some point, I realized I was standing on the sidewalk, staring at the house. The man with crutches was still working on his car, and I saw that he was missing a leg, his pant leg tied at his knee. I walked toward where he was standing, and both of his children glared at me from behind filthy freckled faces.

"Excuse me," I said.

The man looked up but didn't say a word. He did place his wrench down, however.

"Can you tell me who lives in that house?" I asked, pointing at the pink bungalow.

His expression turned suspicious. "What do you want to know for?"

"Because my husband just walked into their house. I want to know whose house he walked into."

That was good enough. "The Martins," he said.

"The Martins?"

"Yes. The Martins."

"And . . . who are they?" It was a ridiculously stupid question.

His left eyebrow cocked. "They're just people. I haven't talked to them more than once or twice. They're just people."

I walked away from the one-legged man and his filthy children. I opened the gate and walked across the lawn. Then I stopped. None of this felt right. And if I knocked on the door? Then what? Instead, I made a beeline to an old pepper tree on the side of their house. I hid behind it, on my haunches. With all sorts of bad ideas, I stared at one of the windows. The curtain was pulled wide open. I could see the Martins' kitchen. There was an old refrigerator and dishwasher. A round wooden table with three chairs surrounding it. A single light bulb dangling from the ceiling. I could see shadows but no people.

From off in the distance, I could hear the sound of a mournful train whistle and then crows cawing. A warm breeze blew, carrying with it a candy wrapper, an old newspaper, a rusted beer can.

I hid behind that tree for ten minutes at least, staring at the window, waiting, waiting. And then I saw a woman—Ms. Martin?—enter the kitchen. She looked to be in her late thirties. She wore a sleeveless shirt and a long floral skirt. Her black hair was curly and tied in a sloppy ponytail. She wasn't very pretty, but when she smiled, I could see how a man might love her or at least fuck her.

A moment later, Doug entered. His suit jacket was gone and his tie was loosened. He looked relaxed and happy. I hadn't seen him look relaxed and happy, not for some time. But most interesting is what he was holding in his arms.

A little girl, two or three years old.

I tried rationalizing. Maybe Ms. Martin's husband had left her, and she was trying to raise a daughter on her own. Maybe Doug was just trying to help.

But why was the little girl hugging Doug's neck so tightly? Why was he kissing her cheek?

Tell Elizabeth that I miss her.

I stepped out from behind the tree. If Ms. Martin or Doug or the little girl had turned toward the window, they would have seen me standing there, a specter in the yellow grass.

Ms. Martin approached Doug and the girl. She extended her arms, hugged both of them. They stayed like that for some time. The three of them, embracing each other.

No. It couldn't be.

But, of course it could. This is where he'd been going for all of his business trips. To Ms. Martin's house. Not for business. For pleasure.

We'd been married for twenty-four years. We had a daughter. We taught her how to swim. At the lake by October Hill. We had a good life. Not a day of despair.

He was having an affair.

I strode toward the front door. The one-legged man and his children still watched me. I didn't have any control of my body. I didn't know why I was walking toward the front door. I didn't know what I'd do when I got there. Maybe I would kill him. Maybe I would kill all of them.

The wind was blowing harder and hotter. My brain was infected by madness. I walked up onto the crumbling porch. The screen door was banging open and shut. I stuck my shoe out to keep it from closing. My hand touched the doorknob and remained there for a moment. Then I twisted it open and stepped inside.

Nobody heard me enter, but I could hear them. Laughing. Talking. I wanted to scream, but I didn't. Instead, I looked around the living room, my breath shallow. It was a working-class house. There was an old couch with the cushions spilling from the corner. An old-fashioned television. Paint peeling from the ceiling. Toys scattered across the floor. I took a few more steps forward. On the walls were photographs. I stopped and stared at one of Ms. Martin and her daughter. The girl's name was Elizabeth.

More rationalizing. Maybe they were just friends. Ha-ha. Of course. High school friends. He'd come to pay her a visit. That would explain why they were hugging. Would explain why he was holding the girl. Of course. He was paying her a visit before he went to his business meeting. How stupid I'd been. I would just turn around and leave the house. I would go back to the car and hide. I'd become paranoid. I should have listened to Dr. Hoover. I should have stayed at the house.

More laughter from the kitchen. Doug telling a story. I backed up a step. And then another. But then I noticed another photograph on the wall. Another photograph of Ms. Martin and her daughter. Only in this photograph, Doug was in it too. It was taken at the same studio, with the same background. They were all smiling. Ms. Martin was holding the girl in her arms. Doug was holding Ms. Martin's hand.

They looked like a family.

They were a family.

I must have shrieked because a moment later, Ms. Martin, the girl, and Doug came rushing into the living room.

Ms. Martin: "Oh, my God."

Doug: "Catherine? Jesus. How did you get here?"

Me: Another shriek.

Pretty soon it was all chaos in that living room. Me shrieking. Ms. Martin shouting at Doug. Doug trying calm me down. The child crying.

My head was aching. I thought my skull might shatter.

How did I get outside? Did Doug carry me? Or did I walk out of my own volition? The next thing I remember is that I was in the car and I wouldn't stop shrieking.

Doug was driving way too fast, skidding around corners. He got on the phone. He said, "Catherine sneaked into the car. She saw me with Ella and Elizabeth. She won't stop screaming. What should I do? What should I do?"

Who was he talking to? Dr. Hoover? Dr. Zagorsky? I couldn't hear the answers on the other end. I stopped screaming. Doug hung up. He looked at me, said, "Take it easy, darling. Nothing's as it appears to be."

I tried speaking, but nothing came out.

He turned toward me, his lips spreading into a friendly grin. "Your accident . . . it was very serious. All of those doctors. Those pills. It's to help you."

"Who was that woman? Who was that girl? Who is Jane Desmond?"

"It's not important," he said. "All that's important is getting you some care. You're going to be all better. Do you believe me? You're going to be all better."

For the next fifteen, twenty minutes, I kept asking about the woman and the girl. He wouldn't give me a straight answer. He kept talking about the accident. About the doctors. About my brain.

We stopped at the same checkpoint that I suspected we had passed through on the way out. Armed guards wearing civilian clothes but camouflage hats sat inside a glass booth. When we arrived, they got out of the booth and approached the car. But no words were exchanged. Doug didn't even roll down the window. The guards nodded knowingly and waved us along the way.

Eventually, we got home. I got out of the car, went inside, and went to bed.

I slept for nearly twenty hours.

CHAPTER 23

Over these last couple of days, I haven't left the house at all. Neither has Doug. He told me that Hoover and Zagorsky would be coming by soon. When, he didn't know. But soon. They would explain everything. They would make everything better.

I asked him if he loved me. He said that he did.

But I knew that he was lying. I knew that he'd been lying the whole time.

I told him that I was going to sleep in Martha's room, that I wanted to smell her scent and remember her laughter.

"I understand," he said.

I kissed him on the corner of the mouth. "Even if you don't love me," I said, "I might love you. Even if you don't have any memories of us, I have so many. They're so clear. They're like movies, constantly playing. They're as real as anything."

"I know," he said.

I rose from the bed and walked out of the bedroom toward my daughter's room. I missed Martha. I missed her so much. Then I thought of the little girl, Jane. Doug had killed her in Topeka, Kansas. Held her head underwater.

Dr. Hoover says I will get better. Dr. Hoover is a liar.

I yanked the chain on the Emeralite lamp, and the light flickered on, shadows weaving against the wall. I sat down at the old wooden desk and, before they could steal my memories again, finished writing these words. I don't know if my story makes sense. I don't know how much of it is real, how much of it is made up.

Here's what I do know. Tonight, after midnight, I'll sneak out of the house. I'll wear my yellow raincoat and my cloche hat. The sky will be black, and the rain will be falling. I'll dance through those slanted raindrops, whistling a tune I've never heard until I reach 328 Maple Street. That's where Veronica Miller lives. I'll leave the journal for her. Maybe with my words added to hers, she'll be able to solve the mystery, be able to understand the true nature of Bethlam, Nevada.

And then tomorrow, before Hoover and Zagorsky come for me, I'll stand on the front porch, and I'll place the paring knife against the soft flesh of my throat, and when my husband and the neighbors are watching and listening and smelling, I'll slice through that soft flesh, and they'll watch the blood, hear the screams, and smell my death. And the whole time, I'll remember.

I'll remember everything.

PART 4

WALTER "WALLY" DALEY

CHAPTER 24

When I finished reading Catherine's journal, I sat on the floor, back to my bed, and stared at the wallpaper that covered the walls of my bedroom. It was a dull blue, the color beginning to fade from the sun that shone relentlessly through the dirtied window. In the corner, where wall met ceiling, a large patch had peeled, and I felt the urge to rise and yank the entirety of the paper from the wall like an old Band-Aid from skin.

I stared at that wallpaper, tears blurring my eyes, and I worried that I was going crazy, worried that my lucidity was approaching sundown.

From down the hallway, I could hear my father singing Frank Sinatra ("*Something in your eyes, was so inviting / Something in your smile, was so exciting*") and muttering non sequiturs ("Julie Andrews and Blake Edwards, a wonderful couple indeed"), and that did nothing to help.

I took a deep breath and then another. I wanted to somehow put all the pieces together, but there were so many of them, and it seemed that they were all chipped or warped or torn.

So what did I know? What did I know for sure? I knew that Veronica Miller had found herself in a strange underground hospital days after being knocked unconscious by an intruder. They forbade her from leaving her room, but one evening, she managed to escape. Exploring the labyrinth hallways, she witnessed a procession of gurneys being pushed by stone-faced nurses. Each of the patients had an arm dangling off the side (wasn't that what they do with corpses?), and one of the patients she saw was Catherine Gordon. But Catherine had no recollection of this experience, none, and had been led to believe that she'd been in a car accident. Once she returned home, a doctor named Hoover checked up on her frequently. The same doctor who checked up on Veronica. The same doctor who checked up on my father.

What else did I know? I knew that Catherine's husband had been living a lie, that he had another wife, another child, in another town. I knew that he kept photographs and documents of a mystery girl named Jane. A girl that had been murdered by drowning. And I knew that it had all been too much for Catherine, that she'd tried to end it all with a blade to the throat.

But she'd survived, and now she was back in her house, back with Doug Gordon, and she didn't remember a thing. She wore a turtleneck to conceal the scar.

Hell, hell, hell.

I hid the journal beneath my mattress. Then I rose to my feet and stood at the window. From across the street, I could see a man standing at the corner, using a handkerchief to dab the perspiration from his forehead. He was watching me. They all were watching me.

I moved to the far wall, where the blue-and-yellow wallpaper drooped, and I gazed at my reflection in the mirror. I touched my chin, and it was like I was touching a stranger's chin. I touched my cheeks, and it was like I was touching a stranger's cheeks.

"This town," I whispered, "is full of lunacy. I need to get out. I need to get out."

But not yet. First, I needed to find out the truth. What had they done to Catherine Gordon and Veronica Miller? And why?

———

Over the next several days, I was very cautious; I didn't want to raise any suspicions about my newly launched investigation. I went through my routines, just like a good boy. My alarm clock would go off at seven o'clock every morning, and every morning it would play the same song: "Wouldn't It Be Nice" by The Beach Boys. I would shower and shave and dress. Then I would go to the kitchen and make a hot breakfast. Eventually, the old man would appear, hair disheveled, legs lined with varicose veins, and sit at the table before starting his monologues about Beula and James Dean and Natalie Wood.

The same routines. Leave the house at 8:27. Walk to work. Find Mr. Temeer waiting with the three cartons of mail. Organize the mail into my bag. Say goodbye to Mr. Temeer, Ms. Yeats, and Ms. Keaton. Walk the same route down the same bleached sidewalks with the same mailboxes and the same neighbors watching my every move.

But now when a neighbor would regard me with suspicion, I would only nod my head and smile. If my father could put on a performance, so could I. I could be oblivious. I could be Walter Daley, a good son, a good postman. A good actor.

"Why, hello there, Wally!" Mr. Downing would say each afternoon, pausing from pruning his shrubs to wave at me. "Beautiful afternoon, isn't it?"

"Yes," I would say. "Beautiful."

When Dr. Hoover came over and asked me to recite more memories for my father, I did so without complaint.

Like this one:

"It was late fall and the darkening leaves were tumbling to the ground."

"Tell me more . . ."

"My mother was walking ahead, such a lovely woman, her white dress swaying gently in the breeze. From off in the distance, I could hear faded calliope music."

"Wonderful detail. The carnival must have been in town?"

"Yes. It must have been. The air smelled of wet grass and ripened apples. I was six or seven years old. The world was a wonderful place to live."

"And it still is, Wally. It still is."

"I remember my mother stopping and turning around and smiling.

She was so beautiful, my mother. She beckoned to me, with her finger. I quickened my pace until I caught up to her. Calliope music was playing. But I already mentioned that? The air smelled of wet grass and ripened apples. Imagine the moment! She put out her hand, and I squeezed it. Then she gazed at me, unblinking, her eyes the color of espresso. Her lips parted open and she said, 'Promise me, Wally, that you'll never forget this moment, not ever.' I promised her. And I never did forget. It was late fall."

Dr. Hoover squeezed my shoulder. "That's very good, Wally. Look very closely into my eyes. Do you see those tears?"

———

Was it three days later? Five days? A week? It doesn't matter. I was walking my normal route. Normal things happened: cars drove by; neighbors waved; cats meowed. I arrived at Veronica Miller's house. And even though, as always, all of the neighbors were outside watching, I walked up her path and knocked on the door. It took a minute, but then I heard footsteps echoing. Veronica pulled back the curtain on her window to see who it was. Then she opened the door.

"Why, hello," she said with that phony Southern accent. "How can I help you?"

"I'd like to see more of your paintings," I said.

She glanced around again and then forced a smile. I could tell that, once upon a time, she'd been beautiful. But time had roughened her skin, reddened her eyes, and yellowed her teeth. "Unfortunately, I don't think that's a good idea. My husband made it explicit. No more mailmen at the house. Not even you. You see, he's the jealous type."

I nodded. "I understand."

"But . . . you'll be back tomorrow, won't you? To pick up mail?"

"Yes."

She leaned forward and spoke in a voice barely louder than a whisper. "There will be a letter. Addressed to my parents. Mr. and Mrs. Charles Sundberg. They live in Lexington, Kentucky. Will you make sure you take special care of that letter? Don't let it get mixed up with all your other mail."

"Yes," I said. "I will take good care of that letter."

Veronica nodded her head and smiled. "Thank you, Mr. Daley. Thanks for stopping by. I hope you have a wonderful afternoon."

"You the same."

———

And so it was the next day that I returned to her house and collected her mail and, sure enough, there was the letter addressed to the Sundbergs. I glanced around, waiting until I was sure that nobody was watching, and then I placed the envelope in my back pocket.

Forcing myself to whistle a happy tune ("Zip-a-Dee-Doo-Dah"), I finished my route.

When I got home, my father was sitting in the living room, watching a soap opera. The music was loud and dramatic. His eyes were empty, and there was a white crust at the corners of his mouth.

I stood in front of the television, but he didn't seem to notice. "Hey, Dad," I said. "How are you? How was your day?"

He rubbed his face and then shook both his hands wildly, as if trying to will himself into coherence. He cleared his throat and flashed his idiot smile. "Remind me," he said, "of who you are."

I sighed deeply. "I'm your son. Wally Daley. Unless you need anything, I'm going to lie down for a while. And then I can make dinner. Spaghetti and meatballs. Garlic bread. Applesauce."

"That sounds wonderful. I love spaghetti. But what do you think of Tony Curtis?"

"I'm not familiar with Tony Curtis."

"A fine actor. Wonderful in *The Defiant Ones*. You haven't seen it? Equally wonderful in *Some Like It Hot*. Married to Janet Leigh, best known for her roles in *The Birds* and *Psycho*."

"As I said. I'm going to go lie down."

"Yes. Of course. And remind me again of who you are?"

"I'm the mailman. The goddamn mailman."

I sat on my bed and once again gazed at the wallpaper. Over the past few days, the color had become even duller and sicklier. And the corner was peeling some more, revealing repellent yellow paint beneath.

I rubbed the bridge of my nose and sighed an old man sigh. I grabbed Veronica's envelope from my back pocket, unsealed it, and removed the letter inside. Her writing was slanted so severely that it was difficult to read.

> Dear Wally,
> I liked seeing you yesterday. I'm sorry I couldn't let you inside, but I worried what people would say. Just know that I feel a kinship with you. I'm sure you still have a lot of questions. Meet me tonight at the bridge at Shallow Park. Half past midnight. Maybe people will be sleeping then and won't be watching us, won't be listening to us. You can ask your questions then. I don't know if I'll be able to answer them.

I folded her letter and placed it back in the envelope. Then I grabbed a book of matches with an insignia of the Howling Bar in Denver (when had he been to Colorado?) from inside the chest of drawers and struck a match against the coarse surface. I pressed the flame to the corner of the envelope and watched as the paper turned brown and then black and then to ash. Before the flame touched my fingers, I tossed the envelope in my metallic trash can.

I watched as the fire turned to lazy smoke, and then I lay down on the bed, pulling my legs up to my chest. When I squeezed my eyes shut, I was greeted by more childhood memories, all of them wonderful, colored like Kodachrome film, and I wanted them to go away, I so badly wanted them to go away, but they wouldn't, not until I slept, not until I died.

CHAPTER 25

I cooked dinner, but I didn't have much of an appetite. While my father scarfed down his spaghetti and meatballs, I sat there in silence, studying his face. The Irish skin and narrow green eyes. The pug nose and square jaw. The oversized ears and fleshy jowls. And I got to thinking how he looked nothing like me. Nothing like me at all.

"An actor," I muttered. "And a fine one at that."

He looked up, his chin splattered with tomato sauce. "Pardon me?"

"Nothing," I said. "I was just thinking of Tony Curtis, that's all."

His lips spread into that dumb grin. "Oh, Tony. My favorite. Born Bernard Schwartz. Did you know that? Maybe his name sounded too Jewish. So he changed it. He was wonderful in *Operation Petticoat*, don't you think?"

And that was all he had to say about that.

After dinner, I cleaned the dishes while my father moved to the living room to watch a rerun of *M*A*S*H*. After each crack by Hawkeye or B.J., the canned laughter echoed against the walls. But my father didn't laugh. He just sat there in his La-Z-Boy, his face saturated blue and yellow from the light of the show.

At nine o'clock, after the closing credits and theme song, he turned off the TV and wandered toward his room. I reminded him to brush his teeth, to wash his face, to change his underwear, and he nodded his head, said, "Okey-doke." By ten o'clock, his lights were out, and I could hear him snoring softly.

I returned to my own room and closed the door. I grabbed a photo album from the bookshelf, sat cross-legged on the floor, and began flipping through the pages. On the top of each page, there was a year written in red Sharpie, starting with the year I was born. Beneath the writing were two or three photographs from that particular year. I studied each page, feeling not nostalgia but a sense of dread. It was strange watching myself slowly age from an infant to a toddler to a child. From a teenager to a young man to an older man.

On a whim, I removed one of the photos of my father and me. I must have been ten or eleven. We were standing next to each other on a baseball diamond. I was wearing a Cincinnati Reds hat and had a metal Mizuno bat resting on my shoulder. My father looked proud, that worn-out JCPenney glove on his hand. But the longer I stared at the photograph, the greater was my sense of dread. It wasn't right. None of it was right.

I placed the photo back in the album and placed the album back in the closet.

I sat down on the edge of my bed and set my Mickey Mouse alarm clock for midnight. That would give me enough time to get dressed and walk over to the park for my meeting with Veronica. Then I lay down, above the covers, and folded my hands behind my head. The moonlight filtered through the curtains, and I watched strange shadows flicker on the wall.

I closed my eyes, and soon I was asleep, but my sleep was filled with nightmarish images: a rusted canoe floating down a river of fire; an endless field of blank-faced scarecrows; a silo filled with broken and bloody glass; a woman lying on the forest floor, her mouth filled with moths . . .

When the alarm buzzed, the images dissolved, and I slammed the clock so hard that it toppled to the floor. I sat up in bed. My vision was blurry, and the only sound was my breath, raspy and uneven. I flipped on the light and saw that there were two moths stuck to the wall; I wondered if they'd somehow escaped from my dream.

I got dressed and then tiptoed down the hallway to check on my father. I opened the door just a crack and peered inside. By the light of the moon, I could see that he was dead to the world, his mouth open, his nostrils flaring, his shoulders rising and falling with each breath.

Satisfied, I crept silently toward the front of the house and pushed open the door. I stepped outside, and it seemed forever since I'd been out at night. I stared at the sky, the stars and moon now dulled by a thin mist.

I hurried down the sidewalk, my shoes echoing on the pavement. The streetlights glowed, but all the houses were dark, a row of identical tombs in a graveyard neighborhood.

I had only walked two blocks, maybe three, when I sensed that somebody was following me, that somebody was watching me. I stopped and bent down, pretending to tie my shoe. I glanced over my shoulder and saw a shadowy figure vanish behind a tree. Someone was there. I rose to my feet, called out, "Hey!" but there was no answer. Slowly, I walked toward the tree and peered into the darkness. No movement. I remained where I was for a moment, listening for the cracking of a twig, the shuffling of feet. Nothing. Off in the distance, there was a low rumbling of thunder and then, just a moment later, a flash of lightning in the swirling sky. I left that place.

I arrived at Shallow Park. The blackened trees swayed menacingly, and the tentacles of my fears spread in my chest. I glanced at my watch: 12:28. I hurried across the wetted grass until I came to the bridge. I looked ahead of me, behind me, but I didn't see Veronica. I stepped onto the bridge and leaned against the railing, staring at the darkened water below.

I waited for five minutes, ten, and I began to worry that she wouldn't show. But then I heard footsteps and a voice saying, "Wally." I spun around. It was Veronica. She wore a white dress and white shoes and looked ghostly in the dark and mist. In her right hand, she gripped a pink purse.

"Veronica," I said. "I was beginning to worry. I—"

She touched my shoulder with her hand. "Catherine's journal. Did you read it?"

"Yes. Every page. More than once."

"What did you think?"

"It was interesting. It was frightening."

"Come," she said. "Let's go sit on those rocks near the water."

I followed her down a rocky slope, and we sat, the creek wetting my shoes and the bottom of my jeans. She placed the purse next to her and then reached forward and tapped the water with her fingers. "Sometimes," she said, "I wonder what is real and what is imaginary. Catherine wondered the same thing."

"The water is real," I said. "The sky and the moon. The stars hidden in the mist."

"Maybe. But how would you ever know for sure?"

I, too, placed my hand in the water. It was icy cold. "I mean, we can't know anything for sure, but—"

"I've thought a lot about all of this. The time Catherine and I spent at the hospital. Are we part of some nefarious scientific experiment? Or are we simply in the midst of some collective delusion?"

I picked up a flat stone and rubbed it down with my thumb. Then I flung it into the water. It didn't skip; it just sank to the bottom of the creek.

"I don't think you're delusional," I said.

"I don't think so either."

I turned toward Veronica and studied her face. Maybe it was because it was dark, and I couldn't make out the wariness in her eyes, the imperfections of her skin, but to me, at that moment, she looked like an angel of mercy.

"So what do you think they did to you at that hospital?" I said.

"I don't know, Wally. Something sinister, I think."

After that, she didn't say anything, not for a long time. The blackened trees swayed in the breeze, and an owl screamed. Veronica sat cross-legged, placed her hands on her knees, and closed her eyes. She looked like an idol. The moon was, once again, swallowed up by the mist, and the water darkened. When Veronica finally spoke, her voice was so quiet, I had to strain to hear her.

"There's something else you should know. I'm not sure if I should tell you. After all, it might come as something of a shock."

"What is it?" I asked.

She turned away, leaving me only to see the silhouette of her face. The air around her seemed to have transformed into a somber gloom, and the moon reappeared from the mist, curved and glowing a dull white, as if it were about to be extinguished. And still, she didn't speak.

"What is it?" I said again.

She shook her head slowly, almost imperceptibly. Then she turned back to me, and her eyes were now glistening, although it was hard to tell if it was from tears or the moon. "Catherine wasn't the only patient I saw in the hospital."

"Right. A procession of stretchers. A patient or corpse on each one."

"Yes. And I didn't recognize any of the rest of them. Not until recently." A long pause. "Not until I saw you delivering the mail."

I opened my mouth to speak, but no words came out. Instead, I gazed toward the creek, and despite the light of the moon, the water seemed somehow darker and colder and more foreboding.

"Of course, I can't be sure, but—"

She handed me a piece of paper, and it was one of her drawings, a man on a gurney. His lips were stretched in a scream, and his eyes were open so wide it looked like they might pop. The man on the gurney was me.

"It's impossible," I said. "I was never in the hospital. I would remember. I would—"

"Maybe," she said. "But maybe they performed the same experiments on you as they performed on Catherine and me. And maybe you were made to somehow . . . forget all about it. After all, Catherine didn't recall the details of being in that terrible operating room. And neither do I. So isn't it possible that you were also there? And that they somehow scrubbed your memory clean?"

Scrubbed your memory clean. I thought of the boy who'd pointed at me and said, *I know you. You're one of them. One of the scrubbed.*

I began chewing on the webbing of my hand, a bad habit I'd developed over the years. "Maybe," I said. "Maybe."

Veronica massaged her own shoulders, wincing from the tightness. "Let me ask you something, Wally. Have you been having headaches lately?"

I nodded my head. "Yes. Bad ones."

"And what about your memories? I mean from childhood especially. Are they vivid? Do they seem real?"

"Yes. But I don't understand why you're asking me that. Are your memories vivid?"

She turned toward me and smoothed back her black hair. "Sometimes they are. Overwhelmingly so. Take this bridge, for example. This is where my husband proposed to me. And if I close my eyes, I can recall every detail, every smell and sight and sound. The golden leaves falling to the ground. The creek lapping against the shore. The sounds of birds singing their sweet songs. And then my husband getting down on his knee and placing the ring, his mother's ring, on my finger." Veronica stared at her own hand where the ring glowed in the darkened mist. "But recently, I've noticed some problems with my recall. A memory will appear in my consciousness, and it will be full of details and color and sensory imagery, but then there will be . . . a glitch."

"A glitch?"

"Yes. It's hard to explain. Like sometimes, the memory will skip forward. Or sometimes it will play again and again."

"Faulty software," I mumbled.

"Something like that. I know it sounds crazy."

More lightning flashed in the sky, but there was no thunder. For a moment, I had the strange notion that none of this was real, not the bridge, not the stream, not the words. I shook my head as if trying to will myself awake.

"Ever since my mother died," I said, "my father has been slipping further and further into dementia. His thoughts are muddled, memories mixed up. Dr. Hoover, the same doctor who treated you, the same doctor who treated Catherine, has been coming to our house more and more frequently. From the beginning, I thought it was to help my father. To help him recover his memories. But now—"

I stopped speaking.

"Now what? Now you think that—"

"Now I think that he isn't interested in helping my father at all. In fact, I don't think my father is even sick."

"He's faking it?"

I nodded my head. "Not so long ago, I found some old DVDs in his room. On each of them was a recording of an old B film. I watched them. And there was my father. He had a role in each one."

"I don't understand. He's an actor?"

"Apparently so. It was a part of his life I never knew about. Maybe the Alzheimer's-ridden father I've been dealing with is nothing but his latest role."

"But why would—"

"Because Dr. Hoover isn't interested in my father's memories. He's interested in mine. Just like he was interested in Catherine's. Just like he's interested in yours. I think you're right. I think I was also in the hospital. I think they manipulated my brain."

I gazed at the water reflecting the brooding darkness. I thought of the man who'd been following me, and I wondered if he was watching us right now. I knew that he was. Veronica placed her head on my shoulder, and it felt so nice, so comforting. I closed my eyes.

"So . . . what now?" I said, my voice barely louder than a whisper.

She placed her hand on top of mine, and I could feel the warmth of her skin. "What now? We're going to ask around."

"What do you mean?"

"We start with your father," she said. "Make him admit that he's a part of this . . . plot."

I pressed at my temples. I could feel the makings of that familiar headache. "What's my father going to tell me? And why would he come clean now? Because I ask nicely?"

"No," she said. "Not because you ask nicely." She reached into her purse and pulled out an old revolver, the barrel glinting in the moonlight.

"Jesus," I said. "Where did you find that?"

"In our basement. When Brian was gone, I went exploring. I found a bunch of old Bluebird 78 records in the backroom. Benny Goodman. The Carter Family. Lonnie Johnson. Fred Kirby. And next to the records was an old turntable. You know, one of those fake leather ones that opens like a suitcase? When I opened it, I found another record on the turntable, 'La Cucaracha' by the Mexican Bluebird Orchestra and on

top on the record, this pretty little gun. They must have kept it there
for safekeeping. It probably hasn't been fired in a generation at least."

"Does it work?"

"I don't know. I wouldn't even know how to fire it."

I spun the cylinder, saw that there were three bullets inside. "I guess
it doesn't much matter if it works," I said. "As long as my old man be-
lieves it works."

"That's right."

"So how am I going to do this? Just stick the gun against his temple
and ask him the truth?"

"Yes," she said. "That's exactly what you'll do."

I thought things over. None of it was right. I raised the gun in the air
and pointed it in the opposite direction, toward the park. Could I squeeze
the trigger if I needed to?

"Okay," I said. "I'll do it." And then I dropped the gun to my side.

She smiled. "And if he won't talk, maybe my husband will. Maybe
Dr. Hoover. We'll get to the bottom of this. Maybe there's a simple explanation."

"Maybe."

And so the plan was in place. We remained at the creek for another
twenty minutes, and we barely talked. She told me her phone number
in case I had to reach her. The moon vanished and reappeared and vanished again.

At some point, I leaned over and kissed Veronica on the cheek. She
turned toward me, and her lower lip was trembling. I kissed her again,
this time on the lips. And I began to sob.

A psychiatric ward called Bethlam, and I was a patient.

CHAPTER 26

When I got home, it was nearly two in the morning. I stood in the living room, in the darkness, and my body felt like it would collapse under my own sorrow and angst. On top of the mantel, I noticed an old pocket-knife, one that you might use for whittling a stick or slicing into an apple and eating a piece of it straight from the blade.

The gun was in my pocket, so I don't know why, exactly, I walked over to mantel and grabbed the knife, but as soon as it was in my hand, I knew what I was going to do. Smiling grimly, I crept across the hardwood floor to the bathroom and closed the door gently behind me. I stared at my face in the mirror and felt that familiar sense of revulsion. *Who are you?* I leaned close to the mirror until I could see the specks in my irises. I thought of Catherine Gordon and how she'd bloodied her neck to remove the microchip, and I figured I'd do the same. I took a couple of deep breaths, trying to instill courage, and then I reached around to the back of my neck and, just like she'd done, pressed the knife against the flesh. But as soon as I felt the sting of the blade, I lost whatever bravery I thought I'd had. I dropped the pocketknife into the sink basin, and it clattered against the porcelain. For several moments, I stared at my trembling hands, and a series of disturbing thoughts passed behind my eyes and scraped relentlessly at my consciousness. What if Catherine's journal was a fake? What if Veronica had forged it? What if she was trying to drive me crazy, trying to force me to cut a microchip from my flesh, trying to get me to kill my own father?

But, no. Veronica wouldn't do that to me. I believed her. She was the only one I could believe. This I knew, and this I know: Dr. Zagorsky and his medical staff had held us against our will. They'd performed experiments on us. And my own father was part of this conspiracy.

I picked up the knife. I removed my shirt. And, like in some B horror movie that my father might have starred in, I began cutting.

———

And so it was that twenty minutes later, shirtless and bloody, the flesh-encased microchip buried inside a potted plant, I stood over my father and gazed at his face, half lit by the moonlight. The gun dangled from my hand like a metallic appendage, and the sweat dripped from my forehead and into my eyes, stinging them. My weight shifted from one foot to the other, and the floor groaned in response. My father's eyes opened. He stared at me, eyes adjusting to the darkness, brain adjusting to the situation, and he didn't say a word.

"It's time to wake up," I said, and my voice sounded like that of a stranger, like that of a sociopath.

Still no response.

"Wake up," I said again.

This time, he spoke. "It's not time. The sun is still hiding in the cupboard."

I took a step forward. "Enough of that nonsense. Enough of the act. I want you to tell me some things. I want you to tell me what's happening in Bethlam, Nevada. I want you to tell me what they did to me. I want you to tell me why you've been complicit."

His eyes finally opened, focusing not on me but the wall behind. "Dwight Eisenhower," he croaked. "Supreme commander of the Allied Expeditionary Force."

I was losing my patience. I shouted, "Fuck Dwight Eisenhower! And fuck the Allied Expeditionary Force." I raised the gun and pointed it at his chest. My hand was trembling so badly that I could barely hold it straight.

It took him a moment to recognize the gun for what it was. "But why do you have that violent piece of metal?" he asked. "Why are you pointing it at me?"

"Because I aim to kill you, maybe. Or wound you at the very least."

He sat up in bed. He looked so meek and helpless. He grabbed a pillow and placed it on his chest, as if the feathers might stop the bullet from penetrating his heart.

"But I don't understand. What did I do? Why are you angry? Does it have to do with the parakeet that flew away? Her name was Cookie, and she used to spend all day in her cage, kissing the mirror. I opened the cage to change the newspaper, and away she went."

More nonsense from his mouth. "There's no parakeet, Dad. You ask why am I angry? Well, why do you think? Why don't you tell me?"

"I don't know. I only know that—"

"Your dementia. Your Alzheimer's. It's all an act, isn't it?"

He shook his head. "Your mother. Beula. She—"

"Enough! Stop bullshitting me. I found the DVDs. I saw the movies. Once upon a time, you were an actor. A pretender. And now you're pretending to suffer from dementia. That way Dr. Hoover will come to our house. But he's not interested in you. He's interested in me. Why?"

His mouth opened, ready to deny my accusations, but no words came out. When he did speak, there were no denials, only the timid response of, "I don't know."

I pulled the hammer back. My father shielded his face with his arm. For the first time, I was convinced that he would die.

"Why?" I said again.

"Are they trying to hurt you?" he asked. "Is that what they're trying to do? I'm just a poor old man, suffering against the world."

With my free hand, I scratched at my scalp, scratched at my cheek. Then I spat on the floor. "I was in a hospital," I said. "That's what I know. An underground bunker of some sort. I don't know why, but I think you might. I've read about experiments that the government has performed

without our consent. Like when they injected children with tuberculo-
sis, or Blacks with a syphilis extract, or when Frank Olson went crazy and
jumped from a building after being doped with LSD."

My father didn't seem to understand what I was saying. His lower lip
was quivering, and I could see his teeth, crooked and pale yellow. "When
I was a boy—"

"What did they do to my brain?" I said.

"—my father bought me a pogo stick. I used to bounce like a rabbit,
all through the house. Those were happy days. Did you ever have a pogo
stick?"

I moved closer to my old man, the gun just inches from his head.
I'd never killed anybody in real life, but sometimes in my dreams I killed
them all. All I needed to do was pull the trigger. Life was cheap. Not worth
much more than the loose change in my pocket.

"It's not just me," I said. "There are several of us, I think. They're performing experiments on us. Hoover is monitoring our progress."

I knew I sounded crazy, at least as crazy as my old man, but I believed.

"Hoover," my father said, his eyes rolling back into his head as if he
were recalling somebody from a long time ago. And so he was: "The director of the FBI. How do you know him? He's not a good man."

I started laughing because it was funny. He was an actor, my father,
a good one at that. He should have been cast in better films. Academy
Award–winning films. I laughed, and I laughed some more. And I was
still laughing when I reached my hand back and then jerked it forward,
slamming him in the temple with the barrel of the gun. He didn't react
right away, as if he didn't realize he'd been hit. But then, a few seconds
later, he moaned in pain and grabbed at his face, a bright red welt already visible.

"Why did you hurt me?" he said. "Why?"

"Because I need the truth! No more playing! No more!"

I stuck the gun against his temple, and he knew I had nothing left to
lose. And then, just like that, his act ended. "Okay, okay! Please. Don't
kill me. I'll tell you what I do know. Just . . . put down the gun. Please."

I kept the gun pressed against his temple. I'd shoot him dead if need be. Only if need be. I took a few deep breaths. Then I lowered the gun to my side. "Okay," I said. "Speak."

He nodded his head, resigned to the situation. "I'll speak. But first. Do you mind if I smoke a cigarette?"

My eyes narrowed in suspicion. "You don't smoke. You never have."

"Please, Wally," he said. "It'll make it easier for me."

He was lucid. Completely lucid.

I nodded my head. "Fine. Go ahead."

And so I stood there and watched as he rose from his bed and wandered across the room toward his dresser. He opened up a drawer and pulled out a narrow tin can. He clicked open the can and removed a cigarette paper. He licked the edges and then placed it on the top of the dresser. With his back turned toward me, he pressed loose tobacco into the paper and then sealed it. He took out a matchbook, lit a match, and pressed the flame to the handmade cigarette. He puffed a few times, wisps of smoke rising gently to the ceiling.

He sat down on the edge of the bed and took a few more puffs. The dementia was all gone. It was crazy. He looked at me through hooded eyes, said, "You won't believe me when I tell you."

CHAPTER 27

The old man crossed his spindly legs, blue veins weaving beneath the skin like a road map. He pressed the cigarette to his mouth and sucked down some more smoke, held it for a long moment, and then exhaled through his nostrils. His mouth opened a few times, but no words came out. When he did finally speak, his voice sounded different somehow, tentative, as if he were measuring each syllable to gauge my response. "Let's start a year ago, November. When I was living in Denver."

"In Denver? What the hell are you talking about? You never lived in Denver."

He smiled a half smile. "Please. You must let me speak. Then you can ask questions. I promise."

I pulled back my hair with my hand. I wanted to scream. I wanted to pound the walls with my fists. I wanted to yank the carpet from the floor. Instead, I took a deep breath. Instead, I said, "Okay. Speak."

He nodded his head. "There's a lot you don't know about me. In fact, just about everything. You know I'm an actor. But you don't know all the parts I've played."

"Shlock," I said. "Pure shlock."

He ignored me. "Let's start in Denver. In a shithole apartment out on East Colfax. It was nighttime, a day or two after Thanksgiving. The moon hung low in the sky, and I was drinking gulps of whiskey chased by cheap beer. Every so often, I'd rise to my feet and stare down at the sidewalk below where the whores and pimps and addicts screeched and cackled and hollered. I was in a bad place, Wally, physically and mentally and emotionally and every other way, hopes and dreams vanished. Have you ever been so lonely, Wally? Can you relate?"

I shrugged my shoulders. It didn't sound like my father. It sounded like someone else. A stranger. A devil, maybe. *A movie starring Hal Barker.*

He continued. "A record amount of rye, and I had passed out in my chair, the bottle somehow balancing on my lap. I heard a pounding on the door. I wasn't expecting any visitors, and I was drunk as hell, so I started shouting, telling them to go away. But they didn't go anywhere. Instead, the knocking continued. I was scared and angry. Confused and desperate. I rose from my seat, the bottle crashing to the floor, and staggered to the door. My eyes burning, I peered through the peephole and saw a group of men, three in all. They all wore suits and grim expressions. 'Mr. Barker,' one of them said. 'Please. Don't be alarmed. We'd like to talk to you. We've got an opportunity for you. A job. We've seen your work in'—and he looked down at his notes—'*The Blood House.* Among others. We think you're wonderfully talented. Shamefully obscure. But now we have the role of a lifetime for you. Please. Open the door. Hear us out.' Maybe I should have kept the door closed. Maybe I should have ordered them to leave. But I didn't. Here was opportunity knocking, quite literally. So I did what any desperate and drunken actor would do. I opened the door."

My head was spinning. I had so many questions already. None of this made sense. My father never lived in Denver. He'd always been here with me and Mom. But I kept quiet. My father kept speaking. Hal Barker kept speaking.

"As I said, there were three of them. They all flashed their IDs, even though I hadn't asked. They were government-issued. Two of them were very tall and had identical buzz cuts. Mr. Campbell and Mr. Howard were their names. I could barely tell them apart except that Mr. Campbell had a mole beneath his left eyebrow. The other was short with tomato-red hair. Mr. Langford was his name. Langford was the one who did most of the talking. At first, I was skeptical. This wasn't the way movies worked. They didn't send government men to your house in the middle of the night. But the longer Langford talked, the more interested I became. Especially when he talked about the money. Ten thousand dollars a month. You must understand, Wally, that I was nearly broke. I was living in a shithole apartment above the whores and pimps and addicts. Do you understand?"

"Yes," I said. "I understand."

My father again rose from bed. He wandered to the window and pulled the curtain back. Outside, the sky was dark and menacing. The gun was still in my hand. I could aim it at his back and fire. Maybe it would be better to do that. Maybe it would be better not to hear.

"Anyway. They told me about the job. About my role. It was all in very vague terms. Suspiciously vague."

"Your role . . ."

My father took another long puff from his cigarette and then crushed it out against the windowsill. "Yes, my role. To become some- body completely different. A man named Harold Daley. A man who had lost his wife to pneumonia. A man who had a son named Walter Daley. A man who was slowly succumbing to dementia. You were right when you guessed that the dementia was an act. But what you didn't know is that Harold Daley himself is just a character. He's not your father. I'm not your father."

I laughed. I laughed and laughed and then I laughed some more. "Just stop it," I said. "You're lying. You're trying to drive me crazy."

He shook his head. "No. I'm telling you the truth. I promise."

"This is madness. I know who you are. You're my father. You're—"

He spoke over me. "Over the course of that conversation—and sev- eral others that followed—they explained what was expected of me. They gave me a file, eighty or ninety pages in length. It described my role in detail, far more detail than a director or screenwriter has ever pro- vided me. I learned about Mr. Daley's upbringing, his college years, his courting of Beula Young, and their eventual engagement and marriage.

I learned about the birth of their only child, you, born July 16th, 1987. I learned about Beula's pneumonia, her death, and the devastation it caused for both the elder Daley and the younger one. And I learned about the gradual deterioration of Harold's mind, his deluded thinking, his loss of memory, his reliance on living in another decade completely. It really was a wonderful role, when you stop to think about it. And other than a few instances where I slipped out of character—understandable considering the length of time—I think it was my best performance."

My head ached. My chest did too. "No. You're my father. You look like him. You talk like him. I remember throwing the baseball with you, the slap of the ball against the leather . . ."

"And then there's your mother—"

"Please. Don't."

He took a few steps closer to where I was standing. "Do you remember when she died?"

"Yes," I said. "I remember."

"Do you remember how you sat at her bedside? How you brushed the hair from her face? How her last words were, 'I lived a good life'?"

"Yes. I remember all of that."

He placed his hand on my shoulder and squeezed. "It never happened. False memories. Implants. She never existed, either. I know this is hard to hear."

Through gritted teeth, I said, "You're a liar."

"No," he said. "I'm telling you the truth. You know I'm telling you the truth."

False memories.

I closed my eyes and imagined her face, her voice.

"You're wasting my time," I said.

"I know this must be overwhelming to hear. But I aim to tell you the truth. You deserve it. I've been wrong to withhold it from you."

"But you're not telling me the truth. You've never told me the truth. My mother existed. She was real. I remember her reading me stories in bed. I remember, on cold days, when the snow would fall, her making hot chocolate with marshmallows in it."

"It doesn't snow in Bethlam."

"I remember her and me jumping into a freshly raked pile of leaves and laughing and squealing. I remember following behind her while the calliope music played, remember her turning toward me and saying, 'Promise me that you'll never forget this moment.'"

"No," he said. "You only think you remember."

"And I remember the day she died. October 23rd, 2011. I've got the date tattooed on my arm."

My father / Barker shook his head. "That's not what the date symbolizes."

"Then what?"

"I don't know. They didn't tell me. They didn't tell me anything about your past. About who you really are."

"I know who I really am!"

But my father / Barker again ignored me. He kept talking. "They didn't tell me much about the neurological experiments. Only that your long-term memories had been, essentially, wiped clean. New ones implanted. Your sense of self transformed. They told me that you had agreed to the procedure. That your family had agreed."

"My family?"

"That's all I know, Wally. I'm sorry. I don't know about your past. I don't fully understand the science."

I started pacing back and forth across the room, cursing, mumbling. I didn't know who to trust. Didn't know who to believe. One thing I did know: I sure as hell couldn't trust myself.

"Bethlam. Tell me about Bethlam."

"A fake town. Make-believe."

"No. I grew up here."

"You can't trust your memories, Wally. Don't you understand? What you remember never happened. The place you know of as Bethlam isn't real."

I laughed a nervous laugh and then spat on the floor. "The hell it isn't. It's got houses. It's got stores. It's got toilets. It's real."

"Oh, it's got infrastructure. That's because it was once a real town.

Only, back then, it was called Gilford. It was built as a community for those testing nuclear weapons back in the 1950s. Tourists used to come to watch the testing. They even crowned—"

"Miss Atomic Bomb," I mumbled.

Barker: "But by the end of the twentieth century, the industry and economy had dried up, and only a few people remained. Still, as I said, the infrastructure was in place. And, so, it was the perfect location for the type of grand experiment the government was preparing to do. They were able to use eminent domain to buy out the remaining residents. The town became completely empty. Over the course of several months, the architects restored the buildings and the houses. They did a wonderful job. Not picturesque, exactly, but utilitarian."

Everything my father / Barker was saying was crazy. I didn't believe him. They were all lies. "Lies," I said. "All lies."

"I'm afraid not."

"What about the pet shop and the ice cream store and the diner—"

"Temporary businesses."

"And the townspeople—"

"Actors and doctors. Some armed guards. Some children to add authenticity. All there for your sake, Wally. You should feel proud."

"So Al Denning. The intruder. He—"

"Yes. He was one of the residents of Gilford. The ones who got bought out. This had been his house. He was one of those who'd been paid off. Been paid a fair amount. Made to promise he would go far away. But then his life fell apart. He had second thoughts and returned. It was an unforeseen complication. They took care of him. Truth be told, they probably gave him more money. You know how it is with government waste. The Bridge to Nowhere. Et cetera, et cetera."

I felt sick to my stomach. I didn't know what the hell to do. I wanted to bash my father's—or Hal Barker's, or whoever the fuck he was—head in. I wanted to stick my gun in my nostril and pull the trigger, leave my consciousness in bloody chunks on the wall and floor.

"This is my house. I know it is. I remember, I remember."

"No. The past isn't what it always seems to be. Wally, I met you for the first time a month ago. After you returned from the hospital. After they removed your old memories. After they implanted the new ones."

I thought about Catherine and Veronica. About the others she'd seen in the hospital. I wasn't the only one. "How many?"

"How many what?"

"How many patients? In Bethlam?"

"I don't know. They didn't tell me."

I scratched at my face. Then I touched the back of my neck. I looked at my fingers. Fresh blood. *A little water clears us of this deed.* I had wanted the truth, but that desire had been misguided. The truth is never good, not ever. The truth informs us that God is a myth, only created to avoid wallowing in other truths. Like that humans are as purposeless as a housefly banging against the window. Or that we are only biding our time before disease or virus or blade strips away our consciousness. The truth, the truth, the truth.

Give me lies. Forever and for always. Give me lies.

Cinnamon rolls in the oven.

The slap of the baseball against my leather glove.

Faded calliope music.

My mother.

My father.

Myself.

Give me lies.

"Catherine Gordon," I said. "She slit her throat. And then what?"

Barker took a few steps forward. He wasn't my father. Who was my father? "They got her medical treatment. She survived. Some of the project's architects wanted to cut their losses. They thought it would be too much risk to continue with her in the project. But Dr. Zagorsky had the final say. He thought she was too valuable. And so they started over again with her. Once again, wiped her memories clear. Once again, implanted her with new memories, a new soul. There was less planning for the second go-around. They already had her house all set up. Had her husband all set up. My understanding is that she's doing just fine. That the project is proceeding as planned."

That phrase made my skin crawl. "Proceeding as planned? What does that mean?"

Barker shrugged. "I don't know. Like I said, they don't tell me much. They don't tell us what the experiments are for. They only tell us as much as is necessary. That's a good way of living, I think. Too much knowledge can be dangerous."

At this, I once again raised the gun and aimed it at his forehead. "Too much knowledge can be dangerous, huh? What the hell about me?"

"I'm sorry, Walter."

"Aren't you the least bit fucking curious as to why they're doing this to me? Huh? Aren't you?"

But he only shook his head. "No. They gave me a role. I played it. They paid me well. If it hadn't been me in the role, it would have been someone else. And maybe the experiment is to benefit mankind. It's a possibility, don't you think?"

I laughed. I so badly wanted to squeeze the trigger. I so badly wanted to see him die. But, no. Not now. Not yet. "I need to know why they're doing this," I said. "I need to know what happened to my real father. My real mother. My real house. My real town."

But he only shook his head. "I'm sorry, Wally. I already told you. I don't know. And I have no way of knowing."

"What about Dr. Hoover? He'd know. I want you to call him. I want you to have him come here, right now."

"He doesn't know either," Barker said.

"Bullshit."

"Believe what you want to believe. I know it's true. He told me. He's only here to provide medical treatment. To provide research on the trials. But he's not at the highest level."

My head was throbbing, and I gritted my teeth in pain. I could barely keep my grip on the gun. But then a thought, barely formed, appeared in my consciousness. I spoke before the thought vanished for good.

"The bunker."

"What?"

"I need you to take me to the bunker. I need to speak to Dr. Zagorsky. I want to know who I am. I want to know why they did this to me."

Barker looked up, and, for just a moment, his expression was one of panic. But then he looked at his feet and shook his head. "If I take you there, they'll fire me for sure. They'll recoup the money paid. Maybe we could do something different. Maybe I could pay you to—"

I pulled back the hammer. "I don't want your fucking money. I only want the truth."

CHAPTER 28

It wasn't ten minutes later that we stepped inside Barker's car, a lime-green Cadillac Seville with a rusted hood. Barker sat in the driver's seat, and I sat in the back, a fresh flannel shirt covering my still-bloody shoulders, a quilt that my mother had knitted crumpled in my lap. But, no. She hadn't knitted it. She didn't exist.

Considering his role as the doddering old fool, I hadn't known that Barker owned a car or that he even drove. He kept the car parked a few blocks away on Oak Street. He told me that occasionally when I was at work, he'd take it for a drive, head out to the desert to get away for a while.

"There's only one checkpoint on the highway out of town," Barker said, "but they're more concerned with cars coming in than cars going out. As long as you're hidden beneath the blanket, there won't be any problems. You see, the employees of the Bethlam Project are free to leave as we please. We're not prisoners."

"But I am."

He nodded his head. "In a manner of speaking."

Barker hit the engine and drove slowly down the street. He said, "Well, if you ask me, this is all very exciting. A little adventure to break up the monotony. Speaking of which, did you happen to see my film, *The Escapees*?"

"No," I said. "I never saw it."

"Right. You wouldn't have. It went straight to VHS. It was poorly scripted and poorly shot. Just like most of my films, unfortunately. In any case, this reminds me a little of that movie. Only I end up dying. Get shot in the back of the head by a prisoner named Steady Eddie. Quite a death scene. Bloody head leaning against the horn, bystanders covering their mouths in shock. You won't shoot me in the back of the head, will you, Wally?" He laughed. "Son?"

"I make no promises," I said. "Not a single one."

The sun had yet to peek above the Sierra Nevada Mountains, but still the sky was beginning to lighten, the clouds a hazy yellow. We drove through the empty streets of Bethlam, Nevada, or what was supposed to be a representation of Bethlam, Nevada, and memories overwhelmed my consciousness, movie reels playing behind my skull, emotions scraping across my skin like a dulled paring knife. Like this one:

It was Christmas. I must have been eight or nine years old. The tree was beautiful, the lights twinkling, the glass ornaments shining. And beneath that tree, so many presents, but one in particular caught my eye. Big and bulky and colorful. My parents were sitting on the couch, my father with his arm around my mother's shoulder, and both of them smiled as I grabbed the gift and began tearing the red-and-green wrapping paper, scraps covering the floor beneath me. My eyes widened as I saw what was inside: a remote-controlled Tamiya Hotshot 4WD buggy.

I remembered removing the car from the box, and it felt so heavy and powerful in my hands. I remembered placing it on the ground and pushing the lever on the remote and watching as the buggy sped across the floor and beneath the couch until it finally crashed against the wall, flipping upside down, the wheels still spinning. I remembered my parents laughing, and then my father saying, "Easy, Wally. They're going to ticket you for driving a hundred and ten in a school zone." I remembered running across the room and picking up the car and placing it upright and pushing the lever once again . . . but then the memory started fluttering and flashing, like a television losing its reception. Then it all went black.

A glitch.

Another image flashed in my consciousness, and this filled me with no nostalgia. It was of me staring down a blackened well, of those echoed screams, of my hands coated with blood, of me falling to my knees and begging for a God who had long since given up on humanity . . .

"I might kill myself," I muttered. "I might, I might, I might. There isn't much life worth living. And the truth might be the worst outcome of all."

It seemed that we drove for an hour or more—although it was difficult to tell, owing to my dwindling mental state. As we drove, I gazed out the window at the yucca and sagebrush, at the tumbleweed blowing across the graying highway. Barker glanced in the rearview mirror, and his eyes were smiling even if his mouth wasn't.

"Why do you think they chose you?" he asked.

I only shook my head. "I don't know."

"You know your boss? Mr. Temeer?"

"Yeah?"

"Well, that isn't his real name, of course. His real name is Melvin something or other. He used to sneak to our house when you were delivering mail. He'd bring a bottle of rye and we'd have a few sips. He's an actor, like me, but his backlist is even more pathetic than mine. One of the titles I remember is *Mountain Camp Sluts Part IV*. Seen it?"

"No. Not that I remember."

"An early '80s porn. But he didn't even get to bang anybody. He played the camp counselor, warned the girls to stay away from the boys' cabin. They didn't listen to him."

Barker laughed, and it was at my expense. But not only him. Every time the neighbors watched me from their porches, every time I spoke to somebody at church, every time I went into a restaurant or a café, they had all been laughing at me. It was a lousy feeling.

"Those letters you deliver every day. Did you ever open any of them?"

"No. I mean, once the envelope opened on its own and—"

Barker laughed again. He was enjoying every moment of this. Leaving breadcrumbs of information for me to gather. "Well, there's nothing inside those envelopes. Nothing but blank paper. It would have been too time-consuming for them to write the letters. And so they cut corners."

I laughed too. "Hour after hour, delivering empty envelopes. Christ. What a fucking waste of time."

"Yup. Hour after hour. Wasted. But don't worry. Everybody's life is that way."

After that, we drove in silence. It must have been ten, fifteen minutes later that we came to the check point. I quickly huddled beneath the seat and pulled the quilt over me. I growled, "If you say anything about my presence, if you nod your head or blink SOS, I will fire a bullet into the back of your head. Just like that movie you referenced."

"*The Escapees*," he said.

"Yes. *The Escapees*."

He slowed the car down and came to a stop. I could see shadows and hear voices. They asked Barker what his name was, what his business was. He told them he was visiting his daughter for a few hours. He'd be back by early afternoon. He answered confidently. He was an actor. He did a good job. They waved him on.

I waited a few minutes before removing the blanket. "See?" he said. "Piece of cake."

It wasn't more than another three or four miles that my father slowed the car and then came to a stop. I gazed out the window, but I didn't see a thing. Just endless dirt and sagebrush, the devilish sun now shining low in an otherwise blank sky.

"Why'd you stop?" I asked. "Where are we?"

He gripped the wheel tightly. "We're at the clinic."

"I don't see anything."

Barker pointed through the windshield. I shielded my eyes with my hand. "There," he said. "Up ahead. Just past that gully. There's a round panel, barely visible. That's the door to the bunker, to the clinic."

"And there's a handle somewhere? You pull up?"

"There's a panel. There's a code."

"Do you know the code?"

He winked. "I might."

"Get out," I said. "I want you to open it for me."

Barker got out of the car. I walked behind him, vaguely pointing the gun at his back. The wind blew, and his pajama top billowed like a cape. We walked for about fifty yards, Barker a few steps ahead of me. Then, without saying a word, he stopped and dropped to his knees. He began wiping some dirt away, at first slowly and then manically. I watched in fascination. After a few minutes, enough dirt had been wiped away that I could see what was beneath: a round, white, metallic door. On the left side of the door was a plexiglass panel, and beneath the panel, some buttons. Barker pressed in the code, five numbers, and then the lock clicked open. He stuck his hand in the gap and pulled upward, grunting. I took a step back. Eventually, he managed the pull the door open, and it banged against the dirt. Beneath the door was a concrete staircase that disappeared into darkness.

He rose to his feet and wiped the filth from his pajamas. Then he nodded at me. "I can show you down there. Although there's nothing much to see."

But I only shook my head. "Close the door."

"I don't understand."

"Close the door."

Barker did as he was told.

"Walk back to the car."

A few minutes later, we were back in the car. I waited until Barker was inside the car, and then I got in the back seat. "Drive," I said.

"Back to Bethlam?"

I shook my head. "East. Until I tell you to stop."

"East? But why?"

"Because I told you so, that's why."

And so that's what he did. He pulled back on the lonely highway, the asphalt sizzling from the Nevada sun. Every so often, he'd speak, tell me about his ex-wife, about his daughter who he hadn't seen in nearly a decade. I told him to shut up, told him I wasn't interested in his past, was only interested in mine.

We'd driven maybe eight or nine miles when I told him to stop. We were in the middle of nowhere, the sun rising higher in the air. Soon it would be ninety degrees and then a hundred.

"Get out," I said.

"Here?"

"Yes. Here. You can start walking. You'll be back at the bunker in less than two hours if you hustle."

"I don't have any water. It's hot."

"You'll survive. That's why I only had you drive this far."

"Please, Wally."

"Want me to shoot you instead?"

He opened the driver's side door and stepped outside. I kept the gun pointed at him until I'd taken his place behind the wheel. "Don't figure I'll be seeing you again," I said.

"Don't be too sure about that."

"You're a pretty good actor," I said. "All things considered. I don't think you should give up. I think one day you might hit it big."

At that, he laughed. "I don't think so. I think this is my final role."

I nodded my head a single time and then put the car in drive and stepped on the gas. I spun the car around, the tires kicking up dirt. I glanced in the rearview mirror and saw Barker, my father, the actor, standing there, as still as a scarecrow. He got smaller and smaller, and then I couldn't see him at all.

CHAPTER 29

A man without a past, I couldn't say for sure the last time I'd driven, and I was unsteady, the car constantly drifting toward the gullied landscape before I managed to jerk it back toward the double yellow line. Everything was mixed up in my head—all the truths were lies, and all the lies were truths. Yes, the more I contemplated, the more convinced I became that the words Catherine, Veronica, and my father had told me *couldn't* be true. Yet, somewhere deep inside, I knew they were. It was infuriating. These uncomfortable thoughts caused my heart to quicken and palpitate, and caused my head to ache, so I turned on the radio and tried to shush them. I flipped through the dial and settled on a station that was playing classical music, but the music was just as terrifying—a cave full of trolls, gnomes, and goblins, the day of wrath, a death shriek. I turned it off. I sighed and stared out the dust-coated windshield, and I felt good and lonely. Out here on this desert highway, there were no other cars, no crows keeping watch from up high, no sign of life at all. They used to test nukes here. They used to grin in excitement as the radiation spread through the air, poisoning lungs and hearts and brains. I shook my head in disgust. This much I knew: The answers I needed were buried in the nuclear bunker, and I aimed to find them, even if that meant spilling some blood, even if that meant a slaughter of the worst magnitude.

Soon, the ominous-looking bunker was visible again, and I parked the car and stepped outside. The heat sucked my breath away. Other than the sound of the wind, everything was quiet, screams muffled beneath the dirt.

I didn't really have a good plan. Enter the bunker, and then what? Break into the medical rooms? Interrogate the nurses? Search for Dr. Zagorsky, even though I'd never seen him before? And what if the premises were heavily guarded? What if they captured me and, once again, performed brutal experiments on me? What if they sliced my throat with a metal wire and watched me bleed out, my face frozen in a forever shriek? What if they buried me in the desert dirt, with all those screams, never to be found again? What if?

I returned to the metallic door that my father—no, no, Barker—had shown me. I opened the filthy plexiglass panel and pressed the buttons I'd seen Barker press, but there was no click. Cursing under my breath, I tried again, and this time, the lock clicked open. I stuck my hand in the gap and yanked upward, grunting. The door opened, banging against the dirt.

I rose to my feet and glanced around, making sure nobody was watching me, but there was only the overwhelming starkness of the landscape and the empty moans of the wind. I spat on the ground before turning and starting down the staircase.

In the oppressive darkness, the stairs seemed to go on forever, but eventually, my surroundings were illuminated by flickering fluorescent lights. Against the concrete walls, my shadow was shimmering and menacing. My footsteps were too loud and so were my breaths. I finally reached the bottom and pushed open a heavy metallic door. Inside the bunker, the floor was also concrete, and catwalks and metallic ladders hung from the ceiling. On either side, there were windowless doors, all shut closed. It was just as Veronica had described it in her letter to Catherine.

Gun dangling from my hand, I walked down the hallways. At each door, I tried the handle, but they were all locked. I continued walking, and there were no nurses rushing down the corridor, no sounds of machines beeping, no anguished shrieks of suffering patients. It seemed the bunker was empty, completely abandoned.

Still, I kept walking, hoping that around the next bend, I would make a discovery, that a room would appear illuminated with truth. But the farther I walked, the more worried I became that I would spend the rest of my life wandering through these bunker corridors, unable to find my way back to the exit. I worried that Barker had tricked me, left me to die underground. I worried that they wouldn't find me for years, decades even, and when they did find me, I'd be rotted, my grin fleshless.

It seemed as if I'd been walking for an hour (although it must have been far less than that) when I became too tired to continue and slumped down against the concrete wall. I placed the gun on the floor next to me and then dropped my head to my knees.

I squeezed my eyes shut, tried to breathe deeply, but the anxiety only got worse, and I felt like I was suffocating. And that's when I heard the screams.

At first, I thought it was only my imagination; remnants of counterfeit memories escaped into my ear canals. However, the longer I listened, the surer I became that the sounds were from outside my consciousness.

Unsteadily, I rose to my feet and moved to where I thought the sounds were coming from, but every time the screaming and the moaning got louder, I would take a few more steps and they would become muted. And then a thought. I got down on all fours and pressed my ear against the floor. Still muffled, but the screams were coming from below.

I got to my feet and spun around a few times before spotting a panel, barely visible, at the edge of the hallway. There was a gap between the panel and the floor, and I was able to yank the panel up. There I found a metal ladder bolted to the concrete wall. The screams were clearer now, and I grabbed the first rung and moved down cautiously, my legs rubbery and unreliable.

Eventually, I came to the bottom level of the enormous bunker. Here, the walls were no longer drab gray concrete. Here, the walls had been painted to look like the ocean, shades of blue and aqua. Hanging from the ceiling were mobiles of deep-sea creatures: jellyfish, octopuses, eels, goblin sharks.

I walked through the corridor, and just like in the level above, it wound around in a perplexing labyrinth. The gun remained in my hand, and the screams and moans became a nightmarish cacophony. Just past a mobile anglerfish, I came toward a windowless room, the door shut. I placed my ear against the door, and this is where the suffering had originated.

I took a deep breath and then another and then I pushed open the door, just a crack.

What I saw startled me.

There were five hospital beds spaced about three feet apart. On each of the beds lay a patient—three men and two women. They were all in purple hospital gowns. Electrodes and wires splayed from each of their heads. A doctor, her long gray hair falling below her waist, paced back and forth, occasionally pausing to adjust the wires on the patients' heads or to press some buttons on the giant metallic machinery that lay flat against the back wall.

But what was most disturbing were the reactions of the patients, all the moaning and screaming and convulsing. One man, a purplish erection poking through his gown, kept trying to sit up and escape, but his wrists and ankles were tied to the bed. Another man, his eyes rolled back into his skull, was speaking terrifying nonsense: "Our Lord is burning in a pit of fire! Tortured princesses surround us! The moon suffers in silence!" An older woman, her black hair streaked with steely gray, alternated between laughing maniacally and sobbing uncontrollably. Blood from her lower lip streamed down her chin. The doctor stopped pacing and stood behind the woman. She stroked her hair and caressed her cheek, shushing her all the while. It didn't do any good. The patient tried to bite the doctor, and she barely managed to pull her hand away.

I remained there for a few minutes, wondering if I had been held captive in this very room. Wondering if they had restrained my hands and feet just like a prisoner.

I closed the door silently and continued walking down the corridor until I came to an office with a yellow smiley face painted on the door. Just below the smiley face was the name Dr. Zagorsky. I couldn't believe my good luck. I knocked on the door. No answer. Glancing behind me to make sure nobody was in the hallway, I twisted the handle. The door was unlocked.

Inside, the office was lit by garish fluorescent lights. Against the far wall was a desk, swept clean of papers, and a short bookshelf. Lining the bookshelf were maybe two dozen jars filled with brains of various sizes and shapes soaking in a grayish liquid.

Heart pounding, I hurried across the office to the desk and began rifling through the drawers. In the top drawer, there was nothing of interest: only pens and pencils and staplers and notecards. But inside the larger side drawers were stacked a multitude of files, each with a name printed in ink. I didn't recognize any of the names.

I opened one at random. Charles Delgado. Paper-clipped to some papers was a mug shot of a white man with a shaved head and a pair of tattooed tears. Behind the photograph were all sorts of official-looking records including a birth certificate, a copy of a passport, and a criminal record. I skimmed through some of the offenses. Armed robbery. Aggravated assault. Sexual assault with an object. Seemed like a nice guy.

I shut the file and picked up another one. James Holliday. Another mug shot. A man who looked like he could be an accountant. But another long rap sheet. Child molestation. Sex trafficking. Child pornography. Among other grotesqueries.

And then a third file. When I saw her mug shot, hair and eyes wild, I felt like I was going to be sick. The placard she was holding said Patricia Holland, but I recognized the face.

It was Veronica Miller.

Feeling an overwhelming panic, I flipped through her file. I came to a grainy photograph of a Black man lying on a linoleum floor, his eyes open, his mouth stretched in a grotesque scream. His T-shirt was soaked with the same blood that had pooled beneath his body. I squinted my eyes, trying to make out his face, but it was too blurry. Had Veronica done this?

Behind the photograph was a police report. The first page was filled with handwritten dates and addresses and names and numbers. Incident Number: 49671. Date of Incident: 7/16/15. Initial Officer Signature: Dale Hudspeth. Offense Name: Homicide (09A). Victim: Holland, Billy. Offender: Holland, Patricia.

On the second page, there was a narrative, written by Hudspeth. I held my breath as I read:

Officer Lauer and I were out on a trespassing call at the Holiday Inn on Brombard Avenue when a call came over the radio about a shooting on the 2800 block of Pella Avenue. Being less than a mile away, we responded to the shooting call. When we arrived at 2804 Pella Avenue, two Black females, both very upset, came from the residence next door, 2802 Pella Avenue. We later learned that their names were Sharell Patterson and Patricia Mae Holland. They are sisters. Ms. Patterson was crying into her hand and saying things that were unintelligible. Mrs. Holland, meanwhile, was covered with blood. She was yelling that she shot her husband and that she killed him. She kept yelling the same thing over and over again. "I shot him! I killed him!" At this point, I went to Mrs. Holland and pulled her aside and tried to calm her down. I asked her if she could tell me what had happened. While she spoke, Officer Lauer went inside to 2802 S. Pella Avenue, where he found the body. Mrs. Holland stated that she and her husband had been drinking alcoholic beverages throughout the night and that they had been arguing off and on for several hours. At some point, she saw that Mr. Holland, her husband, was showing her nephew, Willie Patterson, how to pull a knife and stab somebody. Another argument started between Mr. and Mrs. Holland about the knife. They went to the back bedroom, where he began choking and hitting her. Mrs. Holland showed me several marks that he'd left, including a bruise on her right cheek. The nephew tried to separate them, but Mrs. Holland pleaded with him to leave, and he did. She eventually got away from Mr. Holland and tried to leave the scene, but he came after her again with his fist raised. She grabbed a loaded gun from the nightstand and shot him twice. She ran from the residence to Ms. Patterson's house. During my conversation with Mrs. Holland, she was very upset and kept saying, "I didn't mean to shoot him. I didn't mean to kill him." I placed her into the back seat of our patrol car with Officer Lauer watching her. Ms. Patterson was still standing at this location, and she told me that the gun was on the ground by her porch. I secured the weapon. We drove Mrs. Holland to the station, where she was booked and held in police custody.

I placed the report and the mug shot back in the folder. I rubbed my eyes with my hand. So that was it. Veronica was a murderer. She'd killed her husband. Well, it looked like he had it coming. And the rest of us? Criminals as well?

I was about to continue my search when I heard the office door creak open. I didn't have time to react before an extraordinarily tall man dressed all in red aimed a strange-looking gun at my chest. I felt a jolt of electricity that spread to my arms and shoulders and head, and then, just like that, I was gone.

CHAPTER 30

When I regained consciousness, I was sitting against the office wall. I searched for my gun, but it was missing. A man, his back toward me, was inspecting the jars of brains, muttering something under his breath. Eventually, he turned around, and when he saw my eyes were open, struggling against the glare of the fluorescent lights, he smiled warmly. I'd never seen him before, but I knew who he was. He had a shock of red hair and a thousand and one freckles on a porcelain-white face. Dr. Zagorsky.

He gestured toward the jars and smacked his lips together as if willing the words to come from his mouth. "And now you're awake," he said.

I grunted.

He nodded at the jars. "I know it seems strange. All these brains. But I am a scientist. And a collector."

"But not of stamps," I said, my voice raw.

"No. Not stamps." Dr. Zagorsky straightened his body and grabbed one of the jars from the shelf, a minuscule organ, no more than a couple of centimeters in diameter, trapped inside. "The brain of a mouse," he said. "It's where we started. I know it doesn't look like much, but there are quite a lot of similarities to our own. In fact, most cells identified in the human cortex have corresponding types in mice. And that's why we—"

"I don't care about your goddamn mouse," I said. "You're Dr.

Frankenstein. I'm your monster." I tried standing, but my legs wouldn't work. There was something the matter with my body and soul.

Dr. Zagorsky watched me with curiosity. "Temporary paralysis," he said. "I apologize. Our security guard is quite excitable. But it's just as well. You could have hurt somebody with that gun. You've been out for a while."

"Why are you doing this?" I asked. "Stealing memories? Creating new ones?"

He ignored my questions. "I must say, though, that it is good to see you in person again. The last time I saw you, you were heavily medicated. In a walking coma."

"I saw the files," I said. "The mug shots. I saw how Veronica Miller— or whatever her real name was—killed her husband."

He leaned against the edge of his desk and scratched at his wild red hair. "Yes. But I don't want you to think badly of her. She's been changed. As have you."

"And what about Catherine Gordon?"

He studied the rodent's brain for a long moment before placing it back on the shelf. "Ah, yes, sweet Ms. Gordon. She's been through a lot. She used to be known as Lucinda Desmond."

"Desmond," I said. "I've heard that name."

"Yes. I believe you have. She had a daughter named Jane."

It took me a minute, but then I remembered. Jane Desmond. Catherine had mentioned her in her journal. Mentioned how she'd found a photo of her. And a death certificate. I felt like I was going to be sick.

"She . . . she killed her daughter," I said, and it was a statement, not a question.

"Yes. Drowned her. Nobody knows why. She never did tell the cops. Her husband was at work when it happened. A normal Tuesday. She drew a bath for Jane like she did every morning. She washed her body and shampooed her hair. But then after that? After that, she pushed the poor girl's head under the water and held it there. I wonder how long it took? Two minutes? More? Anyway. Once the poor girl was dead, she removed the body from the bathtub. She dried her off. She brushed her hair. And then she carried her back to her bedroom. She placed her daughter, her dead daughter, in her bed and pulled the covers up to her chin. Then she went to the living room and began knitting a sweater. She was still knitting when her husband came home, still knitting when he screamed in agony, still knitting when the police came to take her away."

I smiled. I don't know why. "Murderers," I said. "Both of them."

"Yes," Dr. Zagorsky said. "Murderers."

I wanted to cry, but I kept it together. "And what about me? Who am I? What did I do? Am I a murderer as well?"

He only smiled. One thing was clear: Dr. Zagorsky was a sociopath who enjoyed watching me squirm. "But first, let me explain why we chose Veronica. Why we chose Catherine. Why we chose you." He cleared his throat. "As you can imagine, neurological experiments of this magnitude aren't without major risks. Indeed, when the project was in its infancy, when we were experimenting on mice and then monkeys, we had a run of bad luck. Seizures. Strokes. Death. Eventually, however, the kinks were ironed out. We learned from our failures. By the time we got to the baboons, our techniques and methods were bearing fruit. We were ready to go to the next stage of the process. But to convince humans to be experimented on? To convince them to let us manipulate their memory? Manipulate their soul? Not so easy. Not easy at all. We offered healthy cash payments—our movement is well-funded—but we quickly learned that those people who needed money the most tended to be the least trustful of the medical industry and scientific experiments in particular. And I can't say I blame them. The Tuskegee Syphilis Study comes to mind. And so we had to think outside of the box, if you will." He watched me, his eyes narrowing to slits. I felt my skin go cold.

"And prisoners," I said, "didn't have a choice."

"There are more than two million people incarcerated in the United States. That's more than the population of Wyoming, Vermont, and Alaska combined. And it's no secret that, throughout history, our government has taken advantage of this population through risky experiments and trials. Hallucinogenic drugs, dioxins, new cosmetics. Hell, Eileen Welsome won a Pulitzer Prize for reporting on the government's testing of the toxicity of plutonium and uranium on prisoners. And so it continues today. In the name of progress, mind you."

I stared at the brains, and I thought of the ridiculousness of evolution, the absurdity of existence. I was having a difficult time breathing, and I soon realized I was crying, filthy tears streaming down my cheeks.

"Who am I?" I asked again.

Dr. Zagorsky didn't answer me. He glanced at his watch. "They'll be coming soon."

"Who? Who will be coming soon?"

"The authorities. To take you back to where we found you in the first place."

"Who am I? What did I do?"

"I think it's best," Dr. Zagorsky said, "that you don't know the answers to those questions."

"Fuck you! Fuck you! You can't do this to me! It's not right! It's not fair!"

I wiped away the tears with the back of my hand. Two weeks earlier, I had been living a normal life. I had been delivering mail. I had been helping my ill father. I had been warmed by the everlasting love of my mother. No longer. Now they were going to lock me up for a crime that another person, another me, committed.

"Of course," Dr. Zagorsky said, pulling back his red hair, "there is another option. Other than sending you back to prison."

"What option? What do you mean?"

Dr. Zagorsky reached into his jacket pocket and pulled out an old professorial pipe which he placed in his mouth. He looked ridiculous. There was no tobacco in the chamber, and he didn't light it.

"Here's the way I look at things. A fellow like you, you'd get destroyed in prison. What with your newly implanted gentle personality and sensitive disposition. Serve more hard time? It would be difficult. It would be very difficult."

"I'd rather serve time than . . ." I didn't finish my thought.

Dr. Zagorsky continued chewing on his pipe, and then he stroked his stubbled chin with his fingers, giving him an air of cultivated pensiveness instead of one of coldhearted manipulation.

"Securing another subject, as you can imagine, would be costly. But with you, all of the red tape has already been cut through. So? Why don't we try it again? With your permission, I think that we could—"

Once again, I tried getting to my feet, but it was no use. I shook my head and clenched my jaw. "I don't know," I said, and the tears had started again. "I don't know."

He removed the pipe and placed it back in his jacket pocket. "Wally, listen to me. There's nothing to fear. When babies are born, they don't question where they come from. And you won't either. Not this time. We'll tighten up the whole operation. That's what we'll do. We got a little bit sloppy this round, that's all. It will be fixed, that I can promise you. You will wake up a new man. You'll be happy. You'll have a good life. I'll see to it that you have an even better life, even better memories. Isn't that better than being locked up until you're an old man? Isn't it?"

I thought for a moment. "And if I don't agree? If you send me back to prison? Aren't you afraid that I'll tell?"

"Tell what?"

"About the experiments. About my brain."

Dr. Zagorsky laughed. "No. I'm not worried. There are a lot of mentally ill people behind bars. Men who are convinced they are the Messiah. Women who are convinced spider eggs are hatching in their esophagi. So what's another crazy person? Nobody will believe you, I'm afraid."

"The whole world is an insane asylum," I said. "That's the way I feel about it."

The doctor smiled. "You may be right, Wally. But before you decide, why don't I tell you why we're doing these experiments in the first place? Why don't I tell you about the Bethlam Project?"

CHAPTER 31

Dr. Zagorsky removed his glasses, huffed them with steam, and wiped them against his shirt. When he spoke again, he sounded almost giddy, conspiratorial. A fellow like him couldn't help himself. He needed to boast about his accomplishments. He needed validation, even from his own science project.

"Just a few years ago," he said, "the notion that we could implant viable memories was thought to be the stuff of science fiction. The notion that we could isolate memories and eliminate them? Equally absurd. The notion that we could create a whole new self, with self-awareness, new traits, and behaviors: impossible."

"But now," I whispered bitterly. "Miracles."

"What you should know," Dr. Zagorsky said, "is that your brain is absolutely fine. No permanent damage whatsoever. One of the benefits of this procedure is that your long-term knowledge, your learned skills, such as walking and talking, all remain intact. There was no need to relearn how to read or add. It was only your memories that were extracted. Only your past self."

From outside the room, I could hear the sound of footsteps marching and a gurney rolling on the concrete floor. As I glared at Dr. Zagorsky, I was filled with a hatred that was neither learned nor implanted. A hatred that had been there for eternity.

"Hell is empty," I whispered. "And all the devils are here."

"Listen to me, Wally. By consenting to this experiment, you—"

"I didn't consent to anything!"

"—helped your country. It's a patriotic sacrifice you made."

"Stop it. I only—"

He moved forward until he was standing directly over me, and I was having a tough time focusing. His face seemed to be all mixed up—a cheap Picasso rip-off. He said, "Listen to me, Wally. You've been out of commission for a while. Not everything you knew, you know anymore. But know this: our country is at war. With Ukraine. With Poland. With Syria. Those wars might end. But new ones will start."

"What does war have to do with me?"

"Not you specifically. But the Bethlam Project. Here's what's crucial for you to know. Our country has interests that we need to protect, democracy that we need to spread. Officials have to make difficult decisions."

I could begin to feel sensation in my legs. The paralysis was fading. If only I could get to my feet and walk across the office, then I could overpower him. He wasn't a big man. Of course, he might have my gun and shoot me in the temple. That was a factor to consider . . .

Dr. Zagorsky continued: "Someone once said that the horrors of war equal the horror of hell. Imagine seeing your platoon mate with his face blown to bits. Or a peasant girl being eaten by maggots. Or a field full of corpses, the soil soaked with blood. It's too much for the human brain to handle. Our hospitals have become filled not just with soldiers with missing limbs, but those with ruptured psyches. Meanwhile, our military is left nearly barren, unable to complete the tasks they have set out to do. Increased recruitment hasn't yielded much fruit. A draft isn't politically appetizing. So they came up with a plan. They asked the scientists if it was possible."

"You're saying that—"

"Better if you could get the same soldiers, the ones who were shell-shocked, to fight again. Better if you could wipe away those traumas and put them right back on the battlefield. Their families would never need to know. They would never need to know."

I let the weight of what he was saying settle. "So that's what this is about? Recycling soldiers? Wiping clear their memories, their trauma, their guilt so they can kill again?"

He nodded his head and grunted. "The government's aim, not mine. Yes, I will give them what they want. I will prove that memories, that traumas can be not just repressed but eliminated. But my vision goes far beyond that. I'm looking at the public health possibilities. The commercial possibilities."

"Commercial? What do you mean? You're going to sell new brains? New psyches?"

"Soldiers aren't the only ones with trauma. It's part of the human condition. The world is a devastating place, don't you think? Filled with hurt and rage, loss and regret. But now we can change all of that. Imagine being able to wipe clear those traumas. Allowing those people to actually live again."

"But that's not what you did with me. You went beyond that. You—"

"That's why I mentioned commercial possibilities. Don't think me cynical. Far from it. We rebuild computers, don't we? Fix and replace motherboards and hard drives. Why not humans? So, yes, we can eliminate trauma. But not only that. We can give people the past that they wanted. Allow them to pick and choose their own memories. A state championship in basketball. The attention you craved from your father. The love of a girl. You don't think people would be willing to pay for that? How much is happiness, real happiness, worth? We don't have the technology to create a time machine, but we have the ability to change the past. That's my aim, Wally."

"It's crazy," I muttered. "All of it."

"Yes," he said, laughing like we were good old buddies. "Crazy as hell."

If I still had my gun, I might have used it. I might have shot him in the belly and watched as he flopped like a carp on the floor. But I didn't have my gun. And the police would be here soon.

"Maybe," I muttered, "some good can come out of this."

"I think so, Wally. I really do."

I nodded my head. I'd made up my mind. "Call off the authorities. I'll do it. I'll consent to treatment."

"That's wonderful, Wally!"

"On one condition."

He raised a single eyebrow. "And what is that condition?"

"That you tell me who I am. That is, who I was. I want to know. I need to know. Even if I only know for a short while."

He studied me for a few moments. Then he reached down and touched my shoulder in an uncomfortably paternal manner.

"Of course, Wally. I'll tell you. I'll tell you everything. You deserve the truth. Even if that truth will only mix with the rain, vanish down the gutters."

"I don't know what I deserve, Doctor. Maybe only death."

He straightened up and returned to his desk. He picked up the phone and dialed a number. Somebody on the other end answered. Dr. Zagorsky said four words, and those words gave me chills: "Mr. Daley has consented."

A moment later, he jerked open a drawer and removed several thick files, all secured with rubber bands. He shuffled through them, dropping a few of them on the desk with a thud.

"The files on Malachi Severin."

I felt my heartbeat quicken and my skin burning. "Malachi Severin?"

He nodded his head. "Who you used to be."

I squeezed my eyes shut and tried my best to remember that name. Nothing. But at that very moment, I noticed that my leg moved forward. I could get to my feet. I knew I could. And then . . .

But not yet. First, I needed to know the truth.

He picked up the files and started across the room, then he stopped. "I could give you this file and let you read. But I have a better idea. I could let you hear who you are in your own words, in your own voice."

I shook my head. "I don't know what you mean."

"Wait here," he said. "It won't take but a few minutes. You'll understand when I get back."

He left the room, locking it shut behind him. As soon as he was gone, I struggled to my feet. My legs felt like spaghetti, but I could walk. I leaned against the wall and staggered forward, toward the shelves with the jars.

I grabbed one of them, labeled "Pig Brain." I turned around and returned to where I had just come from, sliding down against the wall. I placed the jar behind me, out of sight.

A few minutes later, I heard the door unlock, and Dr. Zagorsky entered. He held an old Panasonic cassette player and a single cassette.

He showed me the writing on the cassette: "An interview between Malachi Severin and Detectives Walters and Gardner. October 24th, 2011."

"I think you'll recognize his voice," he said. "But just remember: You are not Malachi Severin. Not anymore."

I didn't respond. I could feel the jar with the pig brain pressing against my back.

Dr. Zagorsky placed the cassette inside the player and pressed play. For several moments there was only hissing and buzzing. But then there was a voice, and it was gravelly and baritone . . .

CHAPTER 32

DETECTIVE WALTERS: Hey, Malachi, how's it going, buddy? They treating you all right in here?

MALACHI SEVERIN: I just got done throwing up.

WALTERS: Sorry to hear that. You want some water or something? Coffee? We could get you a little snack too.

SEVERIN: I drank some water before you came here.

WALTERS: That's fine. Well, if you're still thirsty or hungry or anything, we can get you something to eat or drink.

SEVERIN: Nah, I don't think so.

DETECTIVE GARDNER: But the rest of the department? They've been pretty nice to you?

SEVERIN: Yeah. Most of them.

GARDNER: That's good.

SEVERIN: Who's that one fellow? The bald one with the short tie? Jackson or Johnson?

GARDNER: Johnson.

SEVERIN: Yeah, I don't like him. He's got mean eyes. A mean face.

GARDNER: I know what you mean. Well, we'll keep him away from you if it makes you feel better.

SEVERIN: I think it was just nerves. That's why I was throwing up. I don't get sick too often.

WALTERS: That's a possibility.

GARDNER: Malachi, let me ask you something else. Do you know where you are?

SEVERIN: Police department?

GARDNER: That's right. Lakewood Police Department.

WALTERS: So we just want to make sure you know where you are and that everybody has been treating you nice.

SEVERIN: Everybody but Johnson. Just so you know, my friend Leon might come to pick me up. Take me home. We've known each other since we were kids. He'll be worried about me.

WALTERS: Uh-huh.

GARDNER: Like I said, if you want any water or coffee or fruit, you just ask.

SEVERIN: Yeah. It's annoying that I can't go home. We have a cat, you know? I don't know how long cats can live without food.

GARDNER: We'll let people know about your cat.

SEVERIN: Come to think of it, my throwing up might not be from nerves. It might be from acid reflux.

WALTERS: What we'd like to know is if you feel okay talking to us about what happened.

SEVERIN: What happened?

WALTERS: At your house. And then by the well.

SEVERIN: Oh, yeah. That. Sure, I can talk. There are no secrets anymore. Not anymore.

GARDNER: That's good, Malachi. If you talk, it'll help us understand. We're just trying to help you. We don't want you to be in trouble.

SEVERIN: Yeah, sure. That's kind of you. Now that I think about it, I would like some coffee. But do you have decaf?

GARDNER: Sure we have decaf. I'll let them know. Any cream?

SEVERIN: No. Just black. But, please, decaf. Otherwise, I'll be bouncing around the cell. Caffeine is a drug. It isn't good for you. I've never done drugs. Not even weed. The people I know who've done it got into bad habits. Did poorly in school.

GARDNER: I can see that.

WALTERS: Let me ask you something, Malachi. What kind of a relationship do you have with your father?

SEVERIN: Now isn't that a funny question? Are you a psychologist or some-
            thing?

WALTERS: No. Not a psychologist. Detectives. Like Detective Gardner said,
            we're just trying to help you. Trying to understand why you did
            what you did. So the more we can learn—

SEVERIN: I think I'd rather not say. Every father/son relationship is compli-
            cated, don't you think?

GARDNER: Yeah. That's true, Malachi. But your dad. He didn't treat you well,
            did he? Not you or your mom.

SEVERIN: Well, that depends. When I was ten years old, maybe eleven, he
            bought me a walkie-talkie set. I really liked that set. Me and Leon
            would talk on them. Pretend we were cops. Only the quality was
            poor. After a while, we got frustrated with them. Say, do you think
            me and Leon could ever use your radios? That'd be a lot of fun, you
            know?

GARDNER: We'll see what we can do. But when he wasn't buying you pres-
            ents. What kind of a father was he?

SEVERIN: Ha. You're persistent, ain't you? Well, fine. I can tell you. Like I said,
            no secrets. Not anymore. What do you want me to say? That he
            was mean? Yeah, he was mean. Red-assed bastard. I could tell you
            some things that he done to me. But really, it was all about protect-
            ing Mom. She was never as thick-skinned as me. I think it's because
            she's a woman. And I'm not trying to sound sexist or anything. Hell,
            my mother gave birth to me. That takes guts, you know? I'm only
            saying that she wasn't able to handle my father's meanness as well
            as I could.

GARDNER: I understand. Protecting your mother. That's noble.

SEVERIN: She doesn't weigh more than a hundred pounds. I worry about her.

WALTERS: And that's why I wonder—

SEVERIN: And that's the problem. Who's looking out for her? Who's looking
            out for our cat? These details have been overlooked.

WALTERS: Your mother is—

SEVERIN: But when you take the big view, you know, give yourself some dis-
            tance, it's hard to blame my father, not completely. See, he wasn't

well. Not for many years. Sometimes you have to be empathetic about these things.

GARDNER: He was sick?

SEVERIN: Hell, yeah, he was sick. I mean, mentally.

GARDNER: I see.

SEVERIN: Did you know that he was in Muammar Gaddafi's army?

GARDNER: I didn't know that.

SEVERIN: He tried deserting. Back in the early '70s. He was a pacifist, believe it or not. But they weren't having any of it. They gave him shock treatment to try and fix his attitude. Day after day. Week after week.

GARDNER: That's awful.

SEVERIN: And so by the time he got to America, his brain wasn't functioning properly. He was paranoid. Violent. It wasn't his fault. Gaddafi made him that way. It's a good thing he's dead. Gaddafi, I mean. Otherwise, I might go there, to Libya, and make him pay for what he did.

GARDNER: I see. And so the things your father did to you—

SEVERIN: At some point you feel like you've had enough.

WALTERS: Do you want to tell us what led up to the incident at the house?

SEVERIN: Not yet.

WALTERS: Okay.

GARDNER: What about your mother?

SEVERIN: My mother is beautiful. And I'm not saying that in some incestual way. It's just an objective fact. She and I have always been close. Closer than most mothers and sons. It's because we share similar traumas. Did you know that when I was young, I used to hear voices? Voices telling me to hurt other people. Voices telling me to hurt myself. And I worried that I must be going insane. I didn't want anybody to know. But I told my mother. I told her all of the crazy things the voices were saying. And you know what was incredible?

GARDNER: What?

SEVERIN: She didn't think I was crazy. She said that maybe the voices were real.

GARDNER: And what about you? Did you think the voices were real?

SEVERIN: Yes. Beyond a reasonable doubt. In fact, I still hear them to this day. I figured out some things. The voices are delivered at a high frequency, somewhere around twenty-three kilohertz. Most humans can only hear upward of twenty kilohertz. So if the voices were to start now, I'd hear them, but you wouldn't. Doesn't mean the voices aren't real. It's because my ears have a higher range than almost everybody else. Dr. Whitecomb told me so. He did tests.

GARDNER: It's not in our records.

SEVERIN: A lot of stuff isn't in your records.

WALTERS: What else?

SEVERIN: In my life, I've been involved in more than a thousand fights.

WALTERS: Is that right?

SEVERIN: And I've had sex with more than a thousand women.

WALTERS: That's impressive, Malachi.

GARDNER: You're a young man. I'd have to do the math on that.

SEVERIN: You don't believe me?

GARDNER: I didn't say that.

SEVERIN: Is it in your records when I tore the ear off that soldier?

WALTERS: We know about that, yes.

SEVERIN: I want to tell you about that. Me and my friends were sitting in the graveyard, minding our own business, having a few drinks. I took a piss on one of the graves. Think the corpse cares? This soldier boy approached me and my friends. Told me that it was time for me to stop desecrating the graveyard. I told him I didn't know what desecrating means, even though I did. He told me to stop pissing on the dead. So I pulled out my cock and started pissing on him.

WALTERS: We all do things we regret, Malachi.

SEVERIN: Not me. I don't regret a thing. Well, maybe a few things. But anyway. He came at me. He'd learned hand-to-hand combat in the army. But I'd learned hand-to-hand combat on the streets. And I got him pinned. He kept kicking at me, spitting in my face. I grabbed a hold of his ear. I pulled. It didn't take much force, believe it or not. Anyway. You should have heard him moan and scream. You should have seen the blood on my hands. But, like I said, I don't have any regrets. He's the one who started it. I was just minding my own business. Me and my friends. Sitting in the graveyard. I find it peaceful.

GARDNER: But I don't want you to focus on that. I want you to focus on your parents. You need to help us understand.

SEVERIN: It's like I said. My father would treat us mean. I didn't mind when he treated me badly. But when he beat my mother? I couldn't abide by that.

GARDNER: And so? That night in question? Was he beating your mother?

SEVERIN: Let me tell you something else that he'd do. When I used to do something wrong—at least wrong in his eyes—he'd take me to the garage. First, he'd take off his belt and bend me over. He would whip me but good. But I could handle that. I'd never cry, and that made him even madder. And then you know what he'd do?

GARDNER: What? What would he do?

SEVERIN: He'd tie me from the rafters. I shit you not. By the feet. Boy, that son of a bitch knew how to tie those ropes tightly. Didn't matter how much I wiggled, I couldn't get loose. He'd leave me in there for an hour, sometimes two, sometimes more. And he'd bring my mom in there and show her, and I looked like a cow about to get stuck. It was humiliating. My mom would cry, but there was nothing she could do. I don't blame her. Because he also used to humiliate her. You know what he'd do? He'd rape her. He'd bring me into their bedroom and make me watch. Tell me that I was going to be learning something. He'd lay her on her stomach, and she'd be begging him to stop. And he'd fuck her. And I'd watch. More than her screams, I remember her eyes. Staring right at me. I don't blame her. Not until what happened last night. Was it last night? How long have I been here?

WALTERS: The night before last.

SEVERIN: Yeah. The night before last. That's when everything changed. That's when I became a man. I don't regret it. I don't regret being a man. What else would I be? A coward? Is that what you'd want from me? Just a cowardly little boy? Nah. I couldn't live with myself if I were a coward. Not for a single day.

GARDNER: Nobody can blame you for hating him. Nobody can blame you for what you did to him.

WALTERS: But now's the time for you to tell us. Tell us everything you remember.

SEVERIN: Okay. I'm ready. Can I have a cigarette?

WALTERS: Yes. Get him a cigarette.

GARDNER: (Inaudible)

SEVERIN: He'd been drinking. Not much of a surprise there. Ten in the morning. Jack Daniel's. Straight from the bottle. The more he drank, the meaner he got. He kept calling me a faggot. I didn't respond. I'm bigger than that. Then he started calling my mom a whore. Said that she loves taking it in the mouth, up the ass. A fucking whore, he said. I didn't care much what he said about me. But I wasn't going to let him abuse Mom in that way. I told him to stop. He laughed at me. Said, "Make me." Mom went to cleaning the kitchen. That's what she does when there's conflict. She cleans. She sings Disney songs. "Someday My Prince Will Come." My father told her to shut the fuck up. He drank more whiskey. Mom scrubbed at invisible spots on the counter. That's the way things went for a long time. I went to my room and listened to music. I didn't want to be around him. I hated him. I wanted him to be dead. I'd always wanted him to be dead. Do you know how many times I'd dreamed of killing him? Other kids fantasized about fucking the hot cheerleader chick. I fantasized about slicing open my dad's throat. About bashing his skull with a cinder block. About forcing him to drink Drano. I focused on the music. Cannibal Corpse. Behemoth. Immolation. I played the music loud. And that's when I heard the screaming. I have no idea how I heard over the death metal. But I heard. It wasn't the first time she'd screamed, of course. Only, this time, her screams were different somehow. I rose to my feet. I grabbed my Louisville Slugger. I don't play baseball. I'm terrible at it. But my dad had given me that bat as a birthday present. Funny, isn't it? He gave me the bat. I returned to the kitchen. She was in the corner of the kitchen, shielding her head with her hands. He was pummeling her with his fists. Just letting her have it. "Goddamn whore," he was saying. "Goddamn whore." I didn't stop to think things over. I didn't say my dad's name. I just walked right over there and swung as hard as I could. I connected with the back of his head. He didn't make a sound. He just slumped to the ground.

GARDNER: Did you think he was dead?

SEVERIN: I was pretty sure. I hoped he was. I hoped he was dead.

GARDNER: But he wasn't.

SEVERIN: No. But my mom thought he was dead. That's why she kept scream-ing. She rose to her feet. She said, "You killed him, you killed him." I thought she'd be happy. But she wasn't. She wasn't happy at all.

WALTERS: You loved your mom. You were only trying to protect her. But in-stead of thanking you, she got mad at you. That must have been difficult.

SEVERIN: It was like she went crazy. She started cursing me out. She said, "You killed my husband. You killed the love of my life." But he wasn't the love of her life. He was an abuser. That's what he was.

GARDNER: And so?

SEVERIN: I said, "Mom, he was hurting you. He might have killed you." She shook her head. She said, "He wasn't hurting me, you stupid son of a bitch." Then she spat at me. Spat at me! I was too stunned to respond. She got to her feet and left the kitchen. Left the house. My dad was still in the kitchen. He was bleeding from the head. But I heard him moan. That's when I realized he was alive. I could have helped him. I could have called an ambulance. Instead, I went after my mother. Outside, the rain was falling in sheets, and the trees looked like scary skeletons. I ran through the forest, and ev-erything was silent. No sound of footsteps on the forest floor, no sound of my breathing, no sound of the wind through the thrash-ing branches. The rain fell, and my hair was soaking wet. And then, up ahead, I could see her, and it was like a dream. She was wearing a white dress, and she had a string of lights wrapped around her body. It's strange because that's not what she was wearing back at the house. Was it really her? Or was it a ghost?

GARDNER: But you caught up with her. Eventually, you caught up with her.

SEVERIN: She kept glancing back, my mother, and her expression was one
of terror. Why was she terrified? I'd protected her from a monster.
And then she disappeared into the shadows of the trees. There
were still no sounds, even though I stepped on the fallen leaves,
even though the wind kept shaking the trees. Time passed. Minutes
maybe. Hours maybe. She was sitting against the old stone well. All
around her were towering trees, swaying menacingly. "Mother," I
said. "Mother." Now she was crying, and she looked so beautiful.
But she wouldn't answer me. I kept saying "Mother" over and over
again, but she was mute. Sometimes, when Dad was drunk, she'd
come to my room and sleep in my bed, and I'd hold her. Did I tell
you that? I took care of her in a lot of ways. I should have killed my
father. I am a coward. I hit him once. I caused him to bleed. But I
should have hit him again and again. Why didn't I? Why did I spare
his life, and yet, with my mother, I—

WALTERS: Did your mother finally speak? Did she say something? Did she spit
at you again?

SEVERIN: No, she didn't say another word. Not out loud. But I knew what she
was thinking. I knew. And then I realized that the voices I'd been
hearing over the years, those voices were hers. Because she got in
my head just then. She told me that she loved my father more than
me. She told me that she'd never loved me and she never would.

WALTERS: She did this through thoughts?

SEVERIN: The voices were always her.

WALTERS: And you killed her. You killed your mother.

SEVERIN: I picked her up by the arms. She was a small woman, my mother. She
barely weighed a hundred pounds. I picked her up by the arms, and
she wasn't crying anymore. She looked at me, unblinking, and it reminded me of when my father made me watch her getting fucked in
the bedroom. Somehow, those eyes made me angry. I didn't want to
kill her. I wanted to kill my father. But her eyes made me angry. Her
voices. I placed my hands around her neck, so slender. I squeezed,
and she closed her eyes, and then a smile appeared on her face. It

didn't seem to take a long time. I thought you had to squeeze for longer. She didn't fight. She'd had enough of this world. Her body went limp. I was scared. My father was back at the house. I knew he was alive. I worried that he would come stumbling through the forest. I worried that he'd find me there with my mother. I lifted her in my arms, the way you would carry a bride across the threshold, and I whispered into her ear. I said, "I'm sorry, I'm so sorry," and then I dropped her over the edge of the well, and her body banged across stone walls, and I heard a splash in the water below. I backed away and fell to my knees. And then I did something that I hadn't done in years. I prayed. I prayed to the Lord Jesus and begged for forgiveness. I told him that I couldn't help the fact that I was bad, that I was born bad, that circumstances beyond my control had made me even worse. But he didn't answer—he never answers—and I peered back down the well. And what happened next, well, I don't expect you to believe me because I don't really believe it myself.

GARDNER: We'll believe you, Malachi. Of course we will.

SEVERIN: It don't matter if you don't. I just got to get it off my chest.

GARDNER: Go ahead.

SEVERIN: As I was looking down the well, I saw that my mother had risen to her feet. I saw that she was staring back at me with those demonic green eyes, and then I heard her laugh, and then I heard her whisper into my skull, heard her say, "You're not long for this world." And so I left that place. I went back to the house. I returned to the kitchen. My father was on his hands and his knees. He had a pail of water, and he was cleaning his own blood. He looked up and saw me. He said, "Did you kill her?" I nodded my head, said, "Yes, sir." He said, "Good. She had it coming."

CHAPTER 33

Dr. Zagorsky clicked the stop button, and then everything was quiet. He leaned against the side of his desk and watched me from the corner of his eye.

I was mumbling to myself, saying the words, "She had it coming" over and over again.

"Now knock it off, Wally. You're not that man anymore. We changed you, but good."

"Malachi Severin," I said. "That's who I am. I killed my mother with my bare hands."

Dr. Zagorsky shrugged his shoulders. "I guess it all depends on how you look at it."

"And so what happened to me after the interview? They found me guilty?"

A quick nod of the head. "By the time your lawyer arrived, the damage had already been done. You'd made a full confession, and the confession was admitted at the trial. The trial lasted for five days, but the jury was out for less than an hour. You were convicted of second-degree murder. Sentenced to fifteen years in prison."

I stared at my wrist, at the tattoo. 10/23/11. I hadn't been entirely wrong. It was the day my mother had died. I turned my hands over and gazed at the skin, and I swear to God a thin coat of blood had manifested.

"A killer," I whispered. "A murderer."

I squeezed my eyes shut and tried to remember that awful night, but there were no memories to be had. They'd wiped me clean.

Dr. Zagorsky moved to where I was sitting and, once again, placed his hand on my shoulder in a paternal gesture. "If it makes you feel any better, there were plenty of mitigating circumstances. You take the years of abuse, both emotional and physical. You take Malachi's own mental illness, a precursor of schizophrenia. We can't place the entire burden on his—on your—shoulders."

"I murdered my mother. My own mother." And then I hung my head and cried.

Dr. Zagorsky let me cry. He knew that I was in mourning not only for my mother, but for myself. He waited until I'd drained every last tear from my eyes before speaking again. Somebody kept knocking on the door, but he didn't make a move to answer.

He said, "I know all of this is hard to comprehend, hard to accept. But listen to me for a moment. Because of the Bethlam Project, you were saved from a lifetime of guilt, rotting in a miserable prison. It might be hard for you to see right now, but the Bethlam Project has been an overwhelming success by virtually all metrics. It has taken the devotion and dedication of literally hundreds of people—scientists, researchers, architects, actors—to make the project a triumph. However, I do recognize that some mistakes were made. Hindsight being what it is, the experiment should have been better controlled. Maybe if the confluence of unfortunate events hadn't happened, then you wouldn't be sitting here in this office learning these difficult truths about who you once were. You would still be good ol' Wally Daley delivering mail. You would still be taking care of your father. You would still be blissfully unaware. So for those mistakes, I am sorry."

I shook my head forcefully. "I don't think so. I think I always knew. Whenever I looked in the mirror. Whenever I said my name. Whenever I spoke to my father. Deep down inside, I knew."

"That very well may be so," Dr. Zagorsky said. "But as a scientist, I believe we must go forward. There is no sense in trying to go back. And since you have agreed, once more, to be a subject, we can indeed move forward."

But the remnants of Malachi Severin's voice haunted me: *Those eyes made me angry . . . I placed my hands around her neck, so slender.*

"What now?" I asked, and the words were dripping with despair. "What happens now?"

He adjusted his glasses on his nose. "There will be some paperwork to sign. A taped video confirming your understanding of the process. Then we take you to the basement floor. We give you medicine. You won't wake up for a long time. And when you do, you'll be a new man with a new name."

A new man, he said, but I knew the truth. We can't escape our true nature.

Dr. Zagorsky turned his back to me for just a moment. I struggled to my feet and raised the pig brain high up in the air. He turned back around, but before he could react, I reached back and swung forward, smashing the glass jar against his temple. A grunt escaped from his mouth, and he stood there for a moment as if he were thinking it over before collapsing to the ground.

Like some savage, I dropped to my knees, straddling his body, and raised the glassed pig brain high into the air, ready to crush his skull completely. My hand was trembling, and I didn't know if it was from rage or fear. I could have killed him, I could have. But at the last moment, I let the jar drop to the ground, and it rolled beneath the table. Malachi Severin was a murderer. Wally Daley was not.

Dr. Zagorsky's breath was shallow, he was groaning, and his eyes kept flickering on and off. I didn't have much of a plan. I reached into his pockets to see what I could find. A wallet. A set of keys. An old-school flip phone, fully charged. And my gun. I left the wallet, kept the phone and keys. Pocketed the gun. Unsteadily, I rose to my feet, staggered across the room, and pushed open the door a crack. I wasn't anybody; I didn't exist in this world or in one's past. I peered down the hallway, empty except for a blue medical gown crumpled in the corner. I took a step forward and then another one, shutting the door behind me. There were three keys on the chain, and I tried each one. The final one worked, and I locked the door. I placed my ear against the door, but there was no sound. Dr. Zagorsky was sleeping.

Head down, bile burning my throat, I wandered through those hallways, strangely decorated with oceanic shades of blue. Each time I heard voices, or footsteps, echoes of radios, I darted down a darkened corridor and pressed my body against the cold wall, praying to a blind and deaf God to protect me from my tormentors. Sometimes I would see nurses, their faces half concealed in shadows, pushing old-fashioned gurneys, and on those gurneys were patients, their faces frozen in agonized screams, and I wondered what crimes they had committed, wondered what new identities they would be given.

It seemed as if I had been walking for hours when I finally found the ladder that led back to the main floor. I felt like I had nothing left, but still, I climbed, and whenever I paused, for just a moment, I was sure I could hear an echo of footsteps and voices, and those voices seemed angry, resolute.

Adrenaline and desperation allowed me to keep going, and soon I was on the main floor, all concrete walls and metal catwalks and ladders hanging from the ceiling. I took off in a wounded gallop, and I didn't know where I was going, didn't know if I would escape. I heard ghostly voices, saw hazy shadows.

Like a trapped animal, I wouldn't stop until I found light, until I tasted fresh air, and then, up ahead, I saw the concrete staircase from which I'd come.

My lungs were aching, and my legs were nothing but rubber. I felt that familiar pain in my skull, and I wondered if Dr. Zagorsky was sticking needles into some scientific voodoo doll. With the last remnants of hope, I got down on my hands and knees, and was able to crawl those final concrete stairs. The voices were getting louder, my pursuers getting nearer, and I could make out some of the words, clear as day: "Get him! He's too important to the cause!"

Once, only once, did I glance over my shoulder, but instead of seeing a mob of white-jacketed physicians holding torches and pitchforks, the gray corridors were empty, and I worried that my mind had been swallowed up by some pestilent lunacy.

I reached the top of the staircase. The hatch door was closed. My eyes were darting all over the place, looking for the latch. I found it and, with trembling hands, unlocked it. Then I used my shoulder to shove open the door, which seemed impossibly heavy.

For the moment, I was free. I rolled onto my back, blinked a few times, and witnessed fireflies and moths and dead suns filling the phosphorescent sky. Dry heaving a night's worth of anxiety, I got to my feet and staggered across the red dirt toward where Barker's car shone like a beacon in the night.

But when I reached the car, another bitter disappointment: The key was gone. I checked over and over again, but it was no use. They must have taken it, along with my sanity. I cursed myself, cursed Dr. Zagorsky, cursed the world. I stared at the long dirt road that led to the two-way highway, and I felt discouraged and hopeless. It would take me hours to get back to Bethlam, hours before I could find Veronica and tell her the nightmare I'd woken up to.

And then another thought. I had Dr. Zagorsky's phone. If there was any reception out here in the middle of hell, I could call her. But I'd just removed the phone and was about to dial, when I saw one person and then two and then three crawling out of the bunker. They wiped themselves off, and one of them turned on a flashlight, the beam illuminating the starkness of the desert.

I took off running—*He's too important to the cause!*—dodging the sagebrush and tumbleweeds that filled the barren landscape. I ran and I ran, not stopping for ten, fifteen minutes at least, lungs filled with shards of invisible glass. I couldn't see or hear the doctors anymore, but I'd also lost my sense of direction, and I found myself wandering in circles, searching desperately for the edge of the highway, but more likely drifting farther and farther away.

The wind was blowing cold, and soon I was trembling badly. I thought of all the ways to go and decided that this would be one of the worst, wandering alone through the desert until I collapsed in exhaustion, until I died of thirst or hunger or a venomous snakebite.

Hopeless, I sat down beneath a catclaw acacia, its tiny leaves shivering in the moonlight. I placed the gun on the desert floor then pulled out Dr. Zagorsky's phone and flipped it open. Veronica had told me her phone number once, only once, but somehow I remembered it. Maybe it was because the last four numbers were 2011, the year I'd killed my mother. Hands trembling, I pressed the buttons. I placed the phone against my ear and it rang and rang, but there was no answer. I called again and again. Nothing. Finally, on my fifth attempt, there was a click and then breathing on the other end.

"Who is this?"

"Veronica! It's me. Wally."

"Wally! Where are you? Are you okay?"

"Yes. No. Not really. Listen, after we spoke, I did what you told me. I confronted my father. He told me some things. And then he took me to the bunker. Dr. Zagorsky told me the rest. I know the truth now. All of it."

There was a long pause on the other end. "The truth? What is it?"

"I'm going to tell you. I'm going to tell you everything. From the moment I saw Catherine Gordon slicing her throat to the present time huddled beneath this cursed acacia tree. But I need you to do something for me."

"Of course. Do you need me to find you? I could steal my husband's car. I could—"

"No time for that. No, here's what I need. I need you to listen to my story. Every single word. Then I need you to write it all down. Can you do that?"

"Yes. My husband is asleep. But I'll need to go to the basement where they can't see me. Otherwise—"

"Then go. I'll dictate and you'll remember. And then later, when they're not watching, you'll write it all down."

"Okay, but—"

"And when you're done writing it down, you'll hide the manuscript, so the town can't find it."

"Okay, Wally. But where? Where would I hide it?"

"In my room, my bedroom, the wallpaper is peeling. It'll come right down. You can staple the pages beneath. Then seal the wallpaper so that nobody can tell. Are you listening to me? Do you understand?"

"Yes, I'm listening. I understand. I'm walking down the basement steps. Give me just a moment, and then—"

I squeezed my eyes shut.

And then I started speaking.

PART 5

HENRY "HANK" DAVIES / MALACHI SEVERIN

CHAPTER 34

I'd read the entire manuscript, every excruciating word, while sitting cross-legged in the middle of our bedroom. I hadn't taken a break—not to use the bathroom, not to get water, not to rest my eyes. Once, when the sun had fallen below the desert mountains, and the light had vanished into the ether, I did stand up and turn on the overhead light, but otherwise, I remained in that same position, back tightening, head aching, mind splintering, the crusted pages spread out in front of me like some madman's accordion. As I read page after page, my emotions drifted from ardent curiosity to sickening dread to paralyzed terror. The revelations were too overwhelming and painful for me to grasp all at once, but every so often, I found myself weeping, the words on the page becoming blurred with my tears. In the course of three or four hours, my world had been turned upside down, my pockets emptied of all those pebbles of hope.

I thought about taking a match to the manuscript, watching the pages—and my soul—flutter and twist in the flame. Perhaps by burning the words, I could burn my past, I could return to the present, a life worth living. But I couldn't bring myself to do it. The truth was agonizing, but the truth was necessary. And so, I neatened the pages of the manuscript and pushed them beneath the bed.

I glanced at the clock, ticking menacingly on the wall. It was nearing ten o'clock. That was the time Iris said she would be home.

I tried pulling myself together through self-talk and deep breaths, but it didn't work. Instead, I found myself yanking at my hair, and when I looked in my hands, I saw thick strands wrapped around my fingers. The sense of dread was only becoming more and more overwhelming. I looked at my wrist, at the date tattooed there. I had been tricked into thinking it represented the day my father had passed from natural causes, just like Walter Daley had been tricked into thinking it represented the day his mother had passed from natural causes. But now I knew that October 23, 2011, was the day Malachi Severin had slammed his father's skull with a baseball bat. It was the day he had strangled his mother and thrown her down the darkened well, left her screams echoing into eternity.

Malachi Severin was a victim of circumstances.

Malachi Severin was a murderer.

I was Malachi Severin.

I again stared at my hands, and I could see the blood shivering beneath the skin.

I couldn't remember doing it. But I'd done it. I'd killed her.

With these hands. These bloody hands.

My own mother.

My brain was spasmatic, my mouth was trembling. Ugly thoughts crawled inside my skull like a thousand red spiders. The truth was in those pages. The handwriting was Veronica's, but the words were mine. When I closed my eyes, everything was mixed up, my hippocampus filled with memories that weren't mine. *Pushing the Matchbox car up and down the hallway, zoom, zoom, zoom; playing catch with my father, the baseball slapping against the leather of our gloves; the roses on the passenger seat as the lights of a semi come over the ridge . . .*

The memories of this Hank Davies, all constructed in a lab.

I thought about the woman who now claimed to be my mother, the woman who gave me mementos for my birthday, the woman who wore Chanel No. 5.

Nothing but an actress.

I thought about the woman who claimed to be my wife, the woman who kissed me on the cheek each morning, the woman who slept in my bed each night.

Also an actress.

I wanted to scream. I wanted to laugh. I did neither. I just sat there, rocking back and forth, eyes rolled into the back of my skull.

Yes, an actress. I recalled the other day when I walked into our bedroom and saw Iris holding my dandruff shampoo, pretending that she was in a commercial. *Has your hair lost its shine?* she'd said. *Is it missing its bounce?*

So now I knew, and maybe I'd known from the beginning. She was a hired hand, a part of the Bethlam Project. The kisses had all been for show. The love only pretend. When she smoothed back my hair with her slender hand, when she held me close as the moon waned, when she said, "I love you, darling," it was not for me; it was for hard, cold cash.

I was Malachi Severin.

I rose to my feet, moved across the bedroom floor, and came to the dresser. I pulled open the top drawer and removed a locket, the one that Iris had given to me on my birthday. I stared at the photograph inside, the one of Iris and me sitting on a Ferris wheel. And more of Hank's memories came flooding back, memories of Iris and me getting stuck on top, swaying back and forth, back and forth, memories of me leaning over and kissing her on the corner of her mouth, memories of her shutting her eyes in ecstasy. All counterfeit. I stared closer at the photograph and saw the inconsistencies, telltale signs that it had been photoshopped. I saw how the trees and buildings warped unnaturally. How her hair blended into the background. How her teeth seemed to duplicate and overlap.

I was Malachi Severin.

They'd tried this once before. Named me Walter Daley. Put me in a house with another actor, a man who pretended to be my father, a man who pretended to be suffering from Alzheimer's. But it hadn't worked. I'd discovered the old movies. *The Blood House. The Devil's Skin. Die Before Midnight. Big Mama's Boys. The Magic of Christmas.*

And now they'd tried it again.

They could keep trying. Over and over and over again. Chipping at my brain with an ice pick. Repairing it with grifter's salve. But I was too smart for them, too resourceful. I would always discover my true self.

And now . . .

See my blood spreading on the linoleum floor. See my heart beating on the butcher's scale. See my eyeballs darting across a fishbowl.

I was Malachi Severin.

I tore at my skin, yanked at my hair, gritted my teeth. I was a ghost, but now I could remember, and what I remembered was real. You don't think I can tell the difference between a real memory and an implant? You don't think I can tell the difference between flesh and fairy dust?

This I remembered: The old man was a real bastard. That's where my sickness came from. Was it passed on through genetics or through abuse? Hard to know. He used to hang me upside down from the rafters in the garage, leave me there for hours at a time. I would sing and cry, laugh, and scream. How could I not be sick?

He used to make me watch him rape my mother. He would fuck her from behind, twisting her arm behind her back, and the whole time he would watch me, his lips upturned into a sociopathic grin, and the whole time she would watch me, her eyes sad and defeated.

What I remembered was real.

I was Malachi Severin.

I didn't tell anybody about the things my old man was doing to me and my mom. I should have. Maybe they would have stopped him then. Maybe my mom and I could have escaped from that house of blood and disappeared into the mountains, found a little cabin overlooking a river, and we could have sipped cider and played Uno and laughed and talked and laughed some more.

On that autumnal night, he really let her have it. He punched and kicked her. He left her bruised and bloody. And so I could take no more. I hit him with the baseball bat. A Louisville Slugger. A Mike Trout model. I should have hit him harder. I should have killed him.

Where was he now?

Dead probably. Hanging from a sycamore tree. Or maybe that was wishful thinking?

Remember him sitting in the kitchen, on his hands and knees, scrubbing away his own blood? I do. I remember. That was after I'd killed my mother. I shouldn't have done that. I loved my mother. She hadn't done anything wrong besides marrying the wrong man.

Her name was Gwendolyn Severin.

My name was Malachi Severin.

Not Walter Daley. Not Hank Davies.

Malachi Severin.

And now the question, the important question. What to do next?

I paced around the room, the sense of dread becoming more and more overwhelming. I wiped the fog from the window and gazed toward the street. No sign of Iris. Not yet.

Option #1:

I could play it dumb, play it cool, act like I hadn't learned a thing. I could burn the manuscript, watch the pages fold under a red flame. Some things were better not to know. Most things were better not to know. The truth might fade away; the truth might be forgotten. And within a bucketful of lies, maybe Iris and I could live happily ever after.

But, no.

I was a test subject, a human-sized rat. As soon as the experiment was complete, as soon as the data was collected, I'd be disposed of. Maybe they'd send me back to prison to rot behind the metal bars. Or maybe they'd shoot me full of poison, bury me in the desert.

I needed to be proactive.

Option #2:

I could try to escape. I could wait until Iris was sleeping and then steal her car keys—she left them in that little red handbag that she always hung on the back of the rocking chair. I could drive toward the mountains and then keep on driving some more. Maybe I could find a little cottage buried high in the hills. Maybe a kindly old woman wearing a checkered apron and a red kerchief would take me, would hide me away from the cruelness and confusion.

But I knew that was just a pipe dream. I knew they'd be watching me, tracking me through my microchip. I knew they'd never let me escape, knew they'd fire a trio of bullets into the back of my head as I pulled out of the driveway.

Option #3:

I could confront Iris.

I could squeeze her throat.

I could kill her.

Just like I'd done to my mother.

There was really only one option.

Only one option.

CHAPTER 35

She didn't get home until after midnight. Do you hear that? Not until after midnight.

> *My girl, my girl, don't lie to me*
> *Tell me, where did you sleep last night?*

For the past hour and a half, I'd been sitting in the chair in the darkness, gazing at the shadows shifting by the light of the moon. I heard the tires crunching on the gravel. I heard the car door open and slam shut. I heard her high heels echoing on the pavement. I heard her enter the house while sirens blared in my head.

When the bedroom door creaked open, I didn't say a word. I waited until she'd taken a few steps inside before I turned on the floor lamp.

"It's late," I said.

I must have startled her because she gasped. "Goodness," she said, covering her heart with her hand. "I didn't expect you to be up."

"You said you'd be home at ten. It's past midnight. I started worrying. Worrying that somebody killed you."

"Worried that somebody killed me?" She laughed nervously. "Oh, goodness what an imagination you have. I'm sorry, darling. I should have called. I was just chatting with my parents and the time slipped away. You understand."

"Of course I do. I'm just glad you're home."

She stood there, smiling, but I could tell she was uneasy. I could tell that she knew that I knew . . . something.

"Well," she said, sighing, "I'll guess I'll go brush my teeth and take out my eyes and put on my nightgown."

"Yes," I said. "And then you can sleep."

> *In the pines, in the pines*
> *Where the sun don't ever shine*
> *I would shiver the whole night through*

Iris came out of the bedroom wearing her nightgown. I couldn't stop staring at her. She wouldn't look at me. She was lovely. I was ugly. This was undeniable.

"You're still dressed," she said.

I bared my teeth, not quite a grin. "Yes. I'm not ready to sleep."

"No?"

"I've been sitting here for the last few hours. Just thinking and reading and thinking."

"Oh? What have you been reading?"

I didn't answer her question. "Here's what I think. I don't think you were with your parents tonight."

"Not with my parents? What . . . what are you talking about?"

For somebody who was trying out for a shampoo commercial, she was a wonderful actress, a real Meryl Streep.

I rose to my feet. Iris backed up and pressed against the wall. The damsel in distress.

"I think you were with your lover. Maybe even your husband. Do you have any children?"

"My lover? My husband? Jesus, Hank. Have you lost your mind?"

I shook my head. "No. Far from it. You heard of Malachi Severin?"

"Malachi who?"

"Severin. Malachi Severin."

"No. Hank, what is this all about? Maybe I should call Dr. Hoover. Maybe I should—"

"Fuck Dr. Hoover."

"Hank. You're scaring me. What we need to do is—"

I took a step forward and then another. "What you should know, Iris, what's important to understand, is that I'm Malachi Severin."

"No—"

"Yes. I killed my mother. Strangled her soft throat. Dumped her in a well."

Iris only laughed. "You're not making any sense, darling. You're not Malachi Severin. We should call Dr. Hoover. If only you'd—"

"You're a part of it. The Bethlam Project or whatever they're calling it. You and Dr. Hoover and Dr. Zagorsky and my mother and my boss and—"

"Will you listen to yourself? You have to know how crazy you sound."

"My name is Malachi Severin. Not only did I kill my mother, but I tried killing my father with a baseball bat. Can you imagine? I should have tried harder."

"Oh, Hank! Oh, dear!"

"My name is Malachi Severin. The jury found me guilty. There was nothing my lawyer could do. He was well-meaning. His name was Jerry Harris. I hold no ill will toward Mr. Harris. He did the best he could, but what else could he do? I'd already confessed to my crimes. I was tired of being a coward. The judge was a stern old man with white hair and a white beard. He sentenced me to fifteen years in prison. There was nothing I could say. Nothing I could do. They put the handcuffs around my wrists. They took me out of the courtroom. They placed me in a cell. I was supposed to stay there forever. That should have been the end of it.

"But they had other plans for me."

I could see Iris eyeing the door, looking for a way to escape. If she tried, if she made a dash for it, I would grab her. I would slam her against the wall. That's what I would do. And not only that.

"It was Zagorsky. He was the mastermind. He erased my memories.

Every single one of them. He gave me a new identity. Walter Daley. A postman. His father suffered from dementia."

Iris: "Listen to me, Hank. You need—"

"And when I made the discovery that I wasn't Walter Daley, that I was Malachi Severin, they erased my memories again. They turned me into Hank Davies. They gave me a wife. But she was only an actress. She liked practicing for shampoo commercials."

Outside I could hear the muted whine of police sirens. Were they coming here? Had Iris somehow managed to call the cops when I wasn't paying attention?

"But I was too smart. I wrote everything down. No, that's wrong. Veronica Miller wrote everything down. Only she's not Veronica. Her name is Patricia Holland. She killed her husband. He had it coming. Are you following me, Iris? It all makes sense now!"

"No, Hank. I'm not following at all. We need to get you seen. There's something the matter with your brain. It's not your fault. It's never been your fault. The accident. You—"

"Stop it! Just stop it. You can't trick me. Not anymore. I've got the proof. I've got the manuscript right here."

I got down on my hands and knees. I pulled the manuscript from beneath the bed. The proof.

"Where did you get that?" she asked, and I could tell she was apprehensive. She knew that I knew.

My lips spread into a grin. I would tell her where I found the manuscript, and wouldn't she be impressed?

"The other night," I said, "while you were sleeping, Veronica Miller came to the window. They should have scrubbed her too. Why didn't they? Why? She told me some things. How I shouldn't trust Hoover. How I shouldn't trust my mother. How I shouldn't trust you. And she told me to look behind the wallpaper. In our bedroom. I waited until you were gone. And then I pulled back the wallpaper."

"I'll call Dr. Hoover. I'll tell him that—"

"It was covered with papers, stapled to the wall, all of them covered with microscopic handwriting. I removed each paper, one by one.

I placed them in the proper order. And then I started reading. The tiny, slanted words told a story. They told my story."

Iris opened her mouth as if to speak, but no words came out.

I dropped the manuscript on the bed. "Read it," I said. "It's all there. The truth is all there."

She eyed me and then the manuscript and then me again.

"Behind the wallpaper, you say?"

"Yes. Behind the wallpaper."

She sighed deeply—all part of her act—and then moved toward the bed. And the whole time, I scrutinized her neck and thought about how easy it would be to squeeze it, how easy it would be to break her windpipe. She deserved it. They all deserved it.

I was Malachi Severin. On October 23, 2011, I'd killed my mother.

Iris sat down and picked up the manuscript. She looked at the first page. I had the opening line memorized: *Mailbag slung over my shoulder, sun helmet tipped back on my head, I walked slowly down the empty and sun-bleached streets of Bethlam, Nevada, and I couldn't help but feel uneasy, couldn't help thinking those thoughts.*

I watched her as she read, fingers tracing the words. Her brow furrowed, and her eyes narrowed to slits. She turned to the second page and then the third. And then her expression turned to that of bewilderment.

"Oh, Hank," she said. "Oh, Hank."

"You see? It's the truth. All of it. Written in ink because there wasn't enough blood. Walter Daley recited each word. And Veronica Miller wrote it all down."

Iris continued shaking her head.

"Why do you shake your head when you know the truth?"

"Because that's not what's here."

"What do you mean?"

"Oh, Hank," she said again.

Oh, Hank. Oh, Hank. Oh, Hank.

"What the fuck do you mean?"

She placed the manuscript back on the bed. And then she wiped away some tears.

"Hank," she said. "There is no story on those pages. No story at all."

She was an actress. That's what she got paid to do. And paid handsomely, I was sure. She was acting. Certainly, she was acting. Look at those tears streaming down her cheeks. Look at those swollen eyes. Look at that trembling lip. Wonderful. Brilliant.

"There's a story," I said. "Veronica wrote it all down."

"There's no story. There's no Veronica." She pointed to the manuscript, and there was such melancholy in her voice, such disappointment. "It's only gibberish. It's only chicken scratches."

At this, I laughed. "Gibberish? Chicken scratches? Wrong! Now, I will grant that Veronica's handwriting is tough to decipher, almost illegible. But the story is there. The story is all there."

"No," she whispered, and hung her head. "You're not well, Hank. You're not well at all."

So this was her defense. That I was crazy. That I had taken a ream of paper and scribbled all over it. That I had stapled those papers to the wall myself. That my accident had caused these spastic and lunatic thoughts. This was her defense.

"I'm not crazy," I whispered, barely loud enough for her to hear.

"No, darling. Of course not. I would never say that. Never, ever."

"I'm not a lunatic."

"No. It's just that the accident caused some problems. Your perceptions . . . they might be a little bit off."

"That's what Catherine's husband told her. Those exact words. You know what Catherine's real name was?"

"Hank. Stop."

"Lucinda Desmond. She had a daughter named Jane."

"There's no Catherine. There's no Lucinda. There's none of this. Please."

"And Lucinda drowned her. And once she was dead, she removed the body from the bathtub. She dried her off. She brushed her hair. And then she carried her back to her bedroom. She placed her daughter, her dead daughter, in her bed and pulled the covers up to her chin. Then she went to the living room and began knitting a sweater. Can you imagine? A sweater."

Iris placed her hand on mine. "We will get you help, Hank. Doctors have a great understanding of brains and how they work. Dr. Hoover will come tomorrow. He will adjust your medicine. And then everything—"

I shook my head. "Dr. Hoover isn't going to come tomorrow."

"Why not?"

"Because I'll be gone."

"Gone where?"

"Gone . . . somewhere."

"Let's go to bed. Let's get some sleep. When you wake up, everything will be better."

But I knew she was lying. I knew that they would come for me. I knew that they would take me back to the nuclear shelter. I knew they would wipe clean my memories.

I wasn't crazy.

I was Malachi Severin.

"Nothing will be better tomorrow," I said. "Nor the day after that or the day after that. I am who I am. We are who we are. There's no escaping our essence."

I moved toward Iris. She tried rising from the bed. Music started playing. Lunatic calliope music. From where was the music playing? From Bethlam proper. Not from my head.

My face stretched into a monster mask. There was nowhere for Iris to go. She screamed. The calliope music stopped playing. With a scream of my own, I pounced upon her. I spread my fingers around her throat and pressed my thumbs into her soft flesh. She tried prying away my hands, but she was weak, and it was no use.

"Your name," I said. "What's your real name?"

Her face was turning red, almost purple. Her eyes were bulging like a squeeze toy.

This was my essence.

"What's your name?" I asked again.

She tried speaking, her cheeks filling with blood. "P . . . P . . . Petra . . ."

Petra! Not Iris! Petra! I squeezed harder. Her eyes never closed. She began to twitch. I could smell excrement. And still I squeezed.

But then I heard the sound of the door slamming open. I released my grip and spun around. A group of men, all dressed in white, came charging toward me.

How had they known? How had they arrived so quickly?

I tried bulling my way through them, but they weren't having any of it. One of them tackled me to the ground.

"I'm not crazy!" I shouted. "I know the real story! Malachi Severin. Malachi—"

It took all of them to keep me down. One pinning down each arm. One pinning down each leg. And then another one of them, the biggest of them all, removed a giant syringe out of his jacket pocket. His eyes were empty, his hands steady. I screamed. He plunged the needle into my neck and squeezed out the medicine. He watched me with calm eyes as my body went limp and my brain got muddled.

"There, there," the man said. "Sleep for a little while."

I could hear Iris/Petra gasping and groaning. Then I heard her say, "He would have killed me. If you hadn't gotten here. He would've killed me."

I closed my eyes.

I figured I was dead.

CHAPTER 36

I cycled through a thousand nightmares, unsure if they were mine or not, unsure if I was awake or sleeping.

Like this one: A woman sitting on a sunken bench beneath the glow of a streetlamp, her white dress swaying in the summer breeze, a black veil covering her mournful face. Her legs are crossed, and her hands are resting on her lap. I'm walking down an endless sidewalk, and there is a child on either side of me, both wearing suits far too big for their bodies, both with their faces painted white, like mimes. They're whispering the words, "Slathered in Jesus's blood" over and over again. We reach the woman, and I stand in front of her, my weight shifting back and forth. Even though she is wearing a veil, even though she is quiet, I can tell that the woman is my mother. It's her hands. A man knows his mother's hands. I say her name—"Mother! Mother! Mother!"—but still she doesn't speak. The two children begin to cry, only there is no sound because they are mimes. They are not really sad—it is all an act. It's then that, with trembling fingers, I reach forward to pull up my mother's veil. And I do. But beneath that veil is no face. Beneath that veil is only a fleshless scream. A single moth crawls out from where her eye used to be and then another and another. The child mimes are crying for real . . .

And this one: I'm standing on top of a hill covered in waves of snow. The snow is still falling, and I can't stop shivering. Shielding my eyes with my hand, I look down in the valley below and see a group of a hundred men at least. They all wear black and carry torches and are marching forward, although they barely seem to move. In the midst of all the fire and blackness is an old man dressed in white who is playing some sort of strange organ. The music is beautiful and haunting. I know that they are coming for me. In fact, they are calling my name, although the name itself is muffled in the wind and the falling snow. I know I need to leave, so I turn and begin to walk up the hill, but I am having trouble moving, and every time I look back, the torches are getting closer, and the organ music is getting louder. I look down and see that I don't have any shoes and that my feet are bloody, leaving a red trail in the snow. Each step is full of agonizing pain, and eventually, I can't go anymore. I fall to my knees and begin to crawl. It's not long before the men are upon me. It's not long before the organ is blaring in my ear. The men all disappear and there is only fire and snow, and I am screaming and crying and laughing all at once.

But we wake, we always wake, and when I did, my mind was wreaking havoc, my thoughts disconnected and discombobulated.

As I lay in bed, eyes pulled open by imaginary fingers, I began to notice Iris / Petra coming in and out of the bedroom. Sometimes she would sit at the edge of the bed and try speaking to me, all the while wiping tears from blushed cheeks, but I didn't understand the words she was saying. No, that's wrong. I understood the words, but they didn't make any sense together. "World beneath floors and or leaves of cloth fantastic throughout the music will stop through through through china whales made of purple splinters following night into autumn."

You think I'm crazy?

Crazy do you think?

Remember who I was.

Malachi Severin.

I killed my mother.

She left me food. Plates of sausage and cheese and pickled okra. I don't remember eating, but I must have because the food vanished and I wasn't hungry anymore. But I do remember drinking the water. I was so thirsty, and so I would drink and drink and drink, the water spilling onto my bare chest, and Iris would keep refilling my glass.

She smoothed back my hair with her hand. She wiped the perspiration from my forehead with a cloth. She changed the pillowcase when it became sopping wet from my sweat. My mind began healing. Her words began making sense again. "Everything's going to be okay, Hank," she said. "Don't you believe me? Don't you believe me?"

Don't you believe me?

And then Dr. Hoover stood over me. He said, "You've been in an accident, Hank. A very serious accident. What do you remember?"

Crazy.

"I remember nothing."

"Take another pill, Henry. Just one more."

I tried sitting up in bed, but I was restrained. It was strange. I looked at my hands—they were free. I looked at my feet—they were free. But I couldn't sit up. The ropes were invisible.

"The tattoo," Iris said, "represents the day your father died."

"The tattoo," I said, "represents the day I killed my mother."

"You didn't kill your mother. Your mother is still alive. She loves you very much."

What is real? What is delusion?

"You've been in an accident," Dr. Hoover said. He wore a white doctor's coat and carried a black medical bag. His eyes were too blue, far too blue.

When they weren't in the bedroom, I could hear them talking in the hallway. The door was closed, but my sense of hearing had always been strong and had become stronger in the preceding days. I could hear every word. And in my scabbed brain, I could see them as well.

"He's getting worse, I'm afraid," Dr. Hoover said, slicking back his blond hair with his privilege-smoothed hands. "It's such a shame. I thought the medication would work. I thought the memory therapy would work. But now, he's full of delusions. Talk of government conspiracies, microchips, and nuclear bunkers. Talk of changing identities, implanted memories, and secret messages behind wallpaper."

"Yes," Iris said. "Delusions. And it seemed as if he was making such big strides. His memories were becoming stronger and stronger. I thought that . . . I thought that . . ." As any wonderful actress would do, Iris burst into tears.

Dr. Hoover touched her gently on the shoulder. "We can't give up on him. We can never give up."

Iris wiped away the tears with the back of her hand. She knew I was listening. Of course, she knew I was listening. "Our life," she said, "was wonderful. So many fond memories. Oh, Dr. Hoover, can I tell you about them?"

"Of course you can. Of course."

"Well then. I remember that gentle summer night when we sat on the top of the Ferris wheel, the town glowing beneath us. He leaned toward me and we kissed, and the world was full of faith and magic. I remember holding hands and laughing as we ran across the baseball diamond, leaves fluttering to the ground, the autumn wind blowing cold. I remember swimming at Mapleton Pool, the sky pale blue and cloudless. I remember making love in Shallow Park, the muted sound of a violin drifting through the ash and dogwood trees. I remember kissing at the altar and saying, 'I do.' I remember all of those things."

You've been in an accident, Hank. A very serious accident. What do you remember?

I don't remember anything.

Iris: "I remember making love in Shallow Park, the muted sound of a violin drifting through the ash and dogwood trees."

"We can't give up on him. We can never give up."

———

Nighttime. How many days had passed since I'd read the manuscript? One? Five? A hundred? It didn't matter. The world could only last for so long.

I lay in bed, staring at the ceiling, when I heard a commotion coming from the living room. A banging on the door. Shrill voices.

"Let me see him! Goddamnit! You can't do this to him. To me. It's unethical. It's—"

I recognized the voice. I was sure of it. The woman who'd come to the window. Veronica Miller.

"Dr. Hoover!" Iris shouted. "Help! She's back."

I tried rising from bed, but my hands and feet were still restrained by those invisible ropes and shadow handcuffs. My mouth was sewn shut with barbed wire.

From the living room, I heard the sound of broken glass. Then a scream. Then the front door slamming shut.

Using all my strength, I managed to pull myself from the bed and crashed to the floor. Like a soldier in the jungle, I used my arms to pull myself along the floor until I reached the bedroom door, which was open a crack. I managed to push my way through. Grimacing, I got to my hands and knees and crawled the rest of the way.

But when I got to the living room, Veronica was gone. Dr. Hoover was sitting on the couch, legs crossed, reading a book: *Diagnostic and Statistical Manual of Mental Disorders*. Iris was sweeping up some broken glass. When she heard me, she spun around.

"Oh, darling," she said. "Did I wake you? Clumsy me knocked this vase from the bookshelf."

I tried speaking, but no words came out.

Dr. Hoover smiled and said, "Let's get you back to bed. Rest will do you good."

He rose from his chair and started toward me. But before he reached me, before he lifted me to my feet, I spotted something right next to the front door.

A silver bracelet, shimmering in the light.

———

Over the next several days, Dr. Hoover gave me more and more medicine, and I was dead to the world.

But even though they were drugging me, they couldn't stop me from reliving Malachi's memories. In my mind, I bashed my father's head over and over and over again. I killed my mother over and over and over again. And then I was back in that cold cell, staring straight ahead, a twisted smile on my face.

———

Iris sat on the edge of the bed, and, once again, she was reading the manuscript. She was crying—she cried all the time now. I watched her read, I watched her cry.

"It's all gibberish," she said. "It's all chicken scratch. There is no story here. You've gone crazy. Please. Please. Try to remember. You're Hank Davies. Not Walter Daley. Not Malachi Severin. The tattoo is when your father died. You didn't kill anybody. Not your mother. Not nobody!"

She was lying, but I didn't have the energy to protest.

And then my mother was there as well. The one with a red velour jogging suit, the one with dyed blond hair.

The fake one.

"Of course you didn't kill me!" she said, laughing. "I'm standing right here. Where did you come up with that name? Malachi Severin? It's so exotic! Your name is Hank Davies. I named you after my grandfather. He was a wonderful man. He fought in World War I. He fought for Germany, unfortunately. But how is that his fault? He couldn't help where he was born."

Then she was gone, but Iris was still there.

Now she sat in the middle of the room, reading the manuscript by candlelight.

My head was aching.

"Take another pill, Henry," Dr. Hoover said (where did he come from?). "Just one more."

I took his advice, but I didn't have any water. When I tried swallowing, I choked on the pill. My hacking must have startled Iris. She knocked over the candle with her leg. The flame came into contact with the manuscript, but like Moses's bush, it wasn't consumed.

Iris sat there, cross-legged. She rubbed her hands over the fire. Her face glowed like the devil.

I squeezed my eyes shut.

When I opened them, Iris was sound asleep, her back turned to me. I gazed at the wallpaper, blue flowers on a dull yellow background. The paper was beginning to peel, and beneath it I could see what looked like letters, what looked like the truth.

ACKNOWLEDGMENTS

Writing can be a pretty isolating gig, and I'm sure I would have descended into lunacy by now if not for the encouragement of so many people. In particular, I want to thank my editor, Addi Wright, who has constantly stuck out her neck for me when she could have just as easily shaken her head. I'm forever in debt for her kindness and advocacy.

Thanks to my agent, Becky LeJeune, a Louisiana gal who doesn't take any bullshit. I'm incredibly thankful to be represented by somebody as passionate and professional as her.

Thanks to Celia Johnson, who proved to be an incredible developmental editor. She understood what I was trying to do and made everything right.

Thanks to the entire Blackstone team including Josie Woodbridge, Daniel Ehrenhaft, Ember Hood, Anthony Goff, Candice Edwards, Bri Jones, and Nicole Sklitsis. I couldn't ask for a more supportive publisher.

Thanks to Patrick Hughes and Amy Wilson at Foundation Media, who keep telling me my words are going to turn into a movie someday, and who am I to argue with them? I appreciate your passion and tenacity.

Thanks to Adam Sigal, a creative partner and owner of my favorite Instagram Sphynx cats.

Thanks to Gavin Critchlow, who read an early manuscript and didn't hate it. His positivity gave me a reason to believe.

Thanks to the Longmont High School community, especially the English Department: John Fuller, Courtney Campbell, Annie Falkenberg, Tracy Pearce, Madeleine Angelino, Brian Kenney, Tiffany Greenberg, and honorary member Emily Gibson. It's not easy working with somebody as deranged as me, but thanks for not saying anything to my face.

Most importantly, thanks to my family: my parents, my sister Leah, my wife Tobey, and my children Noah and Anna. The stories don't matter without you.